THE ULTIMATE DRAGON FIGHTING CHAMPIONSHIP

TALES FROM THE LAND OF ONONOKIN BOOK 7

JOHN P. LOGSDON
CHRISTOPHER P. YOUNG

CRIMSON MYTH
PRESS

This is a work of fiction. All of the characters, organizations, and events portrayed in this novel are either products of the author's imagination or are used fictitiously and are not to be construed as real. Any resemblance to actual events, locales, organizations, or persons, living or dead, is entirely coincidental.

Copyright © 2017 by John P. Logsdon & Christopher P. Young

All rights reserved, including the right to reproduce this book, or portions thereof, in any form.

Published by: Crimson Myth Press (www.CrimsonMyth.com)

Edited by: Lorelei J. Logsdon (www.LoreleiLogsdon.com)

Cover art: Amy P. Simmonds (www.amypsimmonds.com)

Thanks to the *Ultimate Dragon Fighting Championship* Reader Team!
(listed in alphabetical order by first name)

Adam Saunders-Pederick, Allen Stark, Bennah Phelps, Bonnie Dale Keck, Carolyn Fielding, Carolyn Jean Evans, Christopher Ridgway, Debbie Tily, Deborah Ankrett, Eddie Williams, Elaina Moore-Kelly, Gabriella Wood, Gary Hart, Hal Bass, Harmony Baddeley, Helen Day, Iam Strabo, Ian Nick Tarry, Jacky Oxley, Jamie Smith, Jan Gray, Jan Holmes, Jeff "Sully" Arnold, Jodie Stackowiak, John Debnam, Kate Smith, Kathy Beaver, Kevin Frost, Laura Stoddart, Lizzie Fletcher, Lynette Wood, Mark Beech, Mark Brown, MaryAnn Sims, Matthew Stuart Thomas Wilson, Megan McBrien, Michelle Wilkinson, Natalie Fallon, Neil Webber, Noah Sturdevant, Pam Elmes, Patricia Wellfare, Paul Hathcox, Rachel Joan Pegrum, Richard Francis Plummer-Pritchard, Ruth Sanderson, Sandee Lloyd, Sharon Robb, Sian Johnson, Stephen Bagwell, Steve Gould

THE DREAM

*G*ungren sat in front of a mountain of rocks.

There were small ones, big ones, round ones, and jagged ones. Each of them had their own advantages and disadvantages, especially to the discerning eye of a giant. A few of them stood out against the grain, of course, but Gungren would gladly launch any of their number far into the distance.

It was a thing with giants, after all.

A small shadow crossed the ground in front of Gungren. He looked down and spotted someone he knew, someone he had once spent a lot of time with, but he couldn't quite place the name. At least not fully. He knew that it sounded something like "Winkiepiddle" or "Waspsniffle," but he wasn't sure.

"Gungren," said the little man while wagging his finger in a chastising way, "you've got to get a hold of yourself. Throwing rocks like this can only lead you down a path of giantism again."

Gungren looked at himself. As far as he could tell, he was a giant already. Then he frowned thoughtfully at the recognition that he had understood the term "giantism." The fact was that he knew giants weren't that bright. This additional rationalization seriously confused him because, again, giants weren't that bright.

He glanced back down at the little old man who was wearing the pointy hat.

"I can't help it, mister," he said in his childlike voice. "I see a rock and I want to throw it."

"I understand that," came the gentle reply, "but you must resist."

Gungren couldn't think of any way to keep himself from his favorite pastime, though. And why should he anyway?

A little voice in his head told him that he was on the road to being a great wizard. That road was being blocked by him morphing back into a giant. The more things he did that were in line with what giants did, the faster his transformation would be.

He gulped.

"How do I resist?"

"There are many methods, actually," said the old man.

"Name one."

"Hmmm." The fellow scratched at the pointy hat. This seemed silly to Gungren, but he assumed it was just something that little old men who wore pointy hats did when they were thinking. "Well, you could try aromatherapy."

"What that?"

"I think it's when you smell something bad when you want to do something you shouldn't be doing." The man glanced up, raising his hand to block out the sun. "This way your brain manufactures a learned distaste for the thing you shouldn't be doing."

"Hmmmm." Gungren didn't want to smell bad things. Of course, he had grown up in Restain, which was the land of the giants. They weren't exactly known for smelling like roses. "I not like that one. What else you got?"

"Meditation is supposed to—"

"The only kind of medertation I does is throwing rocks. What else?"

The man took off his hat and threw it angrily on the ground.

"I don't know, Gungren! It's not my job to fix your addictions.

It's my job to tell you *to fix them. I have enough trouble keeping my drinking to only magical support."*

A flicker of memory came back at this mention of drinking. "But you drink all the time, Master."

Master? *thought Gungren. This was so very confusing.*

"My point exactly," said the fellow.

"But I want to throw rocks."

"And you can't."

The man picked up his hat and brushed it off. The color of his hair was red, but it was slowly turning to yellow. Gungren thought this was strange, but it offered up another memory that this elderly fellow's name was Whizzfiddle.

"But I want to," Gungren said in a grumpy voice.

"No."

Gungren banged the ground with his overlarge fist.

"It my life and I want to throw rocks!"

"Gungren..."

"I want to throw them!"

"Gungren!"

"I WANT TO THROW—"

"GUNGREN!"

The little giant bolted upright.

He was in bed in his master's house. It was dark except for the light that was floating just above Whizzfiddle's hand.

"What happened?" asked Gungren as the dream quickly faded from memory.

"You were having that rock-throwing dream again, I'm afraid," answered Whizzfiddle.

"Oh." Gungren was sweating. He sighed sadly. "It getting worse."

"Indeed."

"I not know what to do, Master."

Whizzfiddle patted Gungren on the shoulder and took a deep breath.

It had to have been the middle of the night because the sun wasn't yet up and Gungren tended to go to bed not long after sundown.

"Let's go have some tea and see what we can figure out together, shall we?"

"Is that your way of saying you want tea, Master?"

"Of course not," replied Whizzfiddle as if he'd been slapped. Then he raised his chin a bit. "Okay, maybe, but we should still discuss a plan for your situation."

Gungren climbed out of bed and followed Whizzfiddle out to the kitchen.

His body still felt strange after the adjustment done to him by the Fate known as Heliok. Gungren was in the midst of a three-part Fate Quest that was to help him become a wizard *before* the change spell that rested on him reverted. He had only a short window left to finish that third quest and become a card-carrying magic user. If he didn't succeed in time, he would morph back into a giant. He'd no longer have any interest in doing magic, his thoughts would fill again with dreams of rocks, and everything that he'd learned over his time with Whizzfiddle would dissipate. But Heliok had also been changing Gungren's looks after he completed each leg of the quest. The first change was to his teeth. They used to be bent, gapped, and yellowy. Now they were big, straight, and glowingly white. His body was once rotund, but it had been changed after completing the second quest to being thin. The only thing that still remained "normal," in a manner of speaking, was his head. It was bulbous with bushy hair.

The kettle was boiling water as Whizzfiddle pulled out his new TalkyThingy.

"You like that better than the old one?"

Whizzfiddle nodded. "It's a bit smaller, but not much, so

that's good. It has something called 'video chat' on it, too." He flipped it over and shrugged. "Whatever that is."

"Am there a manual?"

"Why would I need that?"

"To learn how that thing works," answered Gungren while pointing.

Whizzfiddle gave him a studious look. He did this whenever he was about to say something that didn't make any sense. At least that's what it seemed like.

"Gungren, if you need to read a book on something in order to use it, then it's not worth having."

"Uh huh."

"Besides, if you just press buttons and such it'll eventually do what it should."

Whizzfiddle began tapping the little squares on the screen. Apparently, this wasn't the best idea since the TalkyThingy suddenly started to play the sound of a siren. It was an annoying sound, especially when it hit certain frequencies, and it was a fair bit louder than Gungren would have expected possible from such a small device.

"What in The Twelve is that?" yelled Whizzfiddle as he smacked the TalkyThingy repeatedly. "Shut up, you bloody noisemaker!"

Gungren snapped up the manual and started scanning the pages. He jumped to the index and found the word "alarm" listed near the top. He then jumped to the page it referenced, grabbed the TalkyThingy from Whizzfiddle, and pressed the red button that showed a little bell on it.

The siren stopped.

"Hmmmph," said Whizzfiddle, crossing his arms. "I would have figured that out eventually."

"Yep."

"Fine." Whizzifiddle picked up the manual and stuck it in

his robe. "I'll read the blasted book later. For now, let's talk about your rock-throwing issue." He briefly looked away. "Maybe there's a book about that?"

"Could be," conceded Gungren. "I'll check tomorrow at the library."

"Good idea. Aside from that, I would say that maybe you should wear gloves or something."

There was no studious look this time, but Gungren was suspicious about his master's idea anyway.

"What would that do?"

"Well, when you go to pick up a rock, you'll not be able to feel it against your skin. This would serve to remind you that you're not supposed to be touching rocks."

"Actually, that not a bad idea, Master."

Whizzfiddle wore a smug face, clearly feeling rather impressed with himself.

"I do have my moments."

"But what if it's just the throwing that I want to do? I mean, I also like to throw apples and tomatoes and stuff."

His smug face disappeared.

"Valid point." The elderly wizard started tapping the table with his index finger. "How about if I cast a spell on you that will give you a jolt of electricity every time you pick up a rock?"

"That another good idea." Gungren was quite impressed, truth be told. "How would that work?"

"Simple. You touch a rock and you'd feel a jolt of electricity." He shivered as if he were experiencing the feeling himself. "It'd sting something fierce, I can promise you that."

"That might be a good detergent."

"I think you mean 'deterrent.'"

Gungren furrowed his brow. "That what I said."

"Right." Whizzfiddle peered up at Gungren from his chair. "Do you want me to do that, then?"

"Please do, Master. I need to keep the giant in me away for as long as I can."

"Agreed," Whizzfiddle replied with a vigorous nod. "Just drop a couple shots of whiskey in my tea and I'll sort it out."

THE DIAMOND OF JALOOF

*H*eliok knew that time was running short for Gungren. Soon he would be turned back into a full giant and then the three-part Fate Quest would be nothing but a washout. He *could* undo things himself, obviously, but that would go against the Fate interference code. He *could* go against that code, too, but that would just raise the ire of The Twelve, and Heliok had no interest in dealing with their incessant whining.

So he had to hurry.

His crew usually helped with these sorts of things. Unfortunately, there wasn't much going on in Ononokin that would fit the complexity needed to satisfy part three of Gungren's Fate Quest trilogy.

That's when he saw the ticker-tape-style bulletin scroll across his data pad.

The Diamond of Jaloof has gone missing from the Museum of Finer Things in the land of Vaq.

Interesting.

Heliok pulled up information on what had happened and found that a petty thief delivered the diamond to a mob boss by the name of Teggins. He was stationed in Dakmenhem.

This got Heliok thinking. Having Gungren go to the Underworld to retrieve the Diamond of Jaloof from a crime syndicate and successfully return it to Vaq's Museum of Finer Things would indeed be a challenge worthy of his final quest. Possibly *too* challenging.

He walked out of his office and stood at the top banister, looking down on those who worked for him.

"Everyone, stop what you're doing," he called out. They did. "I have found the third quest in the series for our dear Gungren. It seems that the Diamond of Jaloof has been liberated from the Museum of Finer Things in the land of Vaq."

Mooli, a member of his staff who was not the brightest bulb in the cupboard, said, "You mean it was stolen?"

Heliok often wondered how she'd made it this far in the land of the Fates. She was kind and helpful, but her lack of intellect showed at nearly every turn.

"Precisely so," Heliok replied slowly.

"Do you know where it is now?" asked Lornkoo, another staff member who was Mooli's perfect associate, at least as far as brains were concerned.

"Of course I do, Lornkoo," Heliok replied more hotly than was necessary, "and so should you. We're Fates, are we not?"

Lornkoo's shoulders slumped. "Oh yeah, right."

"One of the crime bosses in Dakmenhem has it," explained Heliok. "His name is Teggins."

Misty Trealo's head snapped up at this revelation. She was the dark elf who had been brought up to help Heliok get the Fate's belief numbers back to a respectable amount. Misty was an executive at The Learning Something Channel in the Underworld of Ononokin. She was producing the show *Unreal Makeover: Gift of the Fates*. Gungren was the star.

The idea was that Gungren would have a part of his person altered over three quests. Then there would be a reveal showing his final look. The people in the Underworld would be so impressed that their belief in the Fates would jump by leaps and bounds. That was the hope anyway.

"So you're going to send an apprentice wizard into the den of a crime boss in Dakemenhem?" Misty asked as if Heliok were stupid.

"That's correct."

"You *do* realize how dangerous that is, yes?"

"Fate Quests can be rather dicey, Ms. Trealo," replied Heliok haughtily.

"So is losing the main character in our story for *Unreal Makeover*, Heliok."

Heliok shrugged at her. "I admit it's a risk, but each step of this quest has to progress in complexity, so unless you have something better, I suggest we move along."

She didn't reply.

"Good. I shall speak with Gungren immediately then."

MAKING IT WORSE

Whizzfiddle and Gungren stood in the living room.

It had been a while since Whizzfiddle had done a deterrent spell, so he ran over it in his head. Technically, he had *never* connected the electric shock to someone picking up rocks, but he had once helped a lady who couldn't stop buying jewelry. Every time she got close to her favorite jewelry store, her eyes would go crossed, making her walk into the local winery instead. A month later she'd asked to have the spell removed because she was tired of waking up with a hangover.

"Are you sure you want me to do this, Gungren?"

"I are."

"I *am*," Whizzfiddle corrected.

"You am what?"

Whizzfiddle had sworn off constantly correcting the little man, but he just couldn't help himself.

"Never mind. Let's just get on with it."

He took a sip from his mug, but the hot liquid burned his lip.

"Still too hot. I'll just grab a hit from my flask." He spun open the top and drank in enough booze to fill his reserves. It was a decent hit. "Oooh, that'll do it." He cleared his throat and focused. "FLIPS-UM-FLOPS-UM-FLAPS-UM-FLINGS, TOUCH-UM-ROCKS-AND-OUCH-THAT-STINGS!"

A silvery dust fell upon Gungren's head and slowly sank into his scalp. At least it looked like it did. Whizzfiddle honestly had a difficult time knowing for sure since the little giant had a pretty rough case of dandruff.

"Did it work?" asked Gungren.

"It should have, but I don't have a rock with me for you to test with."

Gungren stood up and started for his room. "I got one in my—"

And that's when the blasted Fate known as Heliok blinked into existence directly in front of Gungren, effectively blocking his way. Whether or not Heliok had planned this was anyone's guess, but Whizzfiddle wouldn't put it past the Fate.

"Hello, hello," Heliok said in his flamboyant voice. "Isn't it grand that I'm here?"

"No," Whizzfiddle replied coldly.

He was not exactly fond of Heliok. The Fate had a way of being a pain. To be fair, Heliok felt the same way about Whizzfiddle. Whizzfiddle knew this because Heliok was not afraid to tell him so.

"Hi, Heliok," said Gungren with a full measure of excitement. "You am have a new quest for me?"

"Indeed, I do."

"Am it a good one?"

"Indeed, it is."

"What am it?"

Whizzfiddle groaned. "What *is* it, Gungren!"

"I don't know," Gungren replied with a squint. "Him not told me yet."

Whizzfiddle sighed.

"The Diamond of Jaloof has been taken from the Museum of Finer Things," Heliok announced with a big grin.

Whizzfiddle looked at the Fate. "In Vaq?"

"You've been?"

"Sure, I've been. Everyone who is anyone knows about the Museum of Finer Things."

"Then why'd you ask where it was?" Heliok asked. "Is there more than one?"

"Well, no...I just…"

"Right." Heliok turned back to Gungren. "So, Gungren, your quest is to retrieve the Diamond of Jaloof and return it to the Museum in Vaq."

"That not sound too hard."

"Ah, but it will be your most challenging quest yet, my dear boy."

"Why?"

Heliok's eyes were glowing happily. That couldn't be good. Whenever a Fate got all giddy about a quest they were about to dish out, it meant that quest was going to be pretty rough.

"Because," Heliok explained, "it was stolen by a crime boss in Dakmenhem named Teggins."

"Teggins?" said Whizzfiddle, spitting out the little amount of tea he'd been able to get past his lips. "Are you insane? He's one of the most sinister crime bosses in the land. Gungren wouldn't have a chance against the likes of him and his goons."

"I can do it."

"No, Gungren, you honestly can't." Whizzfiddle set the cup down and put his hands on Gungren's shoulders. "We're not talking about a simple 'go in and take a jewel back' kind of thing. Teggins is known for being exceedingly protective over the things he steals. And he'd just as soon kill you as look at you."

"But—"

"No buts, Gungren." He spun to face Heliok. "You should be ashamed of yourself pinning a quest like this on someone such as Gungren. He hasn't got enough magical control to manage such a thing."

"Even with his Master along for the ride?" Heliok challenged.

"That'd be different, certainly, but will the use of my magic be allowed in the completion of his Fate Quest?"

"Hmmm... no, it would not."

"No, it would not," Whizzfiddle repeated. "And so there you have it." He threw his hands up in the air and laughed. "Heliok, you might as well have set Gungren up to fight in the upcoming Ultimate Dragon Fighting Championship instead. At least then he'd have a chance."

The glowing of Heliok's eyes increased to the point where Whizzfiddle thought certain the Fate's head was going to explode. This wasn't because Heliok was angry; on the contrary, he looked quite pleased.

"That is a brilliant suggestion, Whizzfiddle," the Fate said while clapping. "I shall set it up immediately!"

"No, wait, I—" was all Whizzfiddle could get out before Heliok disappeared. "What have I done?"

Gungren patted him on the arm. "I think you made it worse."

PLANNING A WAGER

*T*eggins sat in his dark office, leaning back in his brown leather chair. The chair had been specially made to handle a man of his size. He was big, burly, and exceedingly strong. To the typical outsider, he just looked fat. That had worked to Teggins's advantage many times over the years.

He was spinning his latest prize around in his fingers. The Diamond of Jaloof. It was a large diamond that was nearly flawless. Teggins didn't care about the way it looked, though. Its value was all that mattered to him, and it was worth a pretty penny. He had plans for that diamond. Plans that would make him even wealthier than he already was.

Ah, money.

There was just something about it that made Teggins feel all warm inside. He'd often wondered if maybe he had dragon blood coursing through his veins. But that was silly considering that he was clearly human.

Just as the clock struck the top of the hour, Teggins's newly appointed right-hand man, Stillwell, walked in.

Stillwell was a weak man, small and lanky, with a pointed nose and chin. He wore glasses, a button-up shirt with a bowtie, and had neatly cropped hair. The guy used to be an accountant, but ever since he made a bad gamble—using funds borrowed from Teggins—his dreams and aspirations didn't matter anymore. Stillwell was now Teggins' property, and since he was such a weak-minded fool, Teggins had no problem giving him special duties.

Being a crime boss *did* have its privileges, after all.

Following Stillwell was Krag the Destroyer. His real name was Krag Jones, but he was a fighter, and so he'd earned a stage name that was much more impressive. Krag was a mean ogre. This meant that he'd kill you just for giving him the wrong look. But Teggins wasn't afraid of Krag, and the ogre knew it. In fact, whenever the greenish, musclebound grunt was around Teggins, he showed an amazing amount of restraint.

"I have a job for you, Stillwell," Teggins said, motioning for the little fellow to have a seat.

"Yes, sir?"

"You're gonna get Krag here into the UDFC 100 tournament and I'm gonna put a bet on him to win it."

"Yes, sir." Stillwell looked instantly uncomfortable as he shifted in his seat. "Sir?"

"Yeah?"

"I heard last night on the news that all of the fighters have already been selected for the tournament."

Teggins tilted his head. "So?"

"So," Stillwell replied with a look of confusion, "Mr. Krag was not on that list, sir."

One of the problems with new initiates to the mob was that they thought things worked like they did in the regular world. When you wanted something done out there, you were often hemmed in by the rules of society. But when the mob wanted something, they just took it.

"What's your point?" asked Teggins as he leaned forward and put his elbows on the desk.

"That it's too late to get Mr. Krag into the event, sir."

Teggins nodded slowly.

"I would agree that it's too late for some folks, Stillwell, but we're a resourceful bunch. We live by the sword in order to get things done, you know?"

"Yes, sir."

"And when one of my underlings is incapable of accomplishing something I desire, they die by the sword." He trained his eyes on Stillwell's. "Am I making myself clear?"

Stillwell gulped. "Yes, sir."

"Good." He leaned back again and eyed the Diamond of Jaloof. It would make for the perfect wager. "Do whatever you have to do to get it done, Stillwell. And do note that I don't take well to failure."

"I understand, sir."

"You may move along, Stillwell," said Teggins, waving the man away, "and send in Lucille on your way out."

Stillwell scampered from the room like a mouse who was under the watchful eye of a hungry cat.

Teggins wanted to sigh at the man's weakness, but he understood that everyone had their place in his organization. He needed peons to do the grunt work just as he needed goons to do the dirty work. It was the nature of running a kingdom, even one that wasn't officially recognized by the state.

The wizard named Lucille walked in a few moments later. She had reddish hair that was in the shape of a bird's nest, meaning it was roundish with pieces of hair sticking out in various directions. There were a few bald patches mixed in as well, which made sense seeing that Lucille's power source came from pulling out her own hair.

This thought made Teggins grimace. Magic users made him uneasy. His was a world of technology, and magic didn't quite fit with that. But, again, everyone had a use, and as long as Lucille did his bidding, he didn't care what she was.

"Lucille," he said, gesturing at the mean ogre, "my man Krag here claims that he will have no difficulties defeating Crazell in the ring."

Lucille's blue eyes went wide at that comment.

"The dragon?"

"Indeed."

She studied Krag for a few moments, walking around him and poking at his muscles.

"Hmmm," she said finally. "Will he have an army with him?"

"I can do it," Krag replied in a dark voice. "I kill dragon. I kill anything."

"Right," Lucille said with a heavy dose of sarcasm.

Krag's eyebrows fused. "I kill you."

"Cute," she replied.

With a level of speed that demonstrated years of practice, she yanked out a clump of hair, said "YOU-GO-OUT-NOW" and flicked her wand at him.

Krag fell over with a thud.

"Real tough guy you've got there," Lucille said while rubbing the newly added bald spot on her head.

"You may want to save your hair, Lucille. I'm going to need you to make sure that Krag *will* defeat Crazell."

She looked up at him as though he were insane.

"That's a tall order, Teggins."

"Have you ever known me to desire any other kind?" he asked.

"Not often." She grunted a moment later. "Fine. How long have I got and what's in it for me?"

"Not long and a satchel full of gold." He held up a finger. *"If* he wins."

"I love your preciseness, Teggins."

"Thank you."

THE JEWELED LIFE

*C*razell was a dragon who had everything a dragon could ask for in life.

Almost.

She was wealthy beyond the level of fathomability, she had a wonderful cave, and she was tall, powerful, and her red scales marked her as being fierce.

Unfortunately, she'd amassed all of her wealth by fighting in the Ultimate Dragon Fighting Championship. In fact, she was the reigning champion. For nearly 250 years, she held the title. This was good and bad. It was good because it meant that she was revered and feared throughout the world; it was bad because those who wanted to test their mettle did everything they could to get to her. Her only saving grace in avoiding daily battles was the fact that the UDFC didn't allow challengers to mess with her. There were the occasional few who got through because they weren't part of the UDFC, but she was able to quickly snuff them out.

But now she was looking at competing in the 100th running of the event and that made her groan.

The big tournament only happened once every ten years.

There were smaller UDFC bouts a couple times a year, of course. It was how fighters rose up the ranks. But the big event that put the champion's belt on the line only happened at the ten-year mark.

This meant that Crazell had defended her title twenty-four consecutive times. If she succeeded in defending it again, that would make her legacy pretty incredible. It would mark her twenty-fifth title defense at the 100th Ultimate Dragon Fighting Championship!

She had to admit that it gave her chills to think of the glory that would bring. But she also had to admit that it would make her life even harder.

Crazell planned to retire after this event. She'd had enough of the training, the fighting, and the constant attention. She just wanted to stay with her jewels in her cave and live in peace.

But that would never happen if she left the UDFC, because the moment they took off their protection, she'd be challenged relentlessly. She'd *never* get a break.

And so here she was, staring across at the little man who had been her trainer for the last four tournaments. He had her doing wing-ups, rolls, talon grabs, and so on.

His name was Ricky Schmicky and he came from a long line of Schmickys who were all a part of Dragon Martial Arts (DMA). It was Ricky's great-great-great-grandmother who had gotten Crazell into the sport in the first place. If only Crazell knew then what she knew now, she would have turned down the offer in a heartbeat. Thinking again of all the jewels she'd amassed made her second-guess that conclusion.

"You gotta push those wings, Craz," Ricky was yelling. He was your stereotypical trainer mixed with promotions manager. In other words, he pushed Crazell in the ring and with the public. "The competition this time around is fierce. You're never going to get by doing the status quo."

"Maybe I don't want to get by," she said in frustration. "Did you ever think of that?"

Ricky grabbed his chest dramatically. "Don't even say such a thing, Craz! If the press caught wind of that attitude, ticket sales would plummet! People want to see you destroy the field just like you did ten years ago at UDFC 99." He then grinned and wiggled his eyebrows. "This is the big 100, baby! Your name will be etched in UDFC lore for all eternity."

"Yeah, yeah, yeah."

"You're the longest-reigning champ in the history of the sport." He began to pace, which meant he was about to do their historical rundown. "My father managed you, my grandfather managed you, and so on. Heck, it was my great-great-great-grandmother who originally dragged you out of your cave and set you on the path to stardom."

"Ahhhh," Crazell said wistfully, "my cave."

Ricky wagged a finger at her. "Now don't start that again. You weren't made for a life of lying on jewels and doing nothing else."

"Actually, Ricky," she corrected him, "I believe that's *precisely* why I was made."

"Particulars, particulars." He scratched his brown hair. Then he looked up at her with inspiration in his eyes. "You've got a gift, Craz! Yeah, that's it. You're special. You're more than other dragons." His face grew dark. "You're a beast!"

She couldn't help but feel her pulse race when he spoke like this. It was in a dragon's DNA to be strong, seek power, and lord themselves over lesser races.

"Well, that's true, I suppose."

"You'd better believe it's true," Ricky continued. "What other dragon has ever held the UDFC title as long as you?"

"No other dragon has, of course."

"Exactly, Craz. And can you name a single living dragon who could even *hope* to challenge you in the ring?"

She sniffed. "They wouldn't stand a chance."

"What about an orc, an ogre, or even a knight?"

"Mere irritants upon my illustrious personage." Her reply included a flick of a talon.

"You see, Craz? You're the cream of the crop, the top of the heap, the pinnacle, the summit..." He paused and put his hands on his hips. "You're the champ."

"Yes," she replied, feeling somewhat invigorated. "Yes, I am. I *am* the champ."

"That's right. And you want to stay there, don't ya?"

The invigoration died. "I...suppose."

"Great, Craz. Now, let's get back to work."

PRESENTING THE PLAN

*H*eliok appeared back in his office and opened his data pad. He did a bit of research on the UDFC event and his thoughts raced at the numbers the Fates would receive if Gungren won the event.

He walked out and announced the new quest to those beneath him.

"The what?" asked Lornkoo.

"The Ultimate Dragon Fighting Championship," Heliok answered.

"Ah."

"Hmmph," said Corg Sawsblade, who was a dwarf that Misty Trealo had brought along to handle filming and production duties when all of this started. He was bossy, blunt, and very good at his job. Heliok did not like Corg very much because he had a tendency of saying disparaging things about Heliok. "And here I was thinkin' ye were daft before."

"Exactly," Heliok replied, and then said, "Wait, what's that?"

"When I heard ye was after sending Gungren into a den of thieves, I already thought yer wispy brain had lost some wind," answered Corg. "But now that yer plannin' to put the wee lad into an arena with orcs, ogres, knights, dwarves, and then a dragon—assumin' he gets that far, which he won't. It's after makin' me think ye've lost yer senses."

Heliok put the insults behind him. "You don't think he's capable of winning?"

"Of course he ain't! He's not a fighter, he's a wizard." Corg pursed his lips as if thinking things through. "Kind of."

"Then that's how he'll battle."

"Aye, that'd give him a chance, at least. But there's a tiny flaw that ye've clearly missed."

"What?"

"There ain't no casting of magic allowed in the UDFC, ye witless Fate!"

"So there *is* magic allowed?"

"I just said there ain't!"

"No, you said, 'Ain't no casting of magic allowed,' which is a double-negative."

Corg's eyes thinned. "Do ye want me to kick ye in the nethers?"

"Corg is right, of course," Misty said, as she stood up from her desk and began to move around the office. She had a look on her face of someone who was sensing an angle. "The marketing avenues available to us would be enormous, though."

"Yes, see?" Heliok said with his eyebrows raised at Corg.

"Ye mean it'd be good marketing to watch Gungren gettin' killed by the flame of a dragon?"

"No…" Misty paused. "Well, actually, probably yes. But that's not what I mean. This event only happens once every ten years. There is a ton of fanfare around it. It's massive in the Underworld, and that's where we need our numbers."

"Go on," said Corg.

Misty's face was slowly morphing from concern to

excitement. She'd obviously been seeing things the same way Heliok had. Corg always saw the glass as half-empty, but Misty was more like Heliok...except nowhere near as powerful.

"Imagine how many people are going to watch the event, Corg," she started. "Then think about how many people will tune into our *Unreal Makeover* show in order to see Gungren's physical change."

"Aye, okay." Corg started to pace, too. Heliok didn't really care if the dwarf was fully onboard with the plan. He'd do it anyway. But having everyone supporting the idea would be a good thing. "So they'll see him start out squat, with a big head, bulbous body, and horrible teeth, yeah?"

"Right," answered Misty.

"Next they'll see his choppers are nice and pearly white. All fixed up and such, 'cause he was after finishin' up that first quest with the prince."

"Exactly."

"Then they'll see how his body is all normalish because he helped out that Wiggles guy."

Misty was beaming now, which was quite a feat for a dark elf. "Now you've got it."

"And finally," Corg said, spinning and putting his hands on his hips, "we'll show him burned to a crisp because Crazell the dragon ain't never lost." He then added, "Oh, and she ain't likely to be losing to someone the likes of Gungren."

Misty's brightened face fell back to its normal shadow.

"There's got to be a chance that Gungren could win," she said weakly.

"No, there ain't, lass. It's completely impossible."

"Just think of how our numbers will shoot through the roof because people will want to see his story anyway."

Heliok had no desire to side with the dwarf, but it seemed

the fellow was right. The Diamond of Jaloof quest was most likely in Gungren's future. How unfortunate.

"Sadly," admitted Heliok, "I have to agree with Mr. Sawsblade on this. Gungren won't be fit for the camera after a dragon flames him."

"Not only that, he'll be after bein' in the Afterlife," noted Corg.

"Possibly." Misty's face was on the mend again. She glanced at them. "He'll only be in the Afterlife if you don't intervene, Heliok."

"How do you mean?"

"Let's say that Gungren loses—"

"He'll definitely be turnin' into a right crispy critter," stated Corg.

"And he gets burned to a crisp," she continued, clearly ignoring Corg's interruption, "cut in half, stabbed, or worse."

Corg frowned. "There's worse?"

"You, Heliok,"—Misty pointed at him—"could intervene and save him from his wounds, and give him his reward."

Heliok looked taken aback. "But you know I can't do that."

"You can if you change the quest parameters ever so slightly."

She looked downright devious now. Heliok simultaneously worried about this and found it exhilarating. If there *was* a way around this mess while still getting the little giant involved, that would be a win for everyone.

"I'm listening."

"You don't require him to *win* the event," she said, speaking quickly. "You merely require that he *participate* in it fully. He can't quit and he must do his best to win. But he's not *required* to win."

"Hmmm."

It *was* a solid angle, and there was nothing in the Fate

Quest rules that would go against such a tactic. Frankly, if Heliok wanted to, he could simply say that Gungren had to attend the event and that would be solid enough. But he knew the little giant would never go for that. He'd say that it wasn't reasonably challenging to warrant it being a third quest, and he'd be right. Even the Fate council would balk at that level of simplicity, if this quest came up in an audit. A shudder ran through Heliok's body as he remembered his last audited Fate Quest. The questions, finger-pointing and accusations would have been enough to give an Ononokinite ulcers. "How did the wizard end up with the life-extending potion?" they asked. "How did the terminally ill knight end up living to a ripe old age?" It had been dreadful. Heliok thought for sure he was going to end up doing time in a Fate prison.

"Bah," said Corg, breaking the silence. "I hate to admit it, but the lass is right."

"Seriously?" said Heliok.

"If'n ye don't make him have to win the whole shebang, yeah." He then pointed at Heliok. "And assuming you'll also heal him up nice. It'd make for great drama and the like. With any luck the lad won't even be facin' a dragon at all. He'll get knocked on his keister in the first battle."

"That *is* interesting."

This could be one of those cases of having your cake and eating it too. Heliok was never quite sure what this sentiment meant because he didn't much care for cake. Pie, certainly. But cake? No.

"Uh, sir?" said Mooli, raising her hand.

"Yes?"

"There's a bit of a problem I see here." She was pointing at her data pad. "All the slots are taken already. There is no room for Gungren to join the competition."

"Honestly…" Heliok said it with a sigh. He then shook his head and glared at her. "What are we, Mooli?"

"We're in your office discussing the—"

"Not *where* are we, Mooli. I asked *what* are we?"

"Fates, sir."

"And what does that mean?"

"That we're stronger, better, smarter, and so on than everyone else…" She looked up at him questioningly. "Right?"

"Not all of us, it seems," he answered sourly. "The point, Mooli, is that I will make sure Gungren has a position in the upcoming battle because I will use my power as a Fate to make it happen."

He let that sink in with his underling. How were they even allowed to remain as Fates? Not that they could be kicked out or anything. Once a Fate, always a Fate, as the saying went. But there should have at least been some type of placement exam requirement so that the lesser-minded of their bunch couldn't make it into jobs as important as this.

"Wait," Misty said with hope in her eyes. "Are you saying we're a go?"

Heliok grinned back at her. "Most definitely."

CONVINCING WHIZZFIDDLE

hizzfiddle and Gungren were seated at the kitchen table discussing things. Whizzfiddle knew for certain that Heliok was going to run with the Ultimate Dragon Fighting Championship idea. And why wouldn't he? He had no concern for Gungren or his wellbeing. He only had an interest in doing what was best for him and the blasted Fates.

Just as Whizzfiddle was about to have another sip of his tea, Heliok popped into existence.

Eloquen the elf was with him. Where Heliok could essentially look like whatever he wanted, Eloquen could not. He was a tall, thin elf, with white hair and a perfect complexion.

"We've been talking it over, Heliok," Whizzfiddle said before any pleasantries could be exchanged, "and the Diamond of Jaloof quest sounds fine."

Heliok waved at him dismissively. "That's so yesterday."

"You just told us about it this morning."

"Did I?" Heliok pursed his lips and then shrugged. "Well, no matter. We've decided to go with the Ultimate Dragon

Fighting Championship. It is the one hundreth one, you know?"

"Hi, Eloquen," said Gungren, being as he was more polite than Whizzfiddle. At least when Whizzfiddle was in a foul mood.

"Hi."

Whizzfiddle sighed. "Hello, Eloquen."

"'Sup?"

"'Sup?" That was odd. Typically Eloquen's dialect was rather flowery. "Did you just say, 'Sup?'"

"Yep."

Whizzfiddle gave Heliok a sharp look. "What have you done to him?"

"I've done nothing to him, thank you very much. He started speaking like that just recently."

Gungren pulled out a chair and motioned for Eloquen to have a seat. Heliok took this to mean that he could sit down as well, and so he did. This was wholly unnecessary since Fates didn't need to take breaks. Plus, he would not have been seated anyway. He'd just float slightly above the chair.

"You okay, Eloquen?" Gungren asked.

"Sure."

"You not talking right."

Eloquen traced the lines of the woodgrain on the table. "Not feeling like it."

"Why not?"

"Only when an elf in my community feels happy, or at least excited, are they able to speak in our native tongue."

"Which is just like ours but with more floweriness to it," said Whizzfiddle, though he was stating the obvious.

"Correct."

"Why you am not happy?"

"Because it's lonely being without those in my

community. My family, friends, lov—" He glanced up at Gungren and coughed. "Erm, I mean acquaintances."

"We am your friends," said Gungren gently.

"That's true. I guess it's mostly family and, well, other things."

Whizzfiddle didn't want to think about what Eloquen meant by "other things." He *knew* what the elf meant, he just didn't want to think about it.

"So, go home," Gungren said, leaning in. "We can do this quest on our own."

"No, no. I signed up for this and I'm going to see it through."

And with that, Heliok slapped the table. Actually, he smacked *at* the table. His hand went slightly through it. But a sound reverberated throughout the kitchen anyway.

"Right," said the Fate. "Now that we have Eloquen's issue all settled, let's get down to business."

"He is not fighting in the UDFC, Heliok."

"Of course he's not," Heliok replied with a scoff. "He wouldn't last thirty seconds in there, especially if he starts speaking flowery again."

"I'm not talking about Eloquen. I'm talking about Gungren."

"Ah, right." Heliok nodded and smiled. "Yes, he is."

"No, he's not."

"Then he won't succeed in completing all three quests and he won't get his head fixed." Heliok crossed his arms. "It's as simple as that."

"He doesn't care about his head getting fixed."

Gungren frowned. "What wrong with my head?"

"We haven't the time to describe all the particulars, I'm afraid," replied Heliok.

"Anyway," Gungren said after rolling his eyes, "I just care

about being a full wizard." He turned to face Whizzfiddle. "I gotta do this quest, Master."

"But, Gungren…"

"You know we am gonna do it, Master, so why you am fighting about it?"

"We *are* gonna do it, Gungren. We *arrrrrre* gonna do it!"

"That great, Master," Gungren said with a huge smile. "Okay, Heliok, we am gonna do it."

"No, I…" Whizzfiddle's head dropped slightly. "Never mind." Without lifting his head, Whizzfiddle said, "You know he can't win, Heliok. You're leading this boy to his grave."

"On the contrary, I have altered the rules a fair bit."

That got Whizzfiddle's attention. "Oh?"

Heliok tapped on the table and pointed at the little giant.

"Gungren, you do not have to win the tournament. You merely have to participate." He looked back over at Whizzfiddle for a moment. "Full participation. You can't quit, Gungren, and you have to do your absolute best to try and win."

"I always does my best."

"Perfect, then."

So he didn't have to win. What difference did that make? The very fact that he was going to be put on a field of battle against a group of trained killers was enough to end the poor lad.

"They'll kill him, Heliok."

"It's a risk, certainly."

Whizzfiddle sighed. "You know I can't allow that."

"I don't believe it's your choice to make, Whizzfiddle."

That much was true anyway. He had learned over his time with Gungren that when the little giant put his mind to something, that was that. Besides, this was the home stretch for Gungren. If he didn't get his full wizardship, everything he had worked for would be undone.

"I'll say it again, Gungren. You could be killed."

"Better than turning back to a giant."

"Is it?"

"Master, pretend you am a great wizard—"

Whizzfiddle bridled at that. "Pretend?"

"…and then suddenly you am a big dumb giant," Gungren continued. "You think you be happy with that?"

"No," Whizzfiddle answered him after a few moments of reflection, "I suppose not." He scratched his beard thoughtfully. "You're certain, then?"

"I has to do it, Master."

"Fine, but we'll need to get you at least some training so you have a chance." Whizzfiddle grimaced at the Fate. "Unless this is against your rules, Heliok?"

"Not at all. But you only have until this Saturday to get him to the event. I've already got his position secured."

"Well, that's something anyway."

Gungren seemed to be very happy with the turn of events. Only he could look in the face of fighting a bunch of warriors and find a silver lining in there somewhere.

"Who am gonna train me, Master?" Gungren asked. "Can't be you. You don't have no fighting skills."

"There are three people I have in mind for the job," he replied. "I just have to get in touch with them somehow."

*P*ayne Sawsblade was in charge of bringing to life the behind-the-scenes elements of the Ultimate Dragon Fighting Championship. Her budget was tight, but all she needed was her personality, one mute cameraperson, and some choice selections for filming.

The home of UDFC 100 was Sed's Point, which was the land of the dragons on the eastern coast of the Upperworld.

It was a beautiful expanse of flat lands, mountain ranges, large trees, the ocean, and the massive UDFC arena. If ever there was a place worthy to be called breathtakingly beautiful, it was Sed's Point.

After her cameraperson grabbed some B-roll for the final production, Payne walked into Hotel Winged Bastion. It was one of the fancier hotels in the land. Not *the* most fancy, but rather the fanciest one that would allow her to film.

Since the UDFC event only happened once every ten years, and since dragons weren't exactly known for their hospitality, trolls were brought up to help train the dragons. There were to be no killings or any other shenanigans by the dragons, after all. At least not outside of the ring. Technically, nobody was supposed to be killing anybody outside of the ring as a simple matter of course, but dragons were the most likely to engage in such activities.

Payne stood in front of the reception area where a smallish dragon was being taught how to engage in customer service.

"This dragon is being taught how to handle a customer who is a pain in the rump," said Payne to the camera. "Let's watch."

"Snap, snap," said the troll who was in charge of training. He was pointing to a surly-looking orc. "Let's go, let's go."

The orc adjusted his jacket and strolled up to the counter. He dropped his hotel key in front of the dragon.

"What's this for?" said the dragon.

"That's his room key," the troll explained. "You just take it and pull up his bill."

"Oh, yeah," said the dragon. Then he reached out and stuck a talon on the orc's chest. "Stay there."

"No, no, no," the troll said, slapping the dragon's claw down. "You don't stab at a customer."

"Why not?"

"Because you don't." The troll cleared his throat and regained his composure. "You must say, 'Thank you, sir. Did you enjoy your stay?'"

The dragon's face contorted. "Really?"

"Yes."

"Ugh." To his credit, he did not fight any further, but there wasn't much enthusiasm in his voice when he said, "Thank you, sir. Did you enjoy your stay?"

"It was fine, I guess," replied the orc. He then held up his watch and tapped on it impatiently. "I'm in a hurry here. Can you get a move on?"

The dragon's eyes turned crimson-red and began to glow. It didn't take much to irk a dragon. The sound of a bubbling mass of ignitable liquid could be heard rolling around in its belly as smoke began pouring from its nose.

Clearly the troll recognized the impending doom as well, since he jumped forward and placed himself precariously between the orc and the dragon.

"Now, now," he said, wagging his finger. "Calm yourself. Remember that this orc is our friend. He is simply playing the role of difficult customer so that you can practice your control."

The dragon's eyes dimmed slowly, and the rumbling sound diminished.

"Right." It took a few seconds for the scaly beast to fully regain his composure. "Sorry, pal," he said to the orc, "but this is tough."

The orc nodded and the troll smiled in a way that only trolls could. It wasn't pleasant, but it was better than their scowls. Mostly.

"You're doing splendidly."

"You really think so?" the dragon asked the troll.

"I do." He stepped back. "Now, you tell him the amount he owes and he'll hand you a credit card."

"Okay," said the dragon. "You owe us, uh...one hundred gold."

"For this dump?" bellowed the orc.

The dragon began to twitch at the outburst.

"Remember that he's just acting," yelled the troll, obviously expecting this turn of events. "You're doing fine. You're doing just fine. Keep your cool...literally. This is the worst of it. If you can get past this, you'll be home free."

"But I wanna kill him," growled the dragon in response.

The troll stepped up again. "And what will happen if you do?"

"Uh, he'll be dead?"

"No, I mean if you destroy an actual guest when they are

in the hotel, will that increase the stores of jewels you and the other dragons have, or will it deplete them?"

It was difficult for a dragon to remain rational when threatened or irritated, but logic ruled the day whenever the concept of jewels came into the picture.

"Fine. May I have your credit card, sir?" The troll cleared his throat, so the dragon added, "Pleeeeaaasssseeee?" in a very sarcastic voice.

Fortunately, the orc handed over his card without a word.

"Thank you," said the dragon.

The troll clapped his hands genuinely. "That was excellent. Now, you swipe the card."

"But he's watching me."

"I don't mean that you *swipe* the card as in steal it," said the troll while eyeing the dragon, "I mean that you run it through the machine."

"Oh, right. How do I do that?"

"Right there." The troll pointed to a smallish square on the counter. "You see that slot? You just slide it through there."

The dragon did so.

"And then I type in the amount, right?"

"Precisely. Well done."

"This isn't so bad." The box made a couple of noises, the last of which sounded like a buzzer going off. "What's 'declined' mean?"

"It means that his credit card didn't work," explained the troll.

"And?"

"It means that he can't afford to pay his bill."

In a flash, the dragon reached out and grabbed the orc with his talons. He then launched the poor actor across the room, slamming him against the far wall with a horrific thud. The orc slid to the ground, looking rather unwell.

"Oh, whoops," said the dragon with a look of horror. "I'm sorry about that. It's just a natural reaction to someone not paying me."

"This is one instance in which we are in agreement," noted the troll. "However, we will need to determine a more suitable means of handling it should the actual issue arise."

The camera swung back to Payne. Her eyes were wide as she finished the report.

"And that will tell you that you'd better pay your bills in Sed's Point, assuming you want to live."

BOWING OUT

*S*tillwell wasn't exactly a man who was cut out for this sort of job. He was thin, pale, shaky, disliked confrontation, and had ulcers. He'd only taken the job of being the right-hand man to Teggins because he'd had no choice. This was because Stillwell was also a compulsive gambler, and not a very good one. He owed a sizable sum of cash to Teggins, so it was either this or he'd be "Swimmin' with the fishes." It should also be noted that Stillwell wasn't much of a swimmer.

Teggins had instructed him to clear a slot on the upcoming UDFC 100 card for Krag the Destroyer. That meant another contestant had to bow out.

Fortunately for Stillwell, there happened to be a fighter in town who was slated to be on the ticket. Even more fortunate was the fact that this fellow owed Teggins money.

His name was Pazo and he was an orc. A very large, very menacing-looking orc.

"My manager says you wanna see me?" Pazo said in a gruff voice.

"Yes, sir," replied Stillwell, his resolve quickly fading. "I, uh...I need to ask you to, uh...well, you see..."

"Spit it out, guy. I ain't got all day. I'm in training, you know?"

"Right." Stillwell coughed. "It's about that, actually."

Pazo gave him a funny look. "My training?"

"In a manner of speaking. You see..." Stillwell's heart was pounding so hard that he thought certain Pazo could see the pencils in his shirt pocket bouncing. "I'm going to need you to fake an injury so that I can replace you with one of my fighters."

Stillwell cringed, expecting the worst.

It was very unfair of Teggins to send him into such a place and make such demands of a warrior who was planning to fight and kill people in only two days. The "don't kill the messenger" defense never seemed to work out in the Underworld, especially in Dakmenhem.

"You want me to what?" Pazo asked in a confused tone.

"Fake an injury," Stillwell said again, though much weaker than before.

The orc cracked his knuckles. "This some kind of joke, pal?"

"I'm afraid it's not, sir," answered Stillwell as his life flashed before his eyes. He was feeling dizzy. "You see, my boss, Mr. Teggins, he's—"

"Teggins?" Pazo interrupted. "Did you say Teggins is your boss?"

"Yes, I did." Stillwell hoped this was a good thing. "Why?"

"Nothin', nothin'." Pazo's eyes were dancing. He was clearly thinking about something. "So he sent you here to tell me I'm injured?"

"I...uh...yes?"

"Right."

Suddenly the massive orc shrieked, howled, and then hit the ground, gripping his ankle.

Stillwell jumped back as a crew of orcs rushed into the room. One of them went to Pazo's aid while the rest gave Stillwell a stern look. It was all the little man could do to keep his bladder from emptying its contents.

"My leg," yelled Pazo. "My leg just gave out. I was talkin' to this guy and I stepped funny and…" He pounded his fist on the ground. "I think it's busted."

"Whadya do to him?" the trainer yelled at Stillwell.

"He didn't do nothin'," Pazo said, causing the goons to hesitate. "Look at that little twerp. You really think he could take me out?" The orcs all backed off completely at that. "I stepped funny, is all."

"We gotta get you on ice, fast."

"Nah," Pazo said sadly. "I'm done for. No way I can fight in the match with my leg like this."

"But this is a once in a lifetime chance, Pazo!"

"Don't ya think I know that?" Pazo said with a groan. "What am I gonna do, though? My leg's out, see?"

"But—"

"But nothin'. It's out and that's all there is to it." He leaned in and whispered something in the trainer's ear, then he said, "Call the club and tell them they need to find a replacement."

"Yeah, I probably should." The trainer was glancing around at the faces. "His leg *does* look pretty bad, ya know?"

They were all blinking in confusion as the trainer shoved them all out of the room.

Once they were gone, Pazo jumped back to his feet and began hopping around like he was the happiest person on the earth.

"Tell Teggins that this squares us, yeah?" he said, his eyes agleam." No more payments or nothing, right?"

"I…" Stillwell remembered that Teggins had told him to do whatever it took. "Yes, yes. I'll do that."

"Hot damn. Been under his thumb for twelve long years. It'll be great to be out on my own again."

"I'm happy for you," said Stillwell, anxiously wanting to leave.

"Thanks, pal," replied Pazo, slapping Stillwell on the back and launching him across the room. He then rushed over and helped Stillwell back to his feet. "Sorry about that. You okay?"

Stillwell nodded reflexively.

"Great, great. I owe ya one, pal." Pazo then stopped and said, "Well, not really, but you know what I'm saying."

WHEN IS THE INTERVIEW?

*H*eliok felt that Misty had been putting his interview off for too long now. He had been promised that he would be on camera again before this entire ordeal was over, and time was ticking away.

"You said that during Gungren's final leg of the quest, we were going to do another interview."

"And we will, Heliok," Misty replied, "just as soon as Gungren finishes. You'll be asked questions and then you'll go about fixing him up and everything."

"Oh…"

"And imagine the glory of you doing that on the field at the UDFC, too."

"If he wins, you mean?"

She shook her head. "Even if he doesn't. You'd bring him back to life right there, proving on live video that you are a Fate."

"Oh, that's true." He rubbed his hands together excitedly. "That's very, very true!"

Misty got that look again that spelled she was about to do

something worrying. She began walking around Heliok's office with her hands up.

"Imagine Gungren's just come back to life by your hand," she said ominously, "and then we announce the *Unreal Makeover* show to the roaring crowd, and then I interview you right then and there."

She stopped and gave him a sinister stare.

He gulped.

"Something wrong?" she asked in a far too innocent way.

"You want me to speak in front of a crowd that big?"

"Of course," she replied as if it were nothing. "You'll have to."

"But…" The pull of the restroom called to him. "There will be a lot of people there."

"So?"

"So…it's just…well…"

"Ah, I see. Fear of public speaking?"

His eye twitched slightly. She knew damn well he was terrified of being put on the spot in the way she described. He couldn't even handle the cameras during their first interview. Sure, he ended up doing quite well. So well, in fact, that he now craved having those lifeless lenses staring at him. But a crowd the size of the one at the Ultimate Dragon Fighting Championship was a different thing altogether.

"I don't know…"

"May I make a suggestion?" she said.

"Please."

"There's a group of people in the Underworld who get together and help each other overcome their fear of public speaking." She pulled out her GnomePad and searched. "Here it is. They're called the Breadmasters."

"That's an odd name."

"I suppose it is," she replied. "Never thought about it. Anyway, you should join that group and go to a couple of meetings over the next few days. They'll help you, especially if you make a nice donation to their cause."

Going to a place where he was forced to talk in front of people sounded dreadful, but if that was the purpose of the place, how bad could it be? It was very likely that there were many people with the same fear there. Besides, if this place could help him to keep calm at the final interview, then it'd be worth it.

"I'll do it!"

SUPPLIES

$\mathcal{T}$he town of Rangmoon was a bustle of activity today. People were shopping and laughing and even skipping around. Whizzfiddle didn't know why and he didn't much care. From his perspective, there was work to be done and that was a dreadful proposition.

Whizzfiddle did not like to work. It was one of the primary reasons he had embraced becoming a wizard in the first place. That, and the fact that when he drank alcohol he became filled with magical powers.

What he found very unfortunate was how the impoverished folks stuck to the alleys, unwashed, and poking their heads out now and then to ask for a little monetary help. Some were poor because of failed businesses, some because of lost parents…the stories went on and on. While most of those with money just turned up their noses at these people, that wasn't Whizzfiddle's style. He had tons of money and there was little that he needed in order to keep himself going. Hoarding his funds seemed silly, even if he was looking at a very long life. As a wizard he could pick up new cash quickly, especially with his experience. Plus, he had investments everywhere.

And so he set about casting quick spells that put a month's worth of coin in each beggar's pocket.

He didn't stop his walk or anything. He just took out his flask, grabbed a healthy sip, and started transferring coins from his pocketbook to their pockets.

They knew he was doing it, too. They also knew of his standing rule. Each of them had to get a thorough cleaning at the bathhouse at least once a month.

Whizzfiddle, Gungren, and Eloquen passed by the local town's clothier, A Hint of Moon, known for their somewhat transparent clothing, and stopped in front of Gilly's Pub. It wasn't the fanciest bar in town, but it had the best ale Whizzfiddle had ever tasted. This was due to the fact that Whizzfiddle had funded the original Gilly to set up the place and had also tasted each horrifying attempt at ale until Gilly hit the magical mixture.

"Good mornin', Gilly," Whizzfiddle said as he entered the joint as if he owned it. To be fair, Whizzfiddle *did* own one table, which he used whenever he was setting up a new quest for himself. Fortunately, he'd not had to take advantage of that table since Gungren had become his apprentice. "I hope all is well?"

"Master Whizzfiddle, sir," replied the booming voice of the current Gilly. The pub had been handed down from generation to generation, after all. This Gilly looked only slightly different from the last, but vastly different from the first. He was big and burly with greasy black hair and bright rosy cheeks. "Right nice to see you in at such a time of day. Hello to you too, Gungren." He then scanned Eloquen and added, "Got yourself an elf along with you, I see."

"Strong eyes you've got Gilly," Whizzfiddle replied with a hint of sarcasm. "Just like your father's."

"Thank you, sir."

"Right, well, we're going on a bit of an adventure in support of Gungren. I'll need to make sure my backpack is properly filled with ale, meats, and cheese, if you would."

"We normally need a bit of time for such a thing, Master Whizzfiddle, but there's a party in town tonight and we had a few extra barrels built out, just in case."

The party explained why everyone outside seemed to be in a cheery mood. It would also mean that the shop owners in town had a windfall of cash coming. If history was any indicator, that meant Rangmoon would be a jolly place for at least a month.

"Wise."

"I can spare three full barrels and plenty of foodstuffs, sir."

Whizzfiddle calculated in the air using his fingers. "That should do it."

"Boys," Gilly hollered. A few moments later, a couple of Gillys appeared, looking more like their mother than their father. "Get down to the cellar and bring up three triple-x barrels."

"Triple-x?" queried Whizzfiddle as the boys took to the stairs.

"Potency, Master Whizzfiddle," Gilly replied with a wink. "I've been tinkering with alcohol content. It's the same flavor, but it's got more pop to it."

"Is that so?"

"My father'd be proud."

"As will I, should it truly spark my taste buds like the normal stuff."

Alcohol content was important to a man like Whizzfiddle since it directly correlated with how much power he had to do magic. But taste was equally important since he had to drink the stuff in the first place.

"Been serving it for weeks now," explained Gilly as he grabbed a mug and filled it from a tap. "Ain't nobody spotted it, sir. Even me wife was none the wiser, and she drinks our ale like it's water."

"Mostly is."

"Aye."

Whizzfiddle sniffed the contents of the mug. It smelled the same as good old Gilly's ale. It also had the same color, which made sense seeing that the mug was metal and not much light could get in.

He took a heavy sip and let it roll around for a moment in his mouth.

The flavor was indeed the same, though possibly a little sweeter. That could have just been his mind wanting to find a difference. Regardless, it was quite tasty. When it went down, he felt the power fill his body quickly.

"Whoa." Whizzfiddle's eyebrows shot up to the brim of his hat. "That *is* powerful stuff!"

"Aye," Gilly replied proudly.

"Three barrels will be more than enough with that measure of alcohol."

Once the three barrels were up, Whizzfiddle opened his backpack and cast a spell. All three of the containers instantly shrank down and slid comfortably into the pack.

"What about us?" Gungren said. "I not like beer stuff."

"We have ginger beer for you, if you'd like, Gungren," offered Gilly.

"Do it got alcerhowl in it?"

"No, sir. It's just a bubbly drink with a hint of ginger and some sweetness."

"That sound okay." Gungren turned to the elf. "What about you, Eloquen?"

"A drink is a drink."

Gungren looked at Gilly. "Him depressed."

"Right." Gilly didn't seem all that concerned with Eloquen's mental state. "Well, I'll have them add a barrel of ginger beer, if that's okay with you, Master Whizzfiddle?"

"Put in two barrels," Whizzfiddle stated. "I'm going to go outside and make a quick call."

"A what?" said Gilly, looking confused.

"Oh, uh...nothing. I'll be outside." He then dug into his purse and pulled out a bunch of coins, which he then placed on the counter. "Hopefully that'll do?"

"More than enough, sir," said Gilly happily. "Thank you, sir!"

"Best ale in the land." Whizzfiddle took another sip of the triple-x. "Gungren, do you know how to shrink the barrels for the backpack?"

"Yup."

"Good. I'll be outside."

Whizzfiddle walked out and moved to an area that was quiet. It was a little spot between Gilly's Pub and Furnitureland.

After glancing around to make sure the coast was clear, he took out his TalkyThingy and searched through the listings until he found "Murray the Mole." He pressed the video button and the little screen lit up.

It began to ring.

Two rings later the face of a mole filled the screen. He was brownish with red eyes and massive black-rimmed glasses.

"Whizzfiddle?" Murray said in his excited voice. He was *always* excited. "Is that you? Is it really you?"

"Hello, Murray," Whizzfiddle said, knowing that he had to speak quickly if he wanted to get a word in edgewise with the mole. "Can you see me? I can see you, but I don't know how this thing works." He flipped over the TalkyThingy for a second. "Gungren showed me the basics of it, but I don't know if I'm doing it right or not."

"It's fine," Murray replied. "This is so exciting. Do you want to play a game? I would love to play a game. Maybe a riddle or a puzzle or something?"

"Actually, I have a search game for you, if you're interested?"

"Search game? A search game sounds fun. Real fun. I love playing games. How does the game work?"

"There are three people that I need to get messages to," explained Whizzfiddle. "I need all three of them to meet me at the Inn of Sargan at the base of the Kesper's Range tonight, if possible."

"I can do that. I know I can do that. I think I can do that, anyway. What do I win if I get them all?"

"Win?" That was a valid point. Games usually did come with the promise of a prize. "Uh...my thanks?"

"Can't ask for more than that," Murray replied seriously.

"Really? I wonder if that's enough for everyone. Probably not."

"Who am I hunting for? I've got contacts all over the place in this grand network of joy you've hooked me up with. I've more friends than I've ever had in...well, ever!"

"Great. Great." Whizzfiddle rattled off the names and details of the three people he wanted Murray to search for. Then he saw Gungren and Eloquen walking towards him. "Okay, I have to go now. Please do your best and, uh...keep in touch."

"That's it?" Murray said, looking somewhat forlorn. "You're going to hang up already?"

"Hi, Murray," said Gungren, causing Whizzfiddle to turn the TalkyThingy to the little giant.

"Hi, Gungren! You still going to play a game of Space Bingo with me tonight?"

"I can't. Sorry. I'm on a quest thing. Will play when I get back, though."

"Oh, that's okay. There will be like fifty of us on anyway." Murray pushed up his glasses. "So is it a fun quest? Good quest? Exciting? Rescuing a princess maybe? Ooh, ooh, maybe you're slaying a dragon?" He said the last bit with a chuckle.

"That one, yep."

Murray's pace slowed dramatically. "Slaying a dragon? You? Really?"

"Yep."

"Oh. Well, it was good knowing you."

"Okay," Whizzfiddle said, taking the conversation over again. "We have to run, Murray. Please work on that task, if you would?"

"On it. Good luck, Gungren!"

"Thanks."

YOU DID WHAT?

Teggins couldn't help but want to reach out and strangle Stillwell.

"You did what?" he said, fighting to keep his calm.

"I spoke with Mr. Pazo and convinced him—"

"I heard what you said, Stillwell," Teggins interrupted. "The problem is that you didn't have authorization to make that deal with him."

The perspiration was beading on Stillwell's forehead like water on a hot griddle. It wouldn't take much to break the guy, literally, and there were undoubtedly another ten who could take the scrawny worm's place, but Stillwell was decent with the books and he was mostly harmless. At least up until now.

"Begging your pardon, sir, but you said that I had to do whatever it took to get the job done."

"Damn. I did, didn't I." Teggins relaxed, leaning back in his chair. He glanced back at Stillwell, who was still visibly shaking. "Well, I suppose you didn't know any better. Besides, it won't be long before Pazo comes to me again for money. He always does."

"As you say, sir," Stillwell replied in a hoarse voice.

"All right, all right. Calm down, Stillwell." He waved at him. "You didn't do anything outside of what I told you to do. As long as you keep it that way, you're fine."

"Thank you, sir."

"Yeah, yeah, yeah." He scratched at the sides of his face. "Look, I want you to handle all of the arrangements for our travel and hotel stay at the event. I want the best. Price doesn't matter." He paused and remembered who he was talking to. "Scratch that. Knowing how you lean on every word, let me alter that last bit. Price *does* matter, but I want something nice."

"Of course, sir."

He studied Stillwell carefully. The guy *was* decent, but a little training went a long way.

"You know what, bring me some options with pricing and all that. I'll choose from your selections."

NOSTALGIA

Crazell was lying on her bed of jewels, recovering from her workout. This was the only place she felt at peace anymore. The diamonds and rubies and emeralds and sapphires all made for an incredible bed to rest her weary muscles.

"My jewels, my jewels, my lovely jewels," she said to them in a loving way. "If only I could spend all of my time with you and never have to battle again."

She rolled over and looked up at the high ceiling of her cave.

"But I can't," she said with a sigh. "The moment I stop fighting in that blasted tournament, I'll have countless challengers showing up at my cave. They'll never let me rest."

Crazell picked up a few of the larger gems and began casually launching them at the ceiling and then catching them when they fell back to her. She often did this when she was thinking.

"I suppose I could always move."

The thought of transporting all of her jewels was daunting, but if it meant a new cave that couldn't be easily tracked, it would be worth it. Besides, if anyone stole from her, she'd hunt them down and kill them. Of course, that would only mean that she'd be found again.

"No, that won't work. I'll never be free. Never!"

And with that, Crazell turned back over and began to sob.

BREADMASTERS

*H*eliok arrived in the bottom of a church in the land of Hazpen, which was located in the Underworld. Hazpen was considered *the* place to go when you were in your retirement years. This wasn't because it was a great place to live. In fact, it was often too cold or too hot. But the younger generations preferred not to worry about the older generations, and so Hazpen was developed specifically with old folks in mind.

"Everyone shut up," said an ogre with the name-tag "Teef" pinned to his shirt. "We got us a new member."

"We ain't supposed to meet until next week," yelled out an orc. Her name-tag read "Choogah."

Teef held up a bag and shook it a little bit.

"This guy just gave us a bunch of diamonds if we would meet now."

Choogah's eyes lit up. "Well, then what are we waiting for? Start the meeting!"

Teef looked to have once been a mean ogre, or at least that was the tale that his numerous facial scars told. He wasn't very large, but that could have been due to his advanced age.

Heliok noticed that most older Ononokinites were shorter than younger ones.

"Come up here and tell us your name and stuff," said Teef, waving Heliok to stand at the podium.

"Up there?" Heliok said, taking another glance around the room.

It wasn't like the place was packed, but he didn't know any of these people. Sure, he could snuff them all out with a snap of his fingers—were he allowed to, anyway—but that was an entirely different thing than having to *speak* to them. He had enough trouble talking in front of four or five people he didn't know. A quick count showed there was double that number here.

"That's right, pal," Teef said.

"But there are a lot of people in the room."

Teef frowned. "What are you, some kind of chicken?"

"I do believe that it's his fear of speaking in public that drew him to our fine Breadmasters group, Teef, no?"

Heliok searched for the person who said that.

It was a troll by the name of "West," and he didn't quite fit in with the rest of them. Most of the people in the room were wearing polyester suits, but West wore a nice silk number with a red tie. He looked completely out of place...in a good way.

"Oh yeah?" said Teef as he scratched his head.

"What is your name, sir?" asked West.

"Teef, you idiot," responded the ogre.

West took a moment before saying, "I was speaking to our new guest."

"Oh, right."

Heliok felt that all of this was strange. A bunch of grumpy

old folks worrying about talking in front of people seemed pointless. Then again, maybe it was their life's ambition to overcome such a fear? Or, more likely, they were all just bored of playing bingo.

"My name is Heliok," he said finally.

"That's a fine name."

"Thank you," said Heliok, feeling quite comfortable with the way this troll was treating him.

"And what is it you do, Mr. Heliok?"

"I'm a Fate."

"I see," West said with a slow nod. "Could you describe what your job as a fate entails?"

"It's Fate with a capital 'F.'"

"Did I say it differently?"

"It just sounded like you were using a lowercase 'f.'"

West bowed slightly. Heliok liked people who bowed to him. It meant that they knew their place.

"My apologies, Mr. Heliok. Now, what does a Fate do, precisely?"

"We do a lot of things." Heliok thought it would take far too much time to list everything that Fates were responsible for, so he just picked the basics. "We run quests, build worlds, make galaxies, and a bunch of other junk. My group tends to yell at The Twelve a lot."

"Well done, Mr. Heliok," West said, clapping his hands as he held a proud smile. "You have just passed your first struggle."

Heliok looked around the room. "I did?"

"Yes, you did. You've just spoken in front of everyone here."

"I..." His eyes opened wide at the realization that he'd done just as West said. "I did, didn't I? And I wasn't even nervous."

"Nor should you be, Mr. Heliok," West stated firmly. "You're a Fate who runs quests, who builds worlds, who makes galaxies, and who yells at The Twelve a lot."

"That's right. I *am* that guy."

"You are, indeed."

"This group is great." Heliok was feeling fantastic. No, it wasn't like there were thousands of people staring at him from the stands, but it was enough. "Thank you for solving my problem."

"You ain't done," stated Choogah.

"I'm not?"

"Uh uh. You gotta write up a paper and present it to the group." She squinted at him. "If you don't, you don't get your Breadmaster card."

"Is that so?"

Teef nodded. "She's right."

"What if I were to hand you another bag of diamonds?" Heliok asked.

Choogah nearly fell off her chair. She stood up and began walking to the podium while fumbling to get something out of her pocket.

"Well, what do you know," she said, "I happen to have a Breadmaster card right here...all ready to go."

Heliok held it up and inspected it.

"But it says 'Choogah' on it."

"Right, that means, uh, 'Graduated with honors.'"

"But *your* name is Choogah, isn't it?"

"Strange coincidence, eh?" she replied proudly. Then she turned to the audience. "Fastest graduate we've had, eh, gang?"

They all applauded, except West.

"If I may, Mr. Heliok," the troll said, "you are being duped."

Choogah grimaced at him. "Stoolie."

"I, however, would like to proffer my services in exchange for a reprieve from my Old Troll's Home." He looked around and sighed. "Even if only for a few days."

"You mean you'll coach me?" said Heliok.

"Happily."

*P*ayne stood inside the Chateau von der Fiamma, which served various delicacies during the UDFC events. It was the only time the place was opened, since dragons didn't tend to frequent it during the between years.

The restaurant was massive, just like all of the buildings in Sed's Point. It went with the territory. If you looked up at the ceiling when you walked in, you ran the risk of getting dizzy. Even the doors were enormous. Of course, they were built using the door-within-door scheme so that each race, regardless of height, would be easily able to enter.

"This is Payne Sawsblade, coming to you again from Sed's Point," she said into the camera. "Today we'll be visiting Chateau von der Fiamma, an oddly-named restaurant that's been considered the top of the town during past UDFC events."

She spun and pointed at the kitchen.

"As you can see, the famous Guy LaYumyum, head chef from The Credian in Gakoonk is training a local dragon on food preparations. Mr. LaYumyum is considered *the* premiere chef in all of the Underworld, so this should prove interesting."

The camera moved in slowly so as not to interrupt the lesson-in-progress.

"When you slice the carrots," explained LaYumyum in a pedantic tone of voice, "you do so with finesse and precision."

The dragon nodded and snagged one of the carrots, cleaving it in half with one of his talons.

"No, no, no." LaYumyum was waving his hands around madly. "This is incorrect." He pushed his cutting board over. It contained paper-thin sliced carrots. "Compare these two carrots and tell me what you see."

"I see carrot pieces," the dragon answered.

"Well, yes, you do. But do you not notice how mine is sliced finely, each with the exact width?" LaYumyum held up two slices that were so thin they appeared almost translucent. "You'd need a measuring tape to spot the difference."

The dragon held up his two hunks of carrot, side by side. "Same with mine."

"While technically true," LaYumyum conceded, "the object is to slice the carrots thinly. Your carrots are fine for a stew or flavorings for a broth—"

"That's what I'm making, then," interrupted the dragon.

To his credit, LaYumyum kept his cool. This was probably a good thing considering that the dragon could make the troll crispy hot in a matter of seconds.

"We're not making a stew or a broth, as you may recall." He opened a book that looked to have been handed down for generations. "We are making a troll delicacy that involves duck, onion, celery, and thinly sliced carrots."

"Why don't we make a dragon delicacy instead?" asked the dragon.

"Because we're not."

The dragon caught him in a dark gaze. "We're in Sed's Point, not Troll's Edge—or wherever it is you're from."

"It's called Gakoonk," LaYumyum stated as if offended.

"Yeah, whatever. The point is that I don't get why we're making a specialty from *your* country when we're in *my* country." The dragon pointed around. "People are coming *here*, not going to Splatoonk."

"Again, it's Gakoonk," the troll chef said irritably. "And we're making what we're making because I said so, you imbecile!"

The dragon's eyes tightened and one edge of his lip lifted. That familiar rumbling of gas began to bubble.

"Did you want to change what you just said to me, guy?"

LaYumyum didn't budge. This was dumb, of course, but clearly he didn't get the memo about dragons not taking well to being talked to in a negative manner.

"I am here to train you to be a master chef in less than a week," the troll said without breaking eye contact. "You have done nothing but question my methods, chop your carrots in half, overpower everything with too much salt, refuse to tenderize the meats, and generally harbor a negative attitude towards this entire venture!"

There was a growl from the dragon, but he didn't attack yet.

"But fine, fine, fine, Mr. Dragon," Chef LaYumyum said in a boisterous voice, "since you are the chef in this kitchen and I am clearly here doing naught more than wasting my time, why don't you tell me what the main ingredient is in this dragon stew you wish to make?"

The dragon bared his teeth and said, "Troll."

HOTELS

*T*eggins looked over the hotel suggestions that Stillwell had provided. It was a pretty thorough list and the suggestions were solid, but it also demonstrated that Stillwell had lived a privileged life before falling under the debt of Teggins.

"You got some decent picks here, Stillwell," Teggins said with a nod. "Not bad at all. Obviously you've lived a little."

"Thank you, sir."

"You seem to be recommending The Dragon Inn most, but the price is pretty toasty."

"I was merely basing my recommendation on the ratings via the Undernet, sir."

"Yeah, I know, but you gotta think about the money too. Not everything is about living high on the hog."

He glanced over the list again. It wasn't all about the lap of luxury in his estimation. There was something to be said about frugality.

"I think I'll go with the Hotel Winged Bastion. More my kind of place anyway. Looks lived in, you know?"

"Not really, sir," admitted Stillwell, "but I shall make the reservations immediately."

"Good."

Stillwell started to leave the office when a thought struck Teggins. Who was going to run things when he was out? He could have Bank do it, but he'd never really trusted the man. Of course, he never really trusted anyone. It was the primary reason Teggins stayed on top. Anyone who had the hutzpah to double-cross him was kept on a very short leash, or sent to the Afterlife, whichever was the safest route for Teggins.

But Stillwell was weak. He barely had enough courage to stay in the room with the crime boss.

"Hold up a second, Stillwell."

"Yes, sir?" said the man in a shaky voice that proved Teggins' point.

"I've been thinking about things a bit. I'll be gone for a few days and I don't like leaving things unattended when I'm out. So I'm going to put you in charge."

The gulp reverberated throughout the office.

"Me, sir?"

"Yeah, why not? You're my right-hand man, sort of, and it's not like you've got the spine to do anything stupid while I'm gone."

Stillwell opened his mouth a few times before finally saying, "But what if people ask me questions, sir?"

"Simple," Teggins replied. "You just answer them like I would answer them, and if you're not sure about something just tell them they gotta wait." He then shrugged. "If they don't like that, they can take it up with me when I get back."

"I don't know, sir. I'm just—"

Teggins interrupted, saying, "I'm getting this feeling that you think I'm asking you if you want to do it, Stillwell."

"You're not?"

"You know me better than that, I hope." He smiled in his

devilish way. "I don't *ask* people to do stuff. I *tell* them to do stuff."

"Oh, yes." Stillwell looked like a man who would have been happy to be anywhere else at the moment. "I understand, sir."

"Good. Now, get me a nice room at the hotel, Stillwell, and then prepare yourself to run this place for a few days."

"As you wish, sir."

GETTING AWAY

*S*ir Zelbaldian Riddenhaur, or Zel, as his friends knew him, crossed the moat bridge and strode through the main gates to the castle. Guards stood to attention as he walked on by, their saluting hands planted firmly against their chests.

It was a beautiful day in the kingdom and the sun shone down on the immaculate grounds that surrounded the main hall. He would have liked to have spent time in his own garden on this day, but duty called and Zel was not one to shirk responsibility. Honor was primary in his book.

"Sir Zelbaldian Riddenhaur," announced the doorman as he stepped into the hall.

"Sir Zelbaldian," Queen Prafia said from her lavishly adorned chair, "is all well?"

It was difficult for things to be unwell in the presence of the queen, for her beauty was without equal. She had long blond hair, supple skin that contained just the right amount of tanning, and rather large…

Sir Zelbaldian shook his mind back to the task at hand.

"All is well in the kingdom, my queen," he replied proudly, "but I must ask for a brief leave of absence."

She place her hand on her heart. "Is your mother in distress?"

"No, my lady."

"Has your father's heart finally given out?"

"Two years ago, my queen."

"Oh, right. Sorry." She was clearly searching for options at this point. "Your wife, maybe?"

"I remain single, your eminence."

"Excellent," she said with hungry eyes. Then she glanced away. "Uh, I mean that saves me from the obvious follow-up question about children."

"None of those either, I'm afraid." He then frowned and chewed his lip. "I don't think so, anyway."

Zel was not the kind of fellow who would do anything untoward, but in his younger years he partook in drink and played the field some. That is until he'd joined the ranks of the military. From that point forward, his was a straight-laced life.

"Right. May I ask the nature of your request, Sir Riddenhaur?"

"I've a friend in need, my lady. He is the one who aided me when I had been changed during the battle where we helped the elves fight against Ikas."

"Whizzfiddle?"

"Yes, my lady."

"Hmmm." She sat a little taller. "What does he require?"

"I know none of the details as yet, my lady," Zel replied apologetically. "I know only that he has requested my aid, and my honor obligates me to assist."

"Of course, of course. How long will you be gone?"

"Five days at most, my lady."

She nodded as she glanced over a booklet that was on a

stand next to her throne. Her quill moved rapidly for a few moments.

"Travel well, Sir Zelbaldian. May your steed be swift and your sword be straight." She then blanched. "I didn't mean for that to sound like innuendo."

"Oh, no, of course not, my lady."

"I wouldn't want you to think that I..."

"I would never think such a thing, my queen."

She frowned at him. "Why not?"

"Hmmm?"

"I *am* a lady, you know? Flesh and bones." She looked somewhat miffed. "I'm the queen, yes, but I'm also a woman with desires just like any other woman."

"I..."

It was clear that she'd just recognized her admission, because her skin went from white to nearly pure red. Her eyes darted about as well. Zel assumed she was checking the faces of those in chambers. Nobody was looking in her direction, which was wise, even if they *did* find what she'd said odd.

"Uh," Zel said, breaking the silence, "I was hoping I could use the portal system because I'm supposed to meet Master Whizzfiddle near Kesper's this very evening...erm, my lady."

"Yes, fine," she said with haste. "Just tell the guards I've approved it."

Zel pulled out a slip of paper and handed it to her. "They require written authorization, my lady."

"Since when?" she said, studying the parchment.

"Remember when we had a bunch of dark halflings running through the town going door to door selling boxes of chocolates?"

"Oh, yes," she replied with a nod. "They were pretending to be school children who were raising money for new orchestra equipment."

"Correct, my lady. That's when you closed down the portal and required a signed letter from yourself for any travel to and fro."

She nodded and dipped the quill in ink.

"I shall make this a roundtrip ticket for you then, Sir Zelbaldian."

"My humblest thanks, my lady."

"And let's just forget about those things I said earlier." She handed him back the slip of paper. "That goes for *everyone* in here."

~

Bekner Diamondcrusher stood in front of key members of his clan.

Ever since he'd fulfilled the prophecy of being the one dwarf who could break through the diamond wall known as "The Glittering Fortress," he had been their king. To be fair, Bekner had been quite a bit taller on the day that he'd broken through that wall. This was because of the spell that was placed on him by the wizard known as Peapod Pecklesworthy. Instead of being a normal-sized dwarf, Bekner was made enormous. If it hadn't been for the help of Master Wizard Xebdigon Whizzfiddle, Bekner would never had regained his dwarfish height.

Now the wizard was asking for help from him, and a dwarf never turned his back on a friend in need.

"Listen up, ye mangy bunch of mongrels," he yelled out, silencing their yammering. "I'm leaving on a trip and will be after being back in a few days."

"Where ye after goin'?" asked Ozzabo, who happened to be Bekner's mother.

"I'm gettin' to that, Ma."

"Well, hurry about it. I've got a loaf of bread in the kiln."

"Right, well, ye all may remember that before I was yer king, I was just simple old Bekner Axehammer."

"I remember," said his mother.

Bekner sighed. "Well, of course ye'd remember, Ma. Yer still an Axehammer!"

"Which ain't much after bein' fair, now is it?" she pointed out while giving him a glare. "Why'd ye get to be gettin' a new name when yer poor ma is left after bein' stuck with her old one?"

"Do ye gotta do this now, Ma?" Bekner said in a pleading voice. "People are watchin'."

"Oh, don't mind me. I'm just yer ma. It's not like I brought ye into this world or nothin'."

Bekner groaned. "Here we go."

"It's not like I scraped and clawed in order to keep hot food in yer belly after yer father went and got himself killed at that brothel," she said, throwing her hands up in the air.

"He *what*?" said Bekner, not wanting to have heard what he thought he heard.

Ozzabo coughed. "Uh, I mean in that huntin' accident near the town of Brothwell."

"Never heard of no town named Broth—"

"And it's not like I was the one who got yer high school teacher to look the other way when yer grades was barely passin'."

"I thought I was after bein' a straight-C student?" Bekner stated.

"Ye wish." Ozzabo crossed her arms and grimaced. "Anyhoo, just forget about your old ma. I'll make do…somehow."

Why was it that his ma always waited for these gatherings to speak her mind? They had dinner together nearly every night and she never said anything, but once Bekner stood on

73

the stage, she opened her yap and let it all out. It was downright embarrassing.

"Oh, for the love of The Twelve," Bekner bellowed. "Fine, as king of the Diamondcrusher Clan, I hereby dub me ma with the name of 'Ozzabo Diamondcrusher.'" He gave her a stern look. "Are ye happy now?"

"Least you could've done," she replied evenly.

"Right. Well, I'm after goin' now." He then pointed at the woman who ran the day-to-day operations for the clan. "Reebo, you're in charge whilst I'm away."

"Why's she get to be in charge?" Ozzabo complained. "She's not a Diamondcrusher!"

"Don't push me, Ma!"

~

Orophin Telemnar finished up his last appointment for the day. It was a bouffant hairdo for one of his oldest customers. Meaning that she was really old, not that she had been coming to him for a long time.

He cleaned off his station and then checked his TalkyThingy for messages. He wasn't supposed to have a TalkyThingy, and he had to keep it quiet, but since his foray into the Underworld during his quest of undoing, he had become somewhat technically savvy.

There was a message from someone named Murray and it mentioned that Whizzfiddle needed help.

"Galania," Orophin said as he approached the owner of Salon DeHairdo, "I need a few days off."

"Sure, sweetie." Galania raised her eyebrow. "New boyfriend?"

"You know I only have eyes for one," Orophin said wistfully.

"Winchester Hargrath III," said Galania while rolling her

eyes. "I know. But *you* know that's impossible. It's been a long time, honey. Let him go already."

"I'm sure I will, but not just yet."

"Just remember that life is short."

"Not for us," countered Orophin. "We're elves, remember?"

"True. Anyway, how long will you be gone?"

"Just a few days, it seems. I'm helping out a friend in Kesper's."

"Oooh!" Galania reached into her purse and pulled out some coins. "Can you pick me up a bottle of Kesper's Red nail polish while you're there? Nobody makes a red like they do!"

PEP TALK

Crazell had finally gotten some rest after bawling her eyes out. It was a solid nap, and she felt rather refreshed. No, she still wasn't happy, but at least she wasn't crying anymore.

"Knock, knock," bellowed Ricky Schmicky as he approached the mouth of her cave.

"You know I don't like anyone coming into my lair, Ricky," said Crazell in a tired voice.

Anyone else who approached would have been rather crispy by now, but she gave lenience to the Schmicky family since they'd been with her for years. In fact, she wouldn't even have half the jewels she'd amassed if it weren't for the Schmickys.

"I know, I know," said Ricky, tipping his hat. "But I'm a friend, yeah?"

"What do you want, Ricky?"

"I saw how down you were at training…" Ricky had taken his hat off now and was holding it respectfully. "Yeah, it's my job to push you and all that, but I'm also here to give you an ear to chew on."

"Don't tempt me," she replied.

"Aw, now, that's not nice. I'm just doing my job, baby!"

And he was. He was also profiting off everything that came from being her manager. T-shirt sales, hats, posters, and so on were all part of the shared revenue between Crazell and the Schmickys. It was fair, though she hated to admit that. Being a dragon caused an innate amount of greed. It couldn't be helped.

"I know you are," Crazell replied with a sigh as she flicked a jewel casually. "It's just not easy being me."

"You mean being revered and feared in the world of Dragon Martial Arts, having more money than most people could amass in ten lifetimes, and having a wonderful trainer and friend like good old Ricky Schmicky?"

"Well, when you put it that way..."

"Craz," he said with passion, "you're an inspiration to dragons everywhere. Knights dream about conquering you, orcs and ogres—the mean type—train for years to defeat you. You're on top, baby!"

"You don't think I know this?"

"Seems like you need reminding from time to time."

If she could do it all over again, she would have won a few bouts to build up her stash and then thrown a fight and retired in disgrace.

She groaned at the thought because she knew damn well it wouldn't have been possible for her to think that way back then. This was made obvious by the fact that she was still fighting now.

Her perspective had changed quite a lot since she had matured to the point where she grasped her level of incredibleness. But when she started fighting, she was a nobody. She'd had to prove herself. Each win built her up, sure, but it only drove her to want more. At least until she started to understand that there were no *real* opponents out there. They were all piddly in comparison to her.

She had nothing left to prove.

But here she was, stuck going into the arena yet again.

"What I want is to forget it, Ricky, not be reminded of it."

"Exactly, and…" Ricky frowned. "Huh?"

"When this all started I had nothing. I *was* nothing." She ran her talon over an emerald. "Your great-great-great-grandmother yanked me out of my cave, which contained little more than a handful of jewels at the time, mind you, and stuck me on this path. I'm grateful, sure, and everything you said is true, but while you've spent only a few tournaments with me, I've been doing this for a very long time." She rolled over again. "I'm tired. I'm bored. The limelight isn't fascinating for me anymore. I want to retire."

"And you can do just that, right after this bout." Ricky put his hand on his chest. "Cross my heart, Craz. Just win number twenty-five during UDFC-100 and you've made a legacy that can never be replaced."

Crazell snorted at him. "And that's when the real trouble starts."

"Why would you think that?"

"Because the moment I retire, the veil of protection comes off. I'll no longer be covered under the UDFC "hands-off" rule."

"So?" Ricky looked quite perplexed.

"So don't you think that every single knight, orc, ogre, gnome, wizard, and anyone else who wants a chance at glory is going to want to challenge me?"

He rubbed his chin. "Good point."

"I'll never get any rest," she said, slamming her tail against the back wall with a snap. "Never!"

The thwack reverberated through the cave, silencing

almost as quickly as it sounded. The only sound remaining was of Crazell's gentle sobs.

Ricky walked up on the jewels and put a comforting hand on her wing. If anyone else had done this, Crazell would have snapped him in two, but Ricky—faults and all—was an actual friend.

"Honestly hadn't thought about that," he said gently. "I mean, I knew, I guess. You *had* mentioned it before." He cleared his throat. "But maybe I just didn't want to know, you know?"

"Yeah, I know, Ricky. I know."

PRODUCTION

*C*org Sawsblade was working with the Fate named Aniok on filming and post-production.

There was always a lot going on for a perfectionist like Corg. People just didn't seem to understand that, but the "it's good enough" mentality didn't sit well with the dwarf. He had a reputation to uphold. Though there was that one shoot for Barn Hunters that he would like to forget, and he hoped everyone else would as well.

Aniok had started out being nearly as useless as everyone else that Corg had worked with in the past. Fortunately, the Fate was a quick learner. Once he'd let down his "I'm more powerful than you" attitude, they built a fine working relationship. If Corg were being honest, though, he'd admit that it was strange being the boss of a Fate. However, it would look great on his resume.

"Ani," said Corg, using the nickname he'd given Aniok, "we're after needin' somethin'."

Aniok looked back at him. "What do you mean?"

"Some pop," replied Corg in animated fashion. "Some zing. And this last bit needs to have pizza!"

"I think you mean pizzazz."

"Aye." His belly grumbled. "I *could* use some pizza, though."

"What did you have in mind?" asked Aniok, giving Corg a studious stare.

Corg shrugged. "I dunno. Pepperoni sounds good."

"No, I mean what did you want to do with the last episode to make it different?"

"Ah, right."

Corg thought about that for a moment. The truth was that he didn't have a lot of ideas on the subject. This was mostly because Gungren wasn't exactly superstar material. If Corg had been working with a leading man or a leading lady, this would have been simple. Alas, that wasn't going to happen.

He set his chin in his hand and studied the screen for a moment.

They'd already done the majority of post-production work on the first two episodes of *Unreal Makeover: Gift of the Fates*, but now they were putting together film for episode three and it was moving slowly.

Seeing as how the first two quests also lacked excitement out of the gate, Corg wasn't too worried about it. He was certain that things would pick up, but he still had to plan ahead because this episode would be in post-production quickly.

"Not sure," he said, musing. "We've got a dumpy little guy getting his body all fixed up by you lot, and that'll play well, but it won't sell beyond that. There were some excitin' bits in the first two quests, too, I suppose." He then shook his head at the UDFC arena that was on the screen. "This last one, though, is gonna either be great or terrible. I doubt the lad will be after lastin' more than a minute in the UDFC. So what can we do to build tension?"

JOHN P. LOGSDON & CHRISTOPHER P. YOUNG

"We could point out that he won't last a minute in the UDFC?"

"Aye," agreed Corg, "but how do we go about sayin' it?"

Misty must have overheard their conversation because she lifted her head from her work.

"Have you ever seen the movie *Pebbly*?"

Corg glanced at her sideways. "Ye mean the one about the gnome who wanted to be a boxer?"

"Yes."

"Was a good flick. Tugged at me heartstrings, it did."

"So why not do something similar with Gungren?" she asked.

Corg didn't reply. He just squinted at her questioningly.

"Based on the information I'm seeing from watching Whizzfiddle's actions," Misty explained, "it looks like Gungren is going to get some training."

"Right."

"So remember when Pebbly was preparing for her fight?" Misty started jabbing at the air. "She was shadowboxing, running, doing pushups and sit ups, and sweating it out while training for her big bout." Misty's face was glowing, and the memory made Corg think that his may have been too. "There was music and everything."

"Aye, there was." He snapped his fingers and pointed at her. "So yer after saying that Gungren should get a theme song?"

"You got it."

He imagined the parts of the show where Gungren was preparing for the fight. Having a theme song playing during his training would definitely bring things to life.

"It's brilliant, lass." Then, since he was trying to include Aniok more often in these decisions, he asked, "Whaddya think, Ani?"

"I've never seen this movie you're talking about, but it's hard to go wrong with a theme song."

"Aye! Let's do it."

THE INN OF SARGAN

The town at the base of Kesper's Range was stunning.

There were rows of shops, taverns, pubs, and houses all around the area. If you stood back just enough and the lighting was right, you'd swear you were looking at a painting. It was one of Whizzfiddle's most favorite places in all of the Upperworld.

"That place am pretty," said Gungren.

"That it is," Whizzfiddle agreed.

He looked over at Eloquen, almost hopeful that the elf would lay out a lengthy description in his flowery way. If any place deserved that kind of flourish, it was Kesper's.

Nothing.

Whizzfiddle shrugged and started heading off to the Inn of Sargan. The place sat on the left edge of town, which meant the troop had to walk past the bakery, the chocolatier, and the cheese shop. The smells pouring out of each were wondrous, until the cheese shop anyway.

"Now, I expect you to be respectful to these trainers,

Gungren," Whizzfiddle said as they approached the inn doors. "They are very good friends of mine."

"I are always respectful," Gungren replied as though his feelings were hurt.

"Yes, I suppose you are." He nodded. "My apologies."

Whizzfiddle pulled open the door and let Gungren and Eloquen go in first.

The place was well lit compared to the likes of Gilly's Pub. There were many tables and a bar that could easily seat thirty thirsty souls. Reds and browns made up the majority of the decor, which was fitting for the area. The innkeeper looked the part perfectly as well, especially with his handlebar mustache, bright eyes, and properly parted grey hair.

Across the room sat three people that Whizzfiddle had not seen in quite some time. They all looked different than the first time he'd seen them, certainly, for now they were normal. Well, at least as normal as they could manage.

"Master," Gungren said excitedly, "it's Zel, Bekner, and Orphan!"

"It's Orophin," complained the elf. "O-R-O-P..." He stopped and sighed. "Oh, never mind."

The troop all hugged and shook hands. Laughs were shared as Whizzfiddle called for a round of the finest available spirits.

"I not know this is who you was gonna have train me," said Gungren.

"I know, Gungren," Whizzfiddle replied with a giggle. "I know."

Gungren hadn't looked this cheerful in a long time. He nearly always had a nice disposition, but over the last few months his buoyancy had waned. "How you guys been?"

"Still actin' kingly and such, myself," answered Bekner with a touch of pride.

Zel bowed his head slightly. "The Queen's Guard remains my home."

"I'm a hairstylist," said Orophin.

"Really?" said Zel.

"No kidding?" Bekner asked.

"Makes sense to me," Whizzfiddle noted. Then he rubbed his scraggly beard and said, "I don't suppose you could maybe do a little trim-up on my beard and hair, if you get some time?"

Bekner pointed at his own mane. "Aye, mine too. Well, not me beard, of course, but me eyebrows could use a bit of a snip."

"Sure," Orophin said. "Happy to do it. Zel?"

"Thank you, no. We have a barber at the castle who leans towards jealousy when we seek out other grooming options."

"I get it."

Orophin seemed to be enjoying the world. In fact, they all did. This was quite the change from when Whizzfiddle had first met them all. That was a dark time in their lives. It made the elderly wizard feel good to know that he had been able to help them return to their solid foundations, and even improve their positions along the way.

"Gungren," Orophin said, "I'm already planning on doing your hair, and also a uniform design for your upcoming match."

"Why?"

"Because you can't just show up wearing a robe and a pointy hat." Orophin wasn't bound to let this go. Style was his thing, after all. "This is not a magical event. Well, seeing all of those musclebound fellows in tights is pretty magical, but I mean *actual* magic here."

Eloquen had been tasked with getting their rooms for the night while the others caught up, so he had yet to be properly introduced. When he had joined them, he was standing behind Orophin.

Having clearly overheard the elf's remark about musclebound fellows wearing tights, Eloquen said, "Fire tickles the soul at the vision of such delicacies."

"Great, he's talking like that again," said Whizzfiddle into his mug.

Orophin spun around and blushed.

"Well, hello there. You are?"

"Eloquen DaNania."

"You sure are a treat for sore eyes," Orophin said. "I'm Orophin, by the way. And this is Zel and Bekner."

The two men nodded uncomfortably at the new elf, who returned their salutation in kind.

He then took a seat and looked at Orophin with dreamy eyes.

"The alabaster pigmentation rests like tranquil waters under the light of the evening star."

"Him say—" started Gungren.

"Oh, I know what he said, honey."

"The rest of us don't," stated Whizzfiddle.

"Him say that he likes Orphan's skin."

Whizzfiddle nodded. "Not surprising."

"Anyway," Gungren said, obviously ignoring the fact that Orophin was currently in the middle of something, "I'm gonna wear my wizard hat, Orphan."

"Again, Gungren, it's not a magical event."

"I not care about that. My hat and robe is who I am."

Obviously Orophin knew Gungren well enough to understand the little giant wasn't going to change his mind. Unless there was a solid reason that made perfect logical sense to Gungren, he would hold his resolve.

"We'll work around it," Orophin said finally.

Whizzfiddle was certain that whatever Orophin made for

Gungren would be too flashy. He noted correctly that the robe and pointy hat didn't make much sense in the ring, but there was little doubt that whatever the elf developed wouldn't be much better. If anything, it'd be worse. Whizzfiddle could only hope that Orophin remembered that Gungren wasn't built like other people.

"What am you guys gonna teach me?" Gungren asked Zel and Bekner.

"I'm gonna be after teachin' how to punch and kick," answered Bekner.

"You?" Whizzfiddle said, nearly spitting his ale back into the mug. "But you can barely lift your feet off the ground."

"Want to test me skills, wizard?" Bekner replied with a sneer.

He *was* an intimidating fellow. "No, I suppose not."

"I shall teach you the skill of grappling," said Zel, interrupting the uncomfortable moment. "Wrestling a man to the ground and pinning him so that he cannot move."

"Visions of desire percolate like dancing bubbles of a refreshing fizzie," Eloquen said in a singsong kind of way.

"You can say that again," agreed Orophin, "but what's a 'fizzie'?"

"It's a carbonated drink that you can get in the Underworld," Whizzfiddle answered for Eloquen.

"Ah."

Before things could loosen up further, the elderly wizard stood up and rapped his knuckles on the table.

"Now, everyone listen to me." The people at the next table turned to him. "No, sorry, I just meant the people here. I'll speak softer." They turned back. Whizzfiddle cleared his throat and lowered his voice. "Firstly, I appreciate that you have come here to help our Gungren prepare for this event. We have a very short time, though, so I ask that we please focus our efforts and build him up quickly."

"Agreed," affirmed Zel.

Bekner and Orophin nodded their agreement as well.

"I'm ready to start whenever you guys is," Gungren stated.

"Good." Whizzfiddle was still standing as he picked up his mug. "First, though, let's make a toast to old friends!"

The rest of them called out, "hear, hear!" in unison.

"And now let's drink another five or so of these."

This time only Bekner called out, "hear, hear!"

HIGHLIGHTS, PART 3

*P*ayne had been looking forward to this installment of her highlights segment for the Ultimate Dragon Fighting Championship.

Today she was interviewing the judges.

These were the people who would make rulings on any untoward activity during the fights. They also had the final say on who would win should the fight not be stopped before the final bell.

This year there were two wizards and one witch. While Payne came from the Underworld, she was given details on the differences between the two practices of magic.

Wizards were stereotypically flighty, lazy, and chilled. Each had to find their own power source in order to do magic. It wasn't something that they could choose, though. The source was preset and they had to figure it out. Some learned their source by pure happenstance, such as the poor wizard apprentice who found her magical essence the day she'd eaten her first peanut. Sadly, she was allergic to peanuts.

Witches, on the other hand, didn't require a power source

to do their brand of magic. They had to put in many hours of study, build up concoctions and potions, and understand the various elements of the world. Plus, if they didn't stay true to their practice, their memories regarding the practice would fade. In other words, they *couldn't* be lazy. If they grew complacent, their witchiness would dissipate. Also, witches were nowhere near as powerful as wizards, but they tended to stick with areas of magic that wizards didn't tend to bother with. Things such as love elixirs, healing arts, and the like. Some witches dabbled more heavily in the wizardish pursuits, but those were few and far between.

"I'm standing here today with the judges for the event," Payne said as the three magic-doers stood behind her. "We have Witch Teresa, Master Wizard Stiermark Argentum, and Master Wizard Sephnedra."

Teresa was originally from the Underworld. She was born to a human mother and a dwarf father. She looked mostly human, though, except for the fact that she had one leg that was sized to fit a dwarf. In order to compensate for this, Teresa had used a wooden prosthetic. This garnered her the nickname "Peg" when she was growing up. Teresa was *not* fond of this nickname. During her youth, she decided that living with the technology of the Underworld wasn't for her. She wanted to pursue magic, but she had learned that her source was to run really fast, backwards. Seeing that her legs were of differing sizes, this was too challenging for her and so she decided on going after witchcraft instead. Once she'd graduated from school, she received approval to move to the Upperworld so that she could study the craft. Teresa did her best to hide her shorter leg, but she always felt that everyone still knew about it, and she was certain they made fun of it behind her back. She would often mishear words to this effect, as well.

Stiermark was a wizard who took being lazy seriously. He

was the king of chill. Even the garden gnomes in the Underworld considered him *too* laid back. He'd been raised to be a blacksmith, but one day in his youth, everything changed. Stiermark had been invited to a big music festival in Ikas. It was called Ikastock, and it had a bunch of bands from all over. They were celebrating love and peace. While there, someone offered Stiermark some mushrooms. Seeing that he was hungry, he partook. But these weren't normal mushrooms. They were the kind that caused all sorts of psychedelic visions. It turned out that they were more than that for Stiermark, though. His response to them was instant. He felt magic filling his veins. A few hours later he saw pink halflings dancing around naked while the trees sang and swayed in unison.

Sephnedra was different from most wizards. She still enjoyed leisurely pursuits, but her pastimes weren't of the standard lay-around-and-do-nothing sort. Instead, she "relaxed" by talking about horses, hanging around horses, and riding horses. Anyone who didn't know her would think that being around horses *was* her power source. It wasn't. Her power came from dancing in ballet fashion, acting as though she were doing some form of figure-skating choreography. This often led to trouble for Sephnedra during quests since suddenly breaking out in dance had a tendency of drawing a lot of unwanted attention your way. Imagine a quest where stealth was a priority, and you can understand why Sephnedra was no longer requested for these sorts of quests.

"Let's start with Witch Teresa," said Payne as she stood by the middle-aged woman who had black hair and the prominent features of a human, though Payne *did* notice some dwarf-like elements, especially as it related to facial hair. "How long have you been a witch?"

"Going on forty years now," she replied.

"Did you ever hope to be anything else?"

Teresa squinted at her. "Did you say 'hop' or 'hope' just then?"

"Uh…hope."

"Ah, well, I always knew I wanted to work with magic. It was a calling for me."

Payne nodded and looked at her biography again, seeing that she was born in the Underworld.

"It's almost as though you'd gotten off on the wrong foot," she noted.

Teresa's face grew dark. "What's that supposed to mean?"

"I just meant having been born in the Underworld, which had to have been challenging seeing that society there doesn't feel comfortable with magic."

"Oh, right. Yes, it was definitely challenging."

Payne smiled uncomfortably and moved over to Stiermark. He wore a grey cape with silver threading around the cuffs. Everything about his outfit was grey, in fact, including the round spectacles that sat over his powder-blue eyes.

"Mr. Argentum, what level of expertise do you feel you bring to this event?" He didn't reply. "Mr. Argentum?" Nothing. Payne waved at him. "Mr. Argentum?"

"Oh, you're talking to me?" he replied in a mellow voice.

"Yes."

"Got it. Just call me Stiermark, yeah? That Mr. Argentum stuff wigs me out."

"Okay, Stiermark," Payne replied with a tight smile. "What do you bring to the event?"

"Mostly a bag of 'shrooms, some snacks, and—"

"Sorry," Payne interrupted. "I don't mean what you *actually* brought to the event. I mean what kind of expertise do you have that makes you worthy of being a judge at the Ultimate Dragon Fighting Championship?"

"Right on," Stiermark said and then looked away.

"Mr...erm, Stiermark?"

"Hmmm?"

Payne gave him a funny look. How this particular judge was selected, she couldn't say, but there was no point dwelling on it. He'd gotten here somehow, so the powers-that-be clearly felt he could bring something to the table.

Looking him over again, she assumed that "something" had to do with bags of funny weed.

She stepped over to Sephnedra and let the camera soak in the tall woman's long blond hair and pale complexion. This wizard looked...elegant. That seemed a bit out of place at an event like this, but it wasn't Payne's place to judge such things.

"Sephnedra," Payne said after a moment, "can you let the audience know the reason you were selected to be a judge at this event?"

"Not a clue," she replied.

This caught Payne by surprise.

"Oh...really?"

"Yep," she said as her eyes focused in on the dwarf. Payne thought it interesting that one eye was brown and the other blue. "I was out riding my horse when my TalkyThingy went off. It was one of the people who run this event. Asked if I wanted to be a judge. Said I had to learn rules and such. I said I wasn't interested, but he offered me another judging opportunity in an upcoming equestrian event if I would do this one." She curtsied. "So here I am."

"*Did* you read the manual?"

"Some of it."

"And what will you do if a rule comes into play that you haven't read about?" Payne asked, furrowing her brow.

"I'll do what I always do," Sephnedra replied. "I'll wing it."

94

HOTEL WINGED BASTION

*T*eggins walked into Hotel Winged Bastion with Lucille and Krag a few steps behind.

It wasn't the classiest joint he'd ever seen, but it fit well with his tastes. In fact, he took a solid glance around so that he could have some contractors who owed him money make some renovations on his place of business. He especially enjoyed the high ceilings.

He walked up to the front desk like he owned the place. If things went his way with this bet—which they would—he may just buy the hotel, so he may as well get the help used to his being in charge.

"Welcome to the Hotel Winged Bastion or whatever," said a green dragon with a surly disposition. "What do you want?"

"Reservation for three, under 'Teggins,'" the crime boss replied without a fuss, recognizing that dragons were known for being grumpy.

"Says here you got a suite for two nights, yeah?"

"Yeah."

"It's only got two rooms, ya know?" the dragon said, peering down at him.

"So?"

It looked past Teggins. "So you got three people."

"So?" repeated Teggins.

"Where are you all gonna sleep?"

"We'll figure it out," Teggins said, thinking how this dragon was being a bit nosey.

"I'm sure you will," the dragon said coldly, "but there are rules—"

"You want me to kill you, dragon?" Krag interrupted with a growl.

While Krag *was* due to fight a dragon in the final match at the UDFC, Teggins wanted to make sure his fighter arrived alive. Regardless of whether or not *this* dragon was currently acting in a customer service role, it wasn't likely that would matter much if it was miffed.

"Excuse me?" the dragon said with a rumble that made Krag's growl sound like a squeak.

"You'll die fast," said Krag, unfazed by the dragon's glare. "Krag the Destroyer takes no prisoners."

The dragon's eyes thinned and Teggins could hear that trademarked sound of flames preparing to be unleashed.

He reached up and grabbed the dragon by the snout with one hand, closing the beast's mouth and held it there. Then he pulled the snout to face him.

"You wasn't about to flame my UDFC fighter, now was you?"

The dragon was clearly not used to this type of treatment because its eyes were very wide.

"Mmmm mmmm," it said.

"Good. I'd hate to have to teach you a lesson, ya know?"

"Mmmm hmmmm."

Two little puffs of smoke exited its nostrils.

"Now here's what's gonna happen," Teggins said in a calm

voice. "I'm gonna let you go, you're going to get my key and hand it over, and then we're going to walk away and think nothing of this incident again." He pulled the dragon in closer. "Capisce?"

"Mmmmpisce."

LEARNING THE ROPES

*G*ungren had a set of makeshift gloves on that Bekner put together for him. They were big, but so were the little giant's hands. Gungren liked the red and green stripes of the tape around his wrists.

They were standing in the basement of the Inn of Sargan.

The barkeep, who also happened to own the place, told them they could workout there as long as they promised not to break anything. He wasn't referring to their bones, but rather his boxes and barrels. At first, he wasn't fond of the idea at all, and were it not for Whizzfiddle's gold coins they would have had to practice outside.

"All right," Bekner said as Gungren hopped around and punched the air, "the first thing ye've got to do is learn to punch the fella in the nethers."

"The what?" asked Gungren.

"Excuse me, Bekner," interrupted Zel, "but I believe that is considered against the rules in the UDFC."

"That's gonna make things tougher."

Bekner started pacing around. He looked to be thinking of other options. Gungren just kept punching the air and jumping around because it was supposed to help him be in shape for the event.

"All right, all right," Bekner said as though a thought had struck. "I've got it. The guy yer after fightin' is gonna have to lean down, yeah?"

"What you mean?"

"'Cause you'll be littler than him."

"Not if him is a halfling," Gungren pointed out.

"Aye, but then you can just stomp him, right?"

"I guess."

"But a big fighter is gonna have to be after leanin' down to knock yer block off." Bekner then made a fist and stuck out his first finger. "When he does, ye poke him in the eye."

"Also against the rules, I'm afraid," Zel noted.

Bekner threw his hands up in frustration. "What in the blazes kind of tournament is this?"

"One that disallows pokes to the eye and punches to the nethers." Zel held up his hand. "And before you ask, kicks to the nethers are also disallowed."

"You're not leaving me much to work with here," complained Bekner.

"Sorry."

"Is he after bein' allowed to hit the guy in the throat with his fingers?"

"No."

"This is impossible."

Bekner plopped down on one of the boxes as Zel continued thumbing through the rule book.

Gungren made a mental note to learn that rule book inside and out. While Master Whizzfiddle was not fond of reading manuals and such, Gungren felt it was the only way to be certain of what you were getting into. Besides, where there were rules, there were exceptions and loopholes.

For now, he would just work on his endurance. He

wouldn't be able to build much up in only a couple of days, and he didn't even have that much time with Bekner and Zel because there was still traveling to do.

"Okay," said Zel, leaning forward. "There is a pretty big list of things he *can* do. He can stab him with a sword, crush his head with a hammer, break every bone in his body, throw him into a flaming pit of doom—if one happens to be available, snap his neck, pull his teeth out one by one, crush his jaw under foot, saw him in half with a razor whip, and many other things that involve weaponry." He spun the book around. "There are at least fifty more items here."

Bekner just blinked. "So he can do all that, but kickin' the guy in the nethers is a no-no?"

"It's considered unsportsmanlike."

"These people are daft."

Zel merely nodded in response.

"Gungren, do ye know how to use a razor whip?" asked the dwarf.

"I doesn't even know what one is," Gungren replied.

"How's about a sword?"

"Nope."

"It's not after bein' that hard," explained Bekner. "Ye take the side with the point on it and stick it in the other guy's nethers."

"Can't do that either," announced Zel.

"What? Ye just said you couldn't punch him or kick him in the nethers. Ye didn't say nothin' about a sword to the nethers bein' out-of-bounds!"

"Anything to the nethers is against the rules," Zel stated.

"Fine." Bekner breathed out heavily. "Anyway, usin' a sword is easy. Ye stick the pointy end of it in the guy's stomach." He tilted his head a Zel. "That's after bein' allowed, right?"

"Oh yes, most certainly," came the emphatic reply.

"Madness."

It *did* seem a little strange that you were allowed to kill someone in the ring in any number of ways, but some things were listed as unsportsmanlike. In Gungren's estimation, the entire sport was a bit twisted. Beating people to a pulp so you could get a belt and some money didn't make sense to the little giant. Killing each other over it was even worse.

"Can ye be after doin' that, Gungren?"

"Doing what?"

"Sticking the pointy end of a sword in another fighter's belly."

"I can, but I not want to do that." He shook his head seriously. "I not want to kill anybody."

"Kill or be killed," argued Bekner. "This is war!"

"He's right, Gungren," Zel said more calmly. "You have to expect that your opponents are going to do whatever they can to take you out of the fight. That includes killing you."

"I know, but that don't mean I got to do that."

Bekner dropped his head into his hands and groaned. "This is gonna take some effort."

"Yes," agreed Zel.

PREPARING FOR THE INTERVIEW

$\mathcal{H}$eliok sat in his office across from West. The elderly troll was the vision of dapperness. His suit was pressed, his posture was straight, and his demeanor was professional.

"The first thing you must do," instructed West, "is hold yourself in proper esteem."

"I'm not sure what you mean," replied Heliok, feeling confused.

"Your confidence, good sir. You must not allow it to wane."

"Ah, right. That should be easy." He leaned back and placed his hands behind his head. "Remember, I'm a Fate."

"A Fate who attended a Breadmasters meeting due to a fear of public speaking, no?"

Heliok resumed a more suitable seated position. "I see your point."

"Not to worry, sir," West said, crossing his legs. "We must merely adjust a few simple aspects of your thoughts and you'll be unfazed at the prospect of gaining the podium."

The troll pulled a card from his pocket. It was rectangular

with lines on both sides. On the front was some writing that West spun to face him. This revealed the back of the card, which read "#1." He then retrieved a pair of reading glasses and put them on.

"First, you will have either memorized what you will say or you will have a teleprompter to aid you along."

"That could be a problem," said Heliok. "You see, Misty asks her questions in real-time. I never know what she's going to ask until it comes out of her mouth."

"I shall remind you again that you are a Fate, sir."

"I don't understand your point."

West lowered the card, dipped his head slightly, and looked over the rims of his glasses at Heliok.

"Are you not able to put a stop to time if you wish?"

Heliok shook his head with fervor. "No, I'm afraid not."

"But you're a Fate," West said with a frown.

"Which merely means that we are far more powerful than The Twelve, who are far more powerful than you." Heliok sighed. "There are always limitations, West."

West removed his glasses and pinched the bridge of his nose. He didn't seem angry or frustrated, but there was clearly an issue.

"This is disappointing," the troll said finally. "I was rather hoping I could find a measure of promise out of aiding you in your cause."

"Is that your concern?" Heliok said, louder than he needed to. "Worry not, then! I shall make this a Fate Quest for you."

"Sorry?" said West, lifting his head.

"If you succeed in assisting me to overcome my fear of public speaking, I shall provide you with whatever you wish...within reason."

"By definition, it would not be whatever I wish if it must be within reason," argued West.

Heliok shrugged. "What would you wish?"

"A young body, long life, and a never-ending supply of money," replied West without hesitation.

"Done."

"Truly?"

"Certainly, my man. That's all within reason." Heliok then grinned and added, "I'd also say that you are rather clever in selecting as you have."

"What do you mean?"

"Well, West, most people ask for only one item. I never correct them, but I do find it amusing when they could have so much more."

West's demeanor changed again. He now wore a face that was a mixture of relief and pride.

This was great for Heliok, since he now knew West would pull out all the stops to help him.

"Right," said West, putting his spectacles back on. "Now that we have that resolved, I have a plan for helping you with card one." He tapped the edge of the card on his knee. "Are you able to increase your rate of thinking?"

"Of course," Heliok answered without delay.

"Is that not effectively the same thing as slowing down time to those who are less powerful than you?"

Heliok often wondered why he didn't understand all of the things that Ononokinites said to him. He assumed it was because he was so much more powerful and intelligent than they were, but wouldn't that mean that he would be able to grasp anything they threw at him?

"How do you mean?" he asked, feeling rather deflated.

"If I were to ask you a question and you had no immediate answer, could you not increase your speed of thought to such a degree that it would give you ample time to come up with a solid answer while making it seem as though only a second had passed from my perspective?"

Why hadn't *he* thought of that? Certainly there must be some reason…

Heliok paused and slowly began to nod. It was because his mind was full of more important things. Coming up with cunning ways around the fear of public speaking was beneath him.

Still, this was an incredibly bright suggestion that West had provided.

"That's sincerely brilliant, West."

"It's a gift," West stated as a matter of fact.

"What's card number two?" asked Heliok as West began tucking the cards back into his pocket.

"Honestly, my good Mr. Heliok, if you can manage thinking faster than the rest of them, you don't need any cards at all."

EXPLORING THE TOWN

hizzfiddle found himself bored with just sitting around as Gungren trained with Zel and Bekner. He would have spent time with Eloquen and Orophin, but he had no eye for design and they both seemed to be enjoying each other's company enough that Whizzfiddle would have felt like a third wheel.

So he headed out to survey the shops and such.

He wasn't much for walking in and out of stores, but now and then there was a gem of a place that sold interesting trinkets. One need only look around Whizzfiddle's home to see that he collected a lot of odd knickknacks. He felt that it livened up his place.

He passed by all of the primary stores, seeing not much more than clothiers and the like.

But then his eye caught a mid-sized gypsy-style building. It was on large wooden wheels, and it was painted in all sorts of colors, giving it a very robust visual for the passerby. The paint job was tastefully eclectic.

A little wooden stand outside said, "Living Audio" on it.

This piqued Whizzfiddle's interest and so he stepped inside and looked around.

There were many boxes lining the walls, each having artwork and a title. It looked as though they were music discs of some sort. This was rather interesting considering that they were in the Upperworld. Whizzfiddle had seen these items in the Underworld many times, and he *did* find them quite interesting, but the locals in this area would have found this as nothing but odd.

"Welcome to Living Audio," said a youngish dwarf with the name "Sonic Missedhammer" sewn into his shirt. He was clearly standing on some type of platform because he wouldn't have been able to see over the counter otherwise. He was also looking at the door, even though Whizzfiddle had moved over to one of the racks of discs. "What can we be after doin' for ye today, madam?"

"First off," Whizzfiddle stated, "I'm over here. Secondly, I'm not a madam."

A tall elf walked in from the back room. The name on his shirt read "Willowy Wordsworth."

"Did you call me, Sonic?" he said in a voice that was made for oration.

"Why would I be after callin' you 'Sonic?'" asked Sonic. "That's my name!"

"I'm asking if you were yelling for me to come out here?"

"Ah, nay." He pointed at the wall. "Someone came in. Nice elderly lady, from the sounds of it."

Willowy looked over and nodded at Whizzfiddle.

"It's a man, Sonic." Willowy then said, "A wizard, if I'm not mistaken?"

"That's right," answered Whizzfiddle.

"Well, why didn't ye say so?" Sonic bellowed. "We've got many audio delights for wizards, ye know?"

"I did not know," Whizzfiddle said, "and I'm standing over here now."

"Ah hah!" The dwarf spun and faced the back wall. "Yes, ye are."

Willowy spun his business partner to face Whizzfiddle.

"Thank ye."

"Don't mention it." The elf placed his hands on the counter and smiled at Whizzfiddle. "So, what are you looking for today, sir?"

"I'm just browsing."

"Ah," said Willowy with a wince, as if he knew something was about to go horribly wrong.

"Just browsing?" yelped Sonic. "Just browsing? Why are people after always just browsing?"

"All right now, Sonic. Let's not irritate our customer."

"What customer? Customers purchase things. It's in the blasted definition of the word!" Sonic harrumphed. "He's not a customer, he's a browser."

Willowy looked confused at this statement. "What? You mean one of those things that you can look at the Undernet with?"

"The underwho?"

"The Undernet," explained Willowy. "I'm sure I've told you about it."

"You know about the Undernet, eh?" said Whizzfiddle. "I know you're an elf, but I assumed you were born and raised in the Upperworld."

"He's an elf?" said Sonic. "That's disheartening." Then Sonic seemed to catch himself. "Wait...did I just hear the voice of a customer?" He turned to the back wall again. "What can we be after gettin' for ye today, madam?"

"It's still me and I'm still not a madam," Whizzfiddle stated, finally grasping that the dwarf was blind.

"Don't mind him," said Willowy. "He's lost his marbles, is all."

"I have not," argued Sonic. "They're right here in my pocket." He fished around for a moment. "Hmmmm, that's strange. They were after bein' here earlier."

Whizzfiddle waved at the elf and pointed at his own eyes as if questioning whether or not the dwarf was indeed blind. Willowy nodded slowly.

"I brought back a case of gnome brownies after one of my travels to Hubintegler," said Willowy a moment later, "and he's been eating two a day for the last week."

"Ah, right."

Whizzfiddle understood that.

Gnome brownies were the type that made you relax quite a bit. They were great for aches and pains. If fact, some places in the Underworld allowed doctors to prescribe them to help treat various ailments. But they *did* have side effects, especially in the way of withdrawal. These side effects had nothing to do with the funny weed. It was completely due to the fact that gnomes used a lot of sweetener in their brownies. Sugar was a very addictive thing, after all.

"Speaking of brownies," said Sonic, "are there any left? I have the munchies."

"See?" Willowy said to Whizzfiddle while raising his eyebrow.

"See? No, I cannot see, and you're after knowin' that, Willowy." The dwarf puffed out his chest as he pointed accusingly at a potted plant near the back wall. "You're fired!"

"Right," Willowy said while shaking his head. "Okay. I'm fired." He leaned in near Whizzfiddle. "Fires me at least three times a day."

"I heard that!"

"And yet you stay?" mouthed Whizzfiddle.

Willowy waved off the point. "He'll forget in a few minutes. Again, they were *gnome* brownies."

"Indeed. It's unusual to see someone get irritated when eating those." He glanced again at Sonic. "Even a dwarf."

"Oh, he was mostly chilled out for the week, but he ate the final one last night before bed, so the withdrawal phase has begun."

"Ah."

Yep, that made sense. If you didn't keep a steady supply rolling after you got hooked, you would indeed become quite irritable. Seeing that dwarves were renowned for being innately grumpy, tacking on gnome brownie withdrawal spelled for a very rough combination.

"Who is that you're after talkin' to, Willowy?" said Sonic suspiciously.

"It's a customer, Sonic."

"A customer? Well, why didn't ye say so?" He spun again. This time he *was* looking at Whizzfiddle. "Welcome to Living Audio. What can we get for you today?"

"Honestly," Willowy said with a hint of remorse, "he was much more with it before the brownies, but he was more relaxed on them."

"You have brownies?" asked Sonic hopefully.

"Why not just order more?" Whizzfiddle suggested.

"Already had a heck of an adventure getting them through customs the first time." Willowy winced, obviously replaying a memory. "I'm not sure if you've ever had a full cavity search, but they're not exactly what you'd call fun."

Whizzfiddle winced too, recalling his own memory of having gone through it during Gungren's prince-retrieval quest.

"In fact, I have, and I would agree with your assessment." He glanced over at Sonic, feeling sorry that the elf had to deal with an aggravated dwarf. "I know a guy who knows a guy who can get you a regular shipment, if that would help?"

Willowy's face registered hope. "Honestly?"

"Sure. They can ship through UUPS, and they never go through customs checks. Too many shipments and not enough customs agents." The elderly wizard shrugged. "They simply scan each box to make sure there are no Underworlders trying to stow away for a trip to the Upperworld. As long as there are no insects or lifeforms detected, it gets past."

"Perfect!"

"What's perfect?" said Sonic, squinting in a way that only dwarves could. "And who is that you're after talkin' to, Willowy? Are ye doin' crazy voices again for some story yer plannin' to read?"

"Again, it's a customer, Sonic."

Whizzfiddle spoke up. "Would it help if I purchased something?"

"It'd help me," announced Sonic.

"Is there something particular you're looking for?" Willowy asked a moment later.

"Me?" replied Sonic. "Not really. I suppose a nice single-story cottage, a tolerable wife, and a bushel full of diamonds would be nice, but that's not going to happen, now is it?" He grunted and then breathed out heavily. "If I were being honest, I'd settle for a brownie."

"I was speaking to our customer, Sonic," Willowy pointed out.

Sonic stood up straight again. "We have a customer?"

ENDURANCE

*G*ungren was running behind a small carriage that contained Zel and Bekner. He was doing all that he could to keep up with them, but he didn't have the longest of legs. Plus, he was already tired from punching and wrestling.

"You've got to put your back into it, Gungren," Bekner yelled from his comfortable position.

"I are trying," Gungren replied, mostly under his breath.

"Maybe we're pushing him too hard?" said Zel.

"He's only after having a couple of days before he's in the ring," Bekner countered.

Zel nodded as Gungren kept sticking one foot in front of the other.

"True," said the knight, "but if he's too sore to fight, it won't do him much good anyway."

"That's why they invented ice baths."

"That's true, but his battle skills are more important than his fitness level." Zel motioned at Gungren. "He'll never outrun anything, so it may be best to just keep teaching him the ropes as it relates to fighting."

"Aye," Bekner said with a critical eye. "Ye may be right. All right, then."

He called out for the driver to stop so that Gungren could get in, but the little giant saw a small hill that looked similar to the one that the fighter in Pebbly climbed. He had never watched a full movie before, but Zel and Bekner thought it would be motivational for him, so he viewed the entire thing. He had to agree with their assessment, too. It *did* motivate him. In fact, there was one scene in the movie that he wanted to reenact right now.

"One second."

He turned and ran up the embankment. It made his legs burn, but once he got to the top, he felt elated and accomplished. He started jumping around like he'd won the day.

A few moments later, he looked down at Zel and Bekner, finding that they were gawking at him as though he had lost a couple of screws.

~

"We'll work on punches again," Bekner announced after they got Gungren's gloves back on.

"I know how to punch already," Gungren complained. "I been doing it all day."

"All right," Bekner said with measured defiance, "let's see it, then."

Gungren looked at his gloves. "What you mean?"

"Punch me in the head."

"I not want to hurt you," said Gungren while shaking his head.

"You'll not be after hurting me, Gungren. Dwarves have heads as strong as rock. Let me show you."

Bekner picked up a loose board that looked to be oak. It

was thick and appeared quite sturdy. He lined himself up with it and then whipped the board against himself. It broke in half—the board, not the dwarf's head.

Bekner grinned.

"See?"

"Yep."

"Good. Now, punch me in the head."

"Okay," Gungren said reluctantly, "if you am sure."

"I am. Now, do it!"

Gungren planted his back foot and threw a right cross while twisting his hips. It was the same type of move he'd learned when throwing rocks as a full giant. That's how he could get the most distance from a rock throw, so he figured it would also be effective in getting the most power from a punch.

He was right.

Bekner fell over and was lying on the ground with his eyes rolled up into their sockets.

"I believe you've knocked him out cold, Gungren," Zel said, looking shocked as he stood over the dwarf.

"I not mean to. Him told me to punch him."

"Yes, he did, but I doubt he had any idea that you had that much power in your fists!"

Zel picked up a small jug of water and dumped it on the dwarf. He roused and sputtered. His eyes were still glassy as he surveyed the area.

"What happened?" he asked while shading his eyes from the lanterns. "I feel like I've been drinking too much, but I don't remember after bein' in a pub." Then he glanced around. "And what's with the sound of little birdies chirping?"

"Gungren punched you in the head," Zel explained, "and knocked you out."

"What'd he do that for?"

"You told him to."

Bekner wobbled. "I did?"

"You were testing his fist strength and punching acumen."

"Oh." His face contorted as he sat up and put his back against a box. "Gungren, you have passed me test, it seems."

"Thanks, Bekner. Sorry for your head."

"Not your fault. I was born with it looking this way."

"No," said Gungren, "I meant punching you too hard."

"Ah, right. Not to worry. It's why we're after being here. Maybe it's time for grappling though, eh, Zel?" He rubbed his head again. "I'm gonna sit down for a while."

"You *are* sitting down," Zel said.

"Am I?" Bekner opened his eyes slightly and checked his surroundings. "Huh, I guess I am. Okay, well, I'll just be after keeping on sitting down for a while. You two go about rolling around and whatnot."

SCOPING OUT THE ARENA

*T*eggins, Lucille, and Krag snuck into the arena to take a look around. They checked the workout facilities, took notes, and then moved out to the field where Crazell was training.

She was flying up and then swooping back down, ripping various dummies in half with her massive talons. Then she'd do a barrel roll and fire flames at suits of armor. Her preciseness worried Teggins.

"That's a very red dragon," said Lucille.

"Meaner than the green ones," Teggins noted, "but they tend to be more emotional."

"So?"

"So, Lucille, where there is emotion, there is weakness."

"Ah." Lucille nodded for a moment and then said, "So?"

"So your job is to exploit that weakness." Teggins watched as Crazell used her razor-sharp teeth to rip into a dummy. "You need to find a way to make sure Krag will win."

"I don't need help," Krag stated darkly. "I'll kill the dragon."

As if in defiance of Krag's statement, which couldn't have been heard on the field, Crazell released a flame that fried all the remaining practice dummies on the field.

Teggins had witnessed dragon flames over his years, but Crazell's fiery belch made them all look like simple candle wicks in comparison.

"You *do* need help and you'll get help," Teggins said to Krag. "Now shut up about it."

Krag turned to face Teggins. "I don't like being spoken to in that way."

Teggins turned to face him.

Krag had the height advantage and he certainly looked more muscular, but Teggins knew his own strength. Teggins also knew how to fight dirty.

"Is that so?" he said menacingly. "You might be able to beat a dragon, but don't mess with me, Krag. I make dragons look like kittens. The cute kind."

"Is there any other kind?" asked Lucille.

Teggins blinked in confusion. "What?"

"You implied that there were kinds of kittens that weren't cute," explained Lucille.

"Yeah, that makes no sense." Krag's irritable disposition had changed to one of contemplation. "I'm more of a dog person myself, but kittens are adorable."

Lucille nodded. "Exactly what I'm saying."

"All right, enough about kittens." Teggins wanted to punch them both, but he held himself in check. "The point, Krag, is that you are going to do this *my* way or I'll string you up by your toenails." Krag gave him a doubtful look. "And before you go judging my ability to do it, note that I've done it before. It wasn't pretty, and those nails did pull out, but the ogre I did it to hung upside down by them for a good four minutes first."

"That's a disturbing image," Lucille said with a sour look.

Teggins spun and pointed at her. "And you, Lucille, are going to figure out a way to make sure Krag wins." He narrowed his eyes. "If you don't, that toenail thing will be a picnic compared to what I'll do to you."

NEED ROOMS

hizzfiddle was enjoying a nice bowl of stew while sitting at the Inn of Sargan. Gungren was seated with him. The rest of the crew were either back in their rooms resting or making a night of it.

"How is your training going, Gungren?"

"It okay, I guess," he answered between bites. "I are pretty sore."

Whizzfiddle wanted to correct his sentence but knew the little giant would just question why Whizzfiddle was sore, so he let it go.

"We'll have to pick up a healing potion from one of the shops. I know you can't use them at the event, but I'm doubtful there's a rule against using them beforehand."

"Nope."

He took another bite of stew, when a thought hit him.

"Oh, no," he said, lowering the spoon. "I've just thought of something."

"What's that, Master?"

"We don't have any lodgings prepared in Sed's Point."

Gungren shrugged. "Can just sleep outside."

"In the land of the dragons?" Whizzfiddle scoffed at the notion. "I don't think so. I know that the dragons are supposed to be on their best behavior, but one slip-up would make us into a meal. No, thank you."

"Maybe Heliok can set up—"

"No, no, no." Whizzfiddle had been down the path of counting on the Fate before. "He'll just make a fuss about it and then, out of spite, he'll put me in a room with a draft."

He took out the TalkyThingy and grunted at it. While it was a marvelous way to communicate, there was just something *wrong* about a wizard using technology. Then again, it *did* allow him to follow the primary pursuit of wizardry. That being laziness.

Back when he'd first visited the Underworld, he found the technological robustness of the place to be rather daunting. Terrifying, if he were being honest. People speaking to each other over vast distances with these little boxes pressed to their heads, large rectangles that showed live animated images of people across the continent speaking about national news, weather forecasts that were never accurate, computing devices that could outpace the fastest orc in mathematics, horseless carriages, and countless other things. But then when he learned that those in the Underworld were just as scared of magic as he was of technology, he relaxed. If *he* wasn't afraid of magic and *they* weren't afraid of all their gadgetry, then neither of them should be worried about the other's mode of operation.

"I'm going to call Murray," he said.

"Him seem to be a good contact you made," Gungren noted, looking very worn out.

"I quite agree."

The TalkyThingy rang and was picked up immediately this time.

"Hello, Whizzfiddle! You're calling me again so soon?"

The mole pushed up his glasses. "I'd not expected to hear from you for a while. Did those guys you asked for get to Kesper's? I told them it was very important. Said that you said they really needed—"

"They're here, Murray," Whizzfiddle interrupted. "You did a great job. So good, in fact, that I was hoping you could help me solve another problem."

"Happy to do it! What are friends for, right?" Murray scrunched his nose. "I mean, sure I'm still getting used to the entire 'having friends' thing and all, but it seems to me that friends help each other. It's what we do."

"Right, right, right! Correct." It was difficult keeping Murray on track. "So, Gungren and I need to have lodgings for the upcoming fight in Sed's Point."

"You haven't got a hotel yet? It's going to be packed. This is the biggest event in all of Ononokin. You really should have planned this out."

"Yes, well, we didn't have much notice."

Gungren spoke up. "Should just get Heliok to do it."

"And I will if it comes to that, Gungren."

"Oh, Gungren's there?" asked Murray.

"Hi, Murray," Gungren called out.

"Hey, Gungren." Murray motioned Whizzfiddle to spin the TalkyThingy around. Whizzfiddle reluctantly complied. "I know you're in training for that fight—good luck, by the way—but if you get out of it alive, I've been thinking of getting an actual poker game going. The kind where people come over and play and have herbal tea and chips."

"That sound fun."

Whizzfiddle spun the TalkyThingy back as he frowned at Murray. "Am I not invited?"

"Huh?" Murray looked suddenly put upon. "Oh, well, yeah, sure you are. It's just that I didn't think you'd want to hang out with a bunch of people who are only a fraction of your age."

"Hmmmm."

"I...uh..." Murray was fishing for ideas. "Oh! I could set up a bingo night for you, if you want?"

"Never mind about that," answered Whizzfiddle, feeling rather old indeed. "Can you get the rooms or do I have to contact that blasted Fate?"

"I can do it," Murray stated confidently. "I have a really good friend at Hotel Winged Bastion. He'll get you in."

PRESENTING TO BREADMASTERS

$\mathcal{H}$e didn't need to do it, but West had convinced him that practicing again in front of the Breadmasters while using his new technique would solidify its effectiveness. This would mean that Heliok could relax when the actual interview occurred.

Another bag of diamonds brought in a large enough crowd to make the Fate nervous.

West was up on the podium explaining the situation to the Breadmasters members. A few of them had already fallen asleep, which was understandable considering the age of the people involved. It *was* past their normal bedtime, after all.

"And so Mr. Heliok will come up and answer questions at the podium," West was saying. "Your questions should be tough but fair."

There were a few nods.

West waved Heliok to join him and then covered the mic for a moment.

"Just do as we said," the troll stated in a supportive voice. "Introduce yourself and ask for questions." Obviously noting that Heliok was a bit pensive, West added, "Remember that you are a Fate who can outthink everyone here."

Heliok nodded and then gulped as he stared out at the sea of faces. He *knew* he shouldn't have any issue speaking to them, but his mouth went dry and his nerves were on edge. His heart was racing like mad, too, making him remove that part of his anatomy. It wasn't like he needed it anyway. He was just using the physical image of a human so that people would accept him. The inner workings didn't matter.

It helped.

How actual people dealt with their blood pressure shooting up was a mystery to him. He *hated* that feeling. It was dreadful.

"You may recall that my name is Heliok and I am a Fate." He cleared his throat and fought to keep his voice from quivering. "I am awful..." He paused, thinking how that was the wrong word. "Erm, I mean, I am *offering* you the chance to ask any questions of me you may have."

He began repeating "I'm a Fate" over and over in his head. If he could just remember that, and subsequently remind himself that the people in front of him were mere mortals, he was confident that his sensibilities would rule the day. His stomach churned, though. He removed it from his innards as well.

"Again," he said with some effort, "anything that I'm *allowed* to answer by way of Fates rules, I will."

Teef stood up.

"If you is a Fate and all, why you gotta come to a Breadmasters meeting to work on talking in front of people?"

"Uhhh...well...it's rather complicated." Heliok took a deep breath. "I...uhh...well..."

"Remember, Mr. Heliok," West whispered from his spot off to the right, "speed of thought."

"Oh, yes. Right." He turned back to Teef. "That's a fair question." Then he kicked up his thought speed until he had a full, well-thought-out response. He slowed his mind back down and said, "You see, Fates are hidden in the background for the most part. We do not seek the limelight, but rather create a God, or gods as the case may be, to garner your praise. Therefore, when we are thrust into a position of needing to discuss matters in a public manner such as this, we tend to get rather flustered."

"If you ain't supposed to be in the limelight," said Choogah, "then why are you doing this at all?"

"Yes, well, that's an excellent question too. We, the Fates, need you to know that we exist, but we don't want you to praise us, if that makes sense?"

"Nope."

"No, I suppose it doesn't at that."

He sped up his thoughts again, built a solid response, and returned to normal. This was actually turning out to be a wonderful idea on West's part.

"Well," he spoke fluidly, "imagine you developed a computing device. Folks took this device and created tons of wonderful applications for it. Those people get a lot of glory for their creations, but you, the one who created the device that made those creations possible, are barely ever mentioned. Would that not bother you?"

"Do I get paid for the computer?"

"I would imagine so, yes."

"Then what do I care?" Choogah said with a shrug. "Money's rolling in. I got a nice place to live, a butler, and all the food I want. The money is praise enough for me."

"Exactly," agreed Teef.

"Okay," Heliok said, pursing his lips. "Imagine you *don't* get paid, nor do you get any recognition. What would you say to that?"

"I'd say that my business manager is gonna be fired," answered Choogah with a serious look, "and quick."

Teef nodded. "Punched in the head, too."

"Yeah, that."

"Obviously this was a bad example..." began Heliok.

"That may be, Mr. Heliok," West interrupted, "but did you notice that once you employed your ability to think speedily, you no longer suffered through your words? In fact, I would imagine that the Breadmasters would even agree that you spoke quite majestically."

"We would?" said Teef.

Choogah appeared uncertain. "I dunno about that."

West pointed at the bag of diamonds that Heliok had provided for the event.

Choogah and Teef glanced at each other with wide eyes.

"I mean, top-notch speaking there," announced Choogah. "Best I've heard in some time."

Teef was quick to agree. "A regular wordsmith, that one."

Heliok felt somewhat deflated, but he had to admit that the general principle was sound. He would just need to practice some more and not simply go with the first thing that came to mind. Speedy or not, his responses needed to be solid.

Still, in the grand scheme of things, this new method was promising, especially the bit about removing his heart and stomach. Just in case, he removed his bladder as well.

"I think I'm good now," he announced. "Let's go, West."

OUTFITTING GUNGREN

*O*rophin and Eloquen completed Gungren's new outfit. It was made of a stretchy material that seemed to be riding up some on the little giant.

"Could you at least make it a color other than pink?" asked Whizzfiddle.

Orophin put his hands on his hips. "What's wrong with pink?"

"Look at him," said Whizzfiddle with a grand gesture.

"I think he looks adorable," Orophin stated, "in a snubbed-nosed-dog kind of way."

"Etchings of frills to float upon the crest of bouncing would ever increase the reflective lights abounding."

"True," Orophin agreed while giving Gungren another look.

At some point Whizzfiddle would have to learn the ins and outs of Eloquen's flowery language. Either that or he could just stop bothering to understand it. Considering the study it would take, he opted to just keep things as they were, relegating himself to continually ask for translations.

"What did he say?"

"Him thinks there should be more stuff hanging from the suit," Gungren replied while pulling the material out of his rear end.

"This isn't the ballet, gentlemen," Whizzfiddle shrieked. "He's going to be out in the middle of the ring fighting for his life!"

"Hmmm." Orophin had turned to holding his chin thoughtfully. "It's a good point. So you think putting in taffeta would be too much?"

"Of course I do." Whizzfiddle just stared at the elf as if he were bonkers. "By The Twelve, man, I think the pink is too much." A thought struck that would solidify his position on the matter. "You're still planning to wear the robe and hat, yes, Gungren?"

"Yep."

"Put them on, please."

The little giant walked over to the table, pulling the stretchy material down multiple times. He then put on the robe and hat and spun around.

"Well, that's just dreadful," Orophin stated in a monotone voice. "He looks like a pimp."

"Daggers of variant hues stab the visual plane in a cacophony of anguished designs," agreed Eloquen, cringing.

"Him say…"

Whizzfiddle nodded at the little giant. "Yes, yes, I got that one." He glanced at Orophin. "Well, then, unless you plan on redesigning his robe and hat, I'm guessing you'll be going with something other than pink."

"Begrudgingly, yes."

FEELING HIS OATS

The entirety of the situation just felt wrong to Stillwell. He wasn't the type of person to sit in this chair. It was the chair of a mob boss, for goodness sakes.

But Teggins had given him this task, and failing Teggins was more terrifying than sitting in the man's chair.

A knock came at the door and an orc walked in, not bothering to wait for a signal to do so.

Stillwell knew the orc as "Bank," which may or may not have been his real name. He was one of the many goons that frequented Teggins's office. While Stillwell was considered Teggins' right-hand-man, he was still new to the position and therefore hadn't fully caught up on whatever everyone's job was. Slowly, though, he'd get there.

"Yes, Mr. Bank?" he said, trying to look the part.

"Name's just Bank."

"Okay," Stillwell replied. "What can I do for you, Bank?"

"Teggins said you was in charge while he's out, right?"

"Yes."

"Seems dumb to me, but I ain't the boss."

Bank paused and studied Stillwell. Was he checking for a

response that may have showed weakness? If so, he was going to be disappointed. At least for now.

"Anyway," Bank said, dropping the study, "we got a guy who wants to borrow some coin for betting on the upcoming match. Says the dragon's gonna win again."

"So what's the trouble?"

"Ain't no trouble that I know of. We just ain't allowed to approve guys borrowing money unless the boss says it's okay."

"Really?" Stillwell said with a laugh. "That sounds like a slow process."

"I been sayin' that for years," Bank agreed.

There had to have been a reason that Teggins didn't just up and approve people for these loans. The first thought was that maybe the crime boss wanted to verify that a person had the ability to pay things back, but Stillwell doubted that. Teggins was known for *wanting* people under his thumb, so collateral didn't seem to matter much.

"Is there some specific reason that Mr. Teggins made this requirement?"

"Other than him bein' a control freak, ya mean?"

"I suppose so, yes."

"We had a guy way back in the day that didn't do any background checks on people wantin' money. Ended up costin' the boss ten gold 'cause the guy ran away and we couldn't find him. Since then, he stopped allowin' us to approve loans without him."

Ah, so it wasn't whether or not they had the wherewithal to pay back the debt, it was to do with their ability to get away untraced.

But ten gold seemed like a small sum to a fellow like Teggins.

"Ten gold?" Stillwell said in disbelief. "That's all?"

"You obviously ain't gotten to know Teggins very well,"

chuckled Bank in a not-so-pleasant way. "He'd sell his own ma for ten gold."

Stillwell crossed his arms. "I find that hard to believe."

"Ask her. You can find her working in the laundry room at Hotel Gakoonk."

"See? She's employed there, so—"

"Ain't no employment about it," interrupted Bank with a slow shake of his head. "Ten gold. It's how Teggins got into the business in the first place."

"You're kidding," replied Stillwell, feeling shocked that Teggins would stoop so low.

"Nope."

Every day it seemed information came out that degraded Teggins' ethics even further. At this point, Stillwell was starting to wonder if the crime boss was even able to spell the word "ethics." It was obvious that he certainly didn't know—or didn't care—what the word meant.

"So, you gonna approve this guy or what?"

"I...uh..."

Stillwell wasn't sure what to do here. Teggins *had* left him in charge, but he'd also told him to just act in accordance to whatever he thought Teggins would do. But Stillwell was too new to all of this. A guy like Bank understood the situation far better.

"I'm going to let you make that call, Bank," Stillwell stated.

Bank stood up straight at that. "Seriously?"

"Yes."

"All right, but it's your neck, not mine," Bank pointed out. "He left *you* in charge, remember?"

"Then I shall have to hope that you'll be thorough."

UPDATING THE BOSS

*M*isty had to return to her office in the Underworld to have her weekly meeting with Knuds Grutch, her boss. He was an orc who had a traditional mohawk, a war tattoo that covered most of the right side of his face, and very thick tusks that stuck up from his lower jaw.

He was not what you would call a pleasant person, either. Then again, seeing that he was a business orc, that was to be expected.

This all came from the fact that orcs used to be ruthless killers, back before Ononokin society threatened genocide. Being rather intelligent, the orcs accepted a treaty that forbade them from attacking with weapons ever again and, as a race, they did. There were small factions now and then that rose up, but that was true of most any race. Since that treaty, orcs had moved from fighting on the battlefield to fighting in the conference room. In other words, they took their warring ways into the world of business. And they were *very* successful at it.

"It's been a few months since you've started this *Unreal*

Makeover project, Ms. Trealo," Mr. Grutch said in his gruff voice, "yet I have not seen it airing."

"That's because it needs to go out with a bang, Mr. Grutch," she replied, trying to sound enthusiastic.

"*You're* going to go out with a bang if it doesn't air soon, Ms. Trealo."

The orc often used threats to make his position known. This was another trick of the trade for orcs in business. Their threats were ironclad, too. An orc worked tirelessly to ensure that all angles were covered before they took steps to squash someone under foot.

But Misty was a dark elf, and that meant she was equally as cunning. Where most races would not see the angles that orcs nearly always left open as they closed their grip on a person, Misty saw quite a few.

So she played her return volley.

"I don't take kindly to threats."

"And I don't make them lightly." Mr. Grutch interwove his fingers as he leaned forward, placing his elbows on the desk. "We've already discussed our positions and how your position is one that can make no demands of my position. Now, when is this show airing?"

She sighed, continuing her part in this act.

"We had to wait for the final leg of the Fate Quest. Now that Gungren is heading off to the UDFC event, we have an end date. This means that commercials are in the process of being built and everything."

"When, Ms. Trealo?" he asked again. "When is the first episode airing?"

"There will be a lot—"

"When?" Mr. Grutch said directly.

Misty wanted to retaliate. She wanted to throw zinger after zinger at the orc. She wanted to pull forth a blade and stick it right in his neck.

But where would that get her?

Jail, likely.

"Two weeks," she answered without inflection.

"Coinciding with the new seasons of countless dramas and comedies on television?" the orc said in a raised tone. "Are you mad?"

"With what we have, sir," she answered, "nobody else will stand a chance."

He stared into her eyes as if surveying her level of honesty.

She didn't waver.

"You'd better hope so, Ms. Trealo," he said finally. "You'd genuinely better hope so."

FAREWELL, MY FRIENDS

*I*t was time for Whizzfiddle, Gungren, and Eloquen to get on the road. The event was right around the corner and they had to get all checked in and ready. Gungren would at least need one good night's sleep before taking the field.

"Do you think he's ready?" Whizzfiddle whispered to Bekner and Zel as Gungren was over speaking with Orophin.

"Who?" said Bekner.

"He's talking about Gungren," Zel answered before Whizzfiddle could.

Bekner scratched his head and then winced. It was obviously still hurting him.

"What about Gungren?"

"That punch really did a number on him, didn't it?" Whizzfiddle asked Zel.

"What punch?" said Bekner.

"Clearly," Zel replied. "Anyway, I would argue that Gungren is as ready as he's going to be with only a couple days of training."

Whizzfiddle took a deep breath and sighed. How could Heliok and his band of Fate idiots think this was a good idea? They had to know Gungren didn't have a chance in the upcoming bout.

But what did they care? Obviously they just wanted to watch some Ononokinite suffer through things. That was abundantly clear by the fact that they were having people film the entire event. It was the primary reason that Eloquen was with them, after all. Not that he was filming or anything, but rather that he....

Whizzfiddle paused his thoughts and looked over at the flowery elf, wondering exactly *why* he was with them. He knew Corg Sawsblade, the dwarf in charge of video and production, wasn't all that fond of the elf, but why not just send him back to the Underworld? It wasn't as though the elf had brought much to the table during all of these quests, except for a funny language that Whizzfiddle could barely understand. Gungren seemed to enjoy the elf's company, and Eloquen *had* stuck by Gungren's side during the entire Major Wiggles incident. Maybe the elf didn't know what to do and so he was just tagging along as a friend? It was the only thing that made any sense.

"I can say that he took very well to grappling," Zel said, bringing Whizzfiddle's thoughts back to the topic of fighting. "I've never seen anyone learn so quickly. He's exceedingly strong. But there is much to learn, so I focused on three moves that should help him." The knight then called out to the little giant, "Gungren, do you remember the three things I taught you?"

Gungren nodded as he walked over. "Arm bar, square choke, and rear-nudie choke."

"Arm bar, triangle choke, and rear-naked choke," Zel corrected him. He then looked at Whizzfiddle and added,

"The names aren't important anyway. He just needs to know how to perform them."

Whizzfiddle shrugged. "I just want him to survive."

"I want that too," Gungren agreed.

Zel patted the little giant on his shoulder. "And as far as you know, Gungren, you will."

"And even if he doesn't, he'll look super," Orophin declared.

Whizzfiddle nodded appraisingly. "I have to admit that the simple black robe you designed is far more appealing against the backdrop of the purple robe and hat."

"He still looks like a pimp," admitted the elf, "but with that robe there's not much of a way around it." Orophin seemed cheery about his work. "I also loosened the lower half some so that he wouldn't have to worry about it riding up on him as much."

Gungren did seem more comfortable than he had in the pink ensemble. At least he wasn't tugging at the fabric anymore.

"Right." Whizzfiddle held out his hands. "I greatly appreciate all of you coming to aid our Gungren in his time of need."

"We are forever bound in honor and friendship," said Zel in his knightly way.

"Aye, that we are," agreed Bekner. He suddenly looked up. "Does anyone else hear bells ringing?"

Zel glanced at him. "Again, it's your head injury, Bekner."

"I've got a head injury?"

"It was delightful seeing you all again," said Orophin. Then he gave a naughty grin to Eloquen. "It was also lovely meeting a new friend."

"The heart soars along the breeze of a cloudless night as precious gems illuminate in the glow of the moon," replied Eloquen with a wink.

Gungren whispered. "That were just lovey talk."

"Right." Whizzfiddle cleared his throat. "Are you all heading back home?"

"Actually," answered Zel, "we are planning to stay here so that we can watch the match together." He pointed to the stairs that led to the basement. "There is a screen of magic down there that the innkeeper said we could use."

"It's called a television."

"Hmmm?"

"The screen of magic," explained Whizzfiddle. "It's called a television."

"Ah. I never know the magical names for things."

"It's not a—" Whizzfiddle stopped.

There was no point in trying to explain it. Zel knew enough about the Underworld to know the device wasn't truly a magical item, but if that's how he needed to view it in order to keep his mind from balking at the concept, so be it.

"Well, I want to thank you all again for your help. You have been true friends, and should you ever have need of our assistance in the future, you need only ask."

And with that, they all shared hugs and goodbyes before Whizzfiddle, Gungren, and Eloquen walked towards the nearest Underworld portal.

STUDYING THE COMPETITION

eggins was sitting on the balcony, watching as workers flowed in and out of the arena.

He wasn't planning to interrupt the flow of things, but once his bet cashed in and Krag was crowned as the new champion, he would start weaseling his way into the system. Within a few months he'd be the majority shareholder, and by the time UDFC 101 started, he'd have everyone working for him.

Lucille stepped outside, holding a roll of paper.

"I've been working on something here that I think you should see," she said as she unfolded it across the small table that Teggins had been using to hold his drink.

"What is it?"

"It's a map of the city."

"I already have a map of the city," Teggins replied, holding up his TalkyThingy. "Shouldn't you be doing research on the fighters instead of building maps?"

"Just look at this." She pointed at the map. "Notice the dots moving around?"

"Ah, yeah," Teggins said thoughtfully. "That's a new piece of technology, eh?"

"It's magic."

"Ah."

Krag walked out and was staring at the map as well.

"Those dots represent each of the fighters who have already arrived in town," she said with a hint of pride.

"Interesting."

Teggins liked this kind of use for magic. It made sense to him. There was no turning people into toads or making them fall in love with someone else. This was the art of manipulating circumstances for *his* benefit. He supposed the toad thing *could* be used for that, too, but he preferred the time-honored snapping of kneecaps when exacting punishment.

"So you're tracking them?" He nodded. "I like that."

"I thought you might approve."

"I do, indeed. Gives us a lot of chances to take out a potential threat, should the need arise."

"Gah!" said Krag before storming off the balcony.

Lucille giggled. "He really doesn't like that we're helping him win, does he?"

"Who cares what he likes?" Teggins said with a flip of his hand. "This is all about me getting a solid payout."

"Right."

"If Krag gets a little glory along the way, so be it."

What did Teggins care? Actually, he thought about that for a moment. If Krag jumped up on a high horse after this event, it would make for a splendid fall in UDFC 101.

One thing at a time.

"I just want to make sure I have the maximum bang for the buck on this venture. That means that we have to make him look good all the way until he wears that belt."

"And this map will help," Lucille agreed, plucking the parchment.

"Yes, I think it may." He nodded appraisingly at her. "Good work. I'll make sure you get an extra silver in your pay."

Her eyes lit up mockingly. "A whole silver?"

"Watch yourself, Lucille. You're easily replaced."

"Only if you're willing to pay more than a silver."

WIMAT STATION

imat station was one of the nicer portal stations. This was due to the fact that the majority of wealthier lands connected to it.

But that didn't mean it was entirely safe.

In fact, Wimat was known for having a problem with scrags. This was the name given to those who hid in the shadows and mugged people if they got off the beaten track. Sometimes, though, when the guards weren't around the actual portal area, the scrags would take advantage of new arrivals.

It was all about timing, and Whizzfiddle wasn't exactly known for having great timing.

"Keep your eyes open for trouble, Gungren."

"You mean scabs?"

"Scrags," Whizzfiddle corrected.

"Sinister intent rests upon the visage of a duo with destinies forthwith."

"Him say there am two bad-looking guys walking over here."

Whizzfiddle glanced over and spotted the two ruffians

headed their way. Neither of them looked all that threatening, but living on the streets had a way of teaching people how to take care of themselves, regardless of their size. Fortunately, money typically made them go on their way since they didn't want to attract too much attention. Guards could easily show up in the area at any moment, after all.

"Indeed," he said with a sigh. "They probably just want coins, but sometimes they can get a little rough."

"We could use magic," Gungren suggested.

"Remember that Wimat doesn't allow magic except in the case of self-defense."

"That what this would be."

"True," conceded Whizzfiddle. "Unfortunately, Wimat officers genuinely dislike magic, Gungren, and that means that we'd be spending a week being questioned." He met the little giant's eyes. "You'd miss your match."

"That not be a good thing." He then began to slowly nod. "Oh, I remember now. We fought them guys in the cafe thing."

"Precisely, and the only reason I got out of the grip of the security team for using magic was because you, Bekner, Orophin, and Zel were there to intimidate the captain."

"Yep."

"The disquietude of our consensus resists lastingness," Eloquen whispered.

"Him said that we am too late."

Whizzfiddle blew out a heavy breath and turned to face the two gentlemen who had arrived. They were both wearing ratty outfits that marked them as being in difficult financial situations. Under normal circumstances, Whizzfiddle would do what he could to assist them, but he was adamantly opposed to their means of procuring funds. Aiding criminals was not something Whizzfiddle felt comfortable with.

"How you gents doin' on this fine day?" asked the taller of the two. He had a greasy smile that matched his hair.

"Look like they's travelin' too heavy to me, Skillz," said the smaller one, who had a similar look to his friend with the exception that one of his eyes appeared to have a mind of its own.

"I think you may be right, Reapy," agreed Skillz.

"Thanks, Skillz." Reapy bowed slightly. "I do what I can."

Even though giving in to criminals was bothersome, Whizzfiddle had to keep focused on Gungren's quest. They had a timetable to keep.

"We don't want any trouble," he said as he begrudgingly pulled out his leather purse, "so how about I give each of you a nice silver from my bag here and we all walk away from this unscathed?"

Skillz's eyes widened. "Probably could've gone about with a silver, except that you made a bit of a judgment error, old fella."

"I did?" said Whizzfiddle, frowning.

"Plain as day, too," Reapy noted.

Whizzfiddle gave Skillz a questioning glance. "What?"

"Ya went and showed us your purse full of coins, gramps."

"Ah, right." Whizzfiddle groaned. Why did he always want to search for the better part of people? "I'll have you note that I dislike being called 'gramps.'"

"Sorry, pops," Skillz amended.

"That's not much better."

"See," interjected Reapy, "the thing is that now we's gonna want more than just a couple of silvers in order to be on our way."

Whizzfiddle could just wait them out. There was bound to be a guard coming through at any minute now. The problem was that he wasn't sure precisely when that would happen. So far neither of these two had pulled a weapon, and seeing that he didn't have his flask in hand, that put him at a disadvantage.

"Fine," he said with a groan. "One gold each, then."

"So you've got gold coins in there, eh?" Skillz said, his eyes twinkling.

"Blast," cursed Whizzfiddle.

"You not very good at this, Master," Gungren noted.

"How's about you just hand over the entire bag, pops," suggested Skillz, "and we'll call it a day's work?"

"I don't think so," Whizzfiddle replied, growing weary of this discourse.

"You wouldn't want things to get rough, would you?" Reapy asked in a dark tone.

"Actually…" He started to reach for his flask, but stopped. "Gungren, do you think you could do what you did to Bekner, but maybe not so hard?"

"Punch them in the head?"

"Right."

"Yep."

"What's a Bekner?" asked Skillz a moment before Gungren's fist connected with his noggin.

It was lights out as the scrag crumpled to the ground with a thud.

His partner in crime had his hands up in an instant, clearly shocked regarding the power that Gungren carried in his fists.

"Hey, hey, hey," he said as he got out of reach of the little giant. "I don't want any trouble."

"You didn't have any problem with it when you were trying to steal my coins," Whizzfiddle spat.

"We wasn't stealing nothin'," retaliated Reapy. "You were giving it to us!"

"Oh, sure, right," Whizzfiddle said with contempt. "Out of the goodness of my heart, no doubt?"

"Right," answered Reapy. "Sure. Whatever you say."

It was Whizzfiddle's turn to give the scrag a dark look. He pointed at the young man with a sinister finger and said, "You've got exactly three seconds to skidaddle or I'll have my young friend here do to you what he did to Skillz."

"All right, all right, I'm going."

And he started going, leaving his friend lying by Gungren.

"Wait," said Whizzfiddle as he pointed at Skillz. "Aren't you going to take him with you? You can't just leave him there."

"I also can't drag him away in three seconds."

"That was just a figure of speech. Take him and go."

"Sure thing, gramps.... Erm, I mean, pops.... Erm, I mean..."

Whizzfiddle threw up his hands. "Just get moving!"

HIGHLIGHTS, PART 4

*P*ayne wasn't allowed inside of Crazell's lair, so she waited for the dragon to exit the arena. Normally, Crazell would just fly home, but her manager, Ricky Schmicky, promised a quick interview in order to help build even more interest in the event.

"We're here with the reigning champion of the Ultimate Dragon Fighting Championship, Crazell, and her trainer, Ricky," Payne said. "Crazell, this is a momentous occasion for you and the UDFC because it's the one hundredth event and you winning it would mark the twenty-fifth in a row. How does this make you feel?"

"Tired," came the dragon's blunt reply.

"Haha," said Payne, finding it excellent that Crazell was using humor. "Very good. But seriously, how do you feel about all of this?"

The response was in the same tone. "Tired."

"Oh."

"What Crazell is saying," Ricky jumped in, "is that she's tired of all these lowlifes thinking they can challenge her."

Payne had the feeling that wasn't the case, but seeing that

147

the dragon wasn't giving her much useful information, she decided to focus in on Ricky. He was her promoter, manager, trainer, and everything else, so he would put a nice spin on things.

"Go on," she urged.

"Right," Ricky said as his hands suddenly got animated. "For two hundred and forty years she's reigned supreme in this event, but they keep comin'. It's a wonder they even bother."

"I'd imagine it's the indomitable spirit of the warrior," Payne debated. "They always seek to challenge themselves."

"That *is* what brings the crowds, eh?" Ricky agreed, rolling with Payne's commentary. "And let's face it, there *could* be that one fighter out there who might be able to best Crazell. You never know."

Ricky was quite the salesman. Even though it was his own fighter he was talking about, he offered up just enough doubt to tighten the hook on any potential viewer who may have been on the fence about forking over ten gold to watch the event live.

"That's very true," she agreed, doing her part to add some influence, "and with this being an anniversary event, the fighters are raising the bar this time around." She then turned back to the enormous red dragon. "There's promised to be some incredibly strong competition this time around. How does that make you feel, Crazell?"

With a groan, she merely replied, "Tired."

A NEW ARRIVAL

"*T*he rest of the fighters have arrived and I'm tracking them all," said Lucille as Teggins walked into the living room.

She had the map on the table and there were tiny dots flying all over it. There were sixteen fighters, not counting Crazell. It was a standard elimination tournament. Sixteen would battle, leaving eight, then four, and finally two. Whoever won that last battle would face the champion. Teggins knew that would be Krag, because if it wasn't, Lucille was going to suffer his wrath.

He had familiarized himself with all the fighters, but there was one missing, seemingly replaced by a new entrant.

"Who is that one?" he said, pointing.

"Oh, one of the fighters became sick and so there was a replacement added," she answered. Then she tapped the dot and said, "His name is Gungren."

"Gungren, eh?" Teggins had heard that name before. "Sounds familiar."

"Does it?"

"Yeah." He couldn't quite place it. "Who is his manager?"

"Xebdigon Whizzfiddle," she answered as if she were familiar with the man.

"Ah," Teggins said at length. "Yeah, that's what I thought. Whizzfiddle was a friend of my old mother. And as I recall, this Gungren fellow was a wizard, of sorts." That made him relax. "No magic is allowed to be cast in the ring, though, so we don't have to worry about that."

"Nope," Lucille agreed.

Teggins rubbed his chin as he lowered himself in a chair that seemed to cry as he did so.

"But why would a wizard go to fight in a UDFC championship? And why, specifically, would Whizzfiddle be involved?"

"That, I don't know," she admitted.

He nodded at her.

Again, it wasn't like this Gungren had a chance of winning, especially since he was disallowed from casting magic in the ring, but Teggins didn't like leaving things to chance. If there was some angle that this Gungren fellow may have, the crime boss wanted to know about it.

"I'm thinking you need to find out," he said to Lucille. "Just in case."

THEME SONG

*C*org and Aniok had all the workout footage for Gungren pieced together, but something was missing.

"It's after needin' somethin', Ani," Corg said while staring at the screen. "I like the footage mostly, but there ain't no oomph."

"I thought it was pretty great the way he knocked that dwarf out," Aniok said, chuckling.

"Didn't see that comin'," agreed Corg. "We dwarves ain't exactly soft on the noggin', ye know?"

"Obviously Gungren's got one heck of a wallop."

Corg nodded. "As much as a smithy's hammer, I'd say. Probably more." He pointed at the screen when Gungren started running away from the little carriage. "I'm after liking the little bit here of him scootin' up that hill and throwin' his arms in the air like he's just won somethin'. But there's just…" He stopped and snapped his fingers. "The theme song we yammered about. Where's it after bein'?"

"Oh, that's right," said Aniok as he grabbed his data pad. "Let me check to see if that's come in yet." He tapped for a moment and then said, "Yep. There are three options. Let me sync the first one, and here we go."

A song came on that sounded like carnival music. There were horns, and bass drums, and what sounded like an accordion. Corg had no clue how that was supposed to fit with this project at all.

"That's awful," the dwarf said. "Sounds like it's after bein' for clowns and whatnot."

"Agreed. Let me try the next one."

It was better than the carnival music, but not by much. The sound was dark and creepy. There were strings playing in discord, using a minor key and everything.

"That's even worse," Corg stated. "He's not after killin' nobody." Actually, it might come to that, but Corg assumed it would be Gungren getting the worst end of the stick. Still, they were looking for excitement, not dread. "What kind of daft twits did ye ask to create these, ya loony Fate?"

"My brother's kid."

"Is he after bein' five years old?"

"In your years he's more like five thousand years old."

Corg scratched his beard. "Do yer type mature slowly or somethin'?"

"Let's try the third one," said Aniok, clearly ignoring Corg's insults.

This one fit the mold. It was upbeat with full orchestration. The vibe was powerful, just as a soundtrack for this type of show should be.

"Now, yer talkin'! That's a right soundin' tune. Gets the blood pumpin' and such."

"It really does, doesn't it?"

"Aye," Corg said with a firm nod. "Now, if'n ye can get your screwy nephew to take that and make it longer than ten seconds, we'll have somethin' to work with!"

MY NEW ASSISTANT

*H*eliok was well aware that he'd promised to give West a fine reward for helping him with public speaking, but there was a chance that the troll might want something even better.

"You have done a wonderful job in helping me, West."

"Happy to do it, sir," West replied with a slight bow. "Once we are through the final interview, you'll be all set."

"And then you'll be young, wealthy, and long-lived," Heliok said.

"Indeed."

Heliok tapped his desk.

"There is another option for you, if you're interested."

"Oh?"

Heliok stood and walked over to the window that overlooked where Lornkoo and Mooli worked. They wouldn't like what Heliok was about to offer the troll, but that only made it sweeter. He did so enjoy toying with his underlings.

"You could work for me for a while." He glanced over his

shoulder. "With all of the privileges that go along with that, of course."

"I'm listening," replied West in a smooth voice.

"Imagine learning how to build worlds and rule over them," said Heliok. "There are many steps involved and loads to learn, but I'd be here to help you every step of the way. Why, if you do well enough, you may even be deemed worthy of ruling a planet much like The Twelve do today."

West looked to be seriously considering this offer. How could he not? It wasn't every day that something like this came along. As far as Heliok knew, it had *never* been offered to a non-Fate before at all. But West had an air about him. He seemed *worthy* of being with the Fates. Heliok couldn't quite place *why* that was, but he felt it.

"Could I not do what it is you do?" the troll asked.

"Sorry, no," replied Heliok as he returned to his seat. "You're not a Fate and I'm afraid there's no such thing as converting to the level of Fate, either. But being similar to The Twelve is not a shabby proposition."

"It *is* interesting, I'll grant you." West was drumming his fingers on his knee. "And how long would I have to serve as your assistant?"

"Until such time that you're ready. There is no specific way to measure that. It's all on you."

"So it could be one year or one million years?"

"More or less, yes," answered Heliok. "Again, it all depends on you. Your honesty, your cunning, your craftiness, and your ability to maintain high standards of work."

"I've never had a fear of working hard." The troll's drumming was faster now. "In fact, I prefer it over being stagnant. Doing nothing is rather dull, even with a young body, a long life, and tons of money."

Heliok had no real point of reference to confirm or deny this claim.

"If you say so," he said noncommittally.

West grinned in a sad way. "Let's just say that I was young once, thought for certain that I'd never grow old, and I inherited a king's ransom at the age of nineteen." He glanced away. "I wasted all of it."

"Ah, yes," Heliok said, coming to terms with what the troll was talking about. "I've seen that story unfold more times than I can count. However, you now have the benefit of wisdom, no?"

"Not where money is involved," admitted the troll.

"Yet you'll have an unlimited supply of money, so you may spend it as freely as you choose."

"That *is* true." He glanced up at Heliok with creased eyes. "Now it almost sounds like you'd prefer I took the money instead."

"On the contrary, I'd rather you didn't. But the fact is that I wouldn't want you here if your heart was somewhere else. I need full commitment."

"Until such time that I can become a god of a new planet, yes?"

"Correct," confirmed Heliok.

This was one sharp troll, that was for sure. He would do well working alongside the other Fates, and he'd already proven himself to be quite a help to Heliok.

"So the question really becomes whether or not I wish to remain young and have eternal wealth," said West, "or if I wish to live forever as a god."

"Sort of," answered Heliok.

"Sort of?"

"Well, gods only live forever if the planet that they're overseeing doesn't destroy itself."

West's eyebrows went up. "And if it does?"

"The god is destroyed with it," answered Heliok seriously. "Failure to do one's job effectively is a serious offense to the Fates."

"Hmmm," said West as his eyes darted about as if seeking reasons for leaving. Finally, he looked at Heliok and said, "I would think that this opportunity would be foolish to pass up."

"Hard to argue that."

"May I have a trial run of one hundred years?"

Heliok tilted his head. "You mean like a probationary period?"

"Correct."

"Interesting." Heliok thought about it for a second. It would actually be a good idea for both parties. Just because West had been a great asset so far, who was to say that would last? "I think we can manage that."

"Then I shall accept your offer."

"Excellent," Heliok said as he walked to the door. "Let me introduce you officially, then."

They walked out of the office and stood at the railing, looking down on Mooli and Lornkoo. Both of them appeared to be playing a game of solitaire on their data pads. It was so hard getting good help these days.

"Listen up, you two," Heliok called down. "Now, you already know that West here has been assisting me as of late, yes?" They both nodded. "Well, I've just offered him a probationary position as my personal assistant and he's accepted."

"That's not fair," yelped Mooli as she set her data pad down. "Why do you get an assistant? We do all the work."

"Yeah," agreed Lornkoo.

Heliok was taken aback by that comment. How could they imagine that they did all of the work? *He* was the one who built The Twelve, not them.

"What? I do more work around here than you two put together, thank you very much."

"Sure you do," said Lornkoo in a sarcastic voice.

Mooli grunted. "Yeah. It's amazing you get any sleep at all."

"Are you two being sarcastic?" asked Heliok.

"I believe they are, sir," noted West.

"This is patently unfair."

"Agreed, Lornkoo," said Mooli, looking at her counterpart. "It's downright ridiculous."

"Your protests have been noted," Heliok said, which meant that he took their complaints and decided to ignore them. "It's the way it is, I'm afraid, and the sooner you accept that, the better things will be."

"Whatever," said Mooli.

"Lame," noted Lornkoo.

These two were ever annoying. They either didn't do their jobs or they did poorly at their jobs. Where they excelled was at complaining. But now that Heliok had a first line of defense, that being West, he would hear a lot less of their whining.

"Anyway, not much will change. You will merely have to schedule all of your meetings with me through West. He will be the keeper of my calendar and such."

"That sounds like he'll have a lot of control," Mooli said.

"Yeah, it does," Lornkoo added.

"Worry not, my friends," West spoke up. "I'm sure we'll get along swimmingly." They were just staring at him, but the troll had a way about him that Heliok found impressive. "I have no wish to stand in anyone's path, and you have all the motivation in the world to make sure not to ruffle my feathers. As long as you don't, I'll have no reason to ruffle yours."

Heliok smiled proudly.

"Oh, yeah," he said, "you're going to work out just fine."

SWEET SUITE

"Welcome to the Hotel Winged Bastion," said the dragon to Whizzfiddle as he approached the front desk. "What do you want?"

Whizzfiddle was used to dragons, having been on numerous quests to swipe jewels from their caves. He'd been asked to go on dragon-slaying quests, but he never accepted those as he felt that hunting was wrong. Now, he had been on a quest to aid in defending a town against a dragon who had been tormenting it, but that was a different thing altogether.

"We have a reservation for three," the elderly wizard said.

The dragon looked past Whizzfiddle. "I only see two."

"Yes, the other is bringing in the luggage."

"So it's really three plus luggage, then?"

"Well, yes," Whizzfiddle said as if judging the dragon's intellect, "but luggage should be considered a standard item, no?"

The dragon squinted. "Are you in hotel management or something?"

"No, but I have stayed at many of the best hotels in the

world, so I have a flair for this sort of thing." He pulled his sleeves up a bit. "Plus, people do tend to travel with extra clothing."

"Okay, I guess that's true." The dragon rolled its eyes. "Whatever. What's your name?"

"Xebdigon Whizzfiddle."

"Well, why didn't you say so?" the dragon said, pulling its head up higher and looking down at Whizzfiddle with big eyes.

Whizzfiddle was confused by this. "Um...I wasn't asked?"

"Murray is a great friend of mine, you know?" the dragon stated.

On one hand, this was quite surprising; on the other hand, Whizzfiddle had been learning that Murray was a dynamo when it came to socializing. He'd only had his computer and connection to the Undernet for a little over a month and he was already networked to more people than Whizzfiddle had known over his life...and that was a lot of people.

"He is?"

"Absolutely," answered the dragon. "You see, the dragon community has been trying to set up an online poker club for years. We have computers because of the UDFC tournaments coming into the area, meaning that people came in from the Underworld and we all became instant online personalities. But we wanted to have our own community for playing cards." He leaned in closer and whispered conspiratorially, "We're not exactly good with being physically around each other or other creatures for very long, you know?"

"You don't say?" Whizzfiddle said in mock surprise.

"It's true." The dragon pulled away. "Well, just a few weeks back this fellow named Murray started to show up in the various rooms. Nice fellow and seems to be an exceedingly fast learner."

"No arguing that."

"Well, he learned of our dilemma and created a private poker site for us dragons. We allow Murray to play, too, of course, but he's the only non-dragon." He leaned in again, this time glancing left and right before saying, "Truth be told, we've been considering making him an honorary dragon."

"Now that would be something."

"I know, right? Anyhoo, any friend of Murray's is a friend of ours."

"That's...great."

And it was.

One of the many lessons Whizzfiddle had learned during his life was that it was *always* a good idea to help others, even if it was difficult or uncomfortable to do so. First off, it just made him feel good to know that he could contribute to someone in need. Secondly, five times out of ten, those people would come back to help him at some point when *he* was in need. Zel, Bekner, and Orophin were proof of that, in addition to Murray the mole.

"Right," said the dragon with a much more amicable demeanor. "We have you set up in the presidential suite with a nice view of the arena."

"That'll be lovely, I'm sure," Whizzfiddle replied, glad that he hadn't gone with Heliok to get him set up with reservations.

"It's our best room," the dragon said proudly.

"Honestly?"

"Only the best for friends of Murray. Note that it's twenty gold a night."

Whizzfiddle choked.

They walked into the presidential suite and Whizzfiddle could readily understand why it cost as much as it did. The room was very large and the furnishings were posh. It should have been named the "King's Suite," from Whizzfiddle's perspective, though he had met a few presidents in the Underworld who appeared to have far more power than kings.

"Majestic visions of ancient promontory stands singularly on distant sands with waters crashing their delight," Eloquen said while dancing around the room.

"Him like the view," explained Gungren.

"At twenty gold a night, he'd damn well better. Charging that much for…" Whizzfiddle grumbled and trailed off.

Gungren yawned. "It a place to put my head."

"Speaking of your head, if you wish to keep it you may want to do that box spell we talked about."

"I guess that okay," Gungren said without much enthusiasm.

Whizzfiddle needed to push him on it, though. It was the only thing that could *possibly* save Gungren's life in the upcoming tournament. He'd only have one he could use, but if used at the proper time it could mean everything.

"It was a brilliant idea on your part, Gungren," Whizzfiddle said encouragingly. "Reading the rule book is not something most people do, you know? Me, for example."

"Yep."

"But you *did* read it, Gungren, and you found a loophole."

"Yep." He looked out the window with tired eyes. "I just not sure if I want to use that thing."

"You can always build it and have it as a just-in-case measure." Whizzfiddle then went to lean on his sensibilities. "You're the one who always talks about being properly prepared, remember?"

"I guess that true."

Gungren must have been tired because he didn't argue back to remind Whizzfiddle that he'd always told his apprentice to just relax and take things in stride. To be fair, that's precisely what Whizzfiddle felt was the proper thing to do in nearly every circumstance. With his apprentice's life on the line, though, he was happy to make an exception.

"I can help, if you want," he said with some difficulty.

"Nope. I gotta do it myself or it breaks the rules."

"Fine, then." He put his hand on Gungren's shoulder. "Well, please do create the box so that I don't worry any more than I need to."

"Okay, Master," Gungren said after another yawn. "I promise I'll do it."

MORE DECISIONS

Stillwell had been taking meetings all day and was starting to really get into the swing of things. His inhibitions were nearly gone, at least as it related to doing this job. The power was simply intoxicating.

"If he doesn't pay up by the end of the week," he was saying to Bank, "we'll just have to bend his fingers into odd angles."

"That's pretty harsh, temporary-boss," Bank replied. "The guy plays the piano for a living."

"Oh, I didn't know that. Toes, then?"

"That's fair."

"Excellent. Now, what other business is on the—"

The TalkyThingy rang and Stillwell saw that it was Teggins calling. His blood ran cold as his bladder threatened to completely seize up.

"Everyone out of the office. Now!"

They all left as if the boss himself had yelled at them. In a manner of speaking, Teggins *had* left him in charge, so technically, Stillwell *was* the boss at the moment.

He fixed his hair, which was dumb seeing that it wasn't a video call.

"Hello, this is Stillwell."

"What took you so long to answer the call?" Teggins said with a hint of suspicion.

"I was indisposed, sir," Stillwell replied smoothly. "The taco truck came by near lunch time and I made the unfortunate decision of ordering two."

"Ah, right." Teggins' tone relaxed. "Four is my limit, but I'm bigger than you. Anyway, how goes things there?"

"Wonderfully, sir."

"Anyone asking you for stuff?"

"Stuff?"

"Decisions on people who ain't payin', new loans people want.... That sort of thing."

"Ah yes, I see." Stillwell cleared his throat. "There have been one or two minor requests. Bank has been assisting in some of the financial decisions. Nothing major, though, I assure you."

"Remember that I didn't put Bank in charge, Stillwell. I put *you* in charge. Got it?"

"Absolutely, sir."

Teggins grunted, but didn't push the point any further. "Any questions for me?"

"Just the one, sir: If I do end up making an unfortunate decision—based on my complete lack of experience doing this line of work—what exactly would happen to me?"

"You talking physically?" Teggins asked.

"Well, yes, sir."

"Nothing."

Stillwell pulled the TalkyThingy away and stared at it for a second. Then he brought it back to his face, thinking he had to have heard Teggins incorrectly.

"Nothing?"

"Not a thing," Teggins answered. "I'm not an unfair person, Stillwell. Kind of hurts to think you could believe otherwise."

"Oh, no, sir! It's just—"

"If you lose me money, I'll not lay a finger on you," Teggins interrupted. He sounded sincere. "Nor will any of my goons. You've got my word on that, Stillwell."

"That's a relief."

The fact was that Stillwell had been making quite a few decisions over the course of the day that Teggins would probably disapprove of, but Stillwell couldn't help himself. Besides, again, Teggins *had* put him in charge.

"I must say that I was somewhat worried you might—"

"What I'd do is just tack my losses on to your debt. That way it's a win-win."

"Win-win, sir?"

"Yeah, I make that money back plus interest over time," explained Teggins, "and you get to kept your kneecaps in one piece."

"Right."

"That sounds fair, don't it?"

"Absolutely, sir!"

"Glad we agree." Even though Stillwell couldn't see the boss, he had a feeling that the man was wearing a sinister grin. "See, Stillwell, you were worried about nothing."

"Yes, sir."

MEETING LUCILLE

The three left the presidential suite the next morning.

Eloquen took Gungren down to the workout facilities to give the little giant some exercise time. Since Whizzfiddle had picked up ample healing potions while they were in Kesper's, Gungren would be able to keep practicing without feeling the repercussions.

Whizzfiddle was planning to head off to the arena to have a look around. His hope was to alleviate some of the stress on Gungren by knowing where things were. It was already going to be a daunting experience for his apprentice, so anything that he could do to help would be worthwhile.

As they parted in the lobby, the front desk dragon waved at him. It was odd, but he waved back since he didn't want to irritate the fellow.

And that's when he spotted something out of place.

It was a woman who was watching Gungren and Eloquen as they walked by. That, in and of itself, wasn't strange; it was when she started to follow them that Whizzfiddle became suspicious. Plus, he recognized her.

Her name was Lucille and she wasn't known for being on the up-and-up with her magical abilities. In fact, her name was on the top-ten list of wizards who were marked as incredibly shifty. That was saying something considering that being shifty was part of a wizard's standard motif.

He spun and began following her.

The hallway was long and adorned with massive paintings of dragon heads. Each had a name underneath them, and those names were often lengthy and full of double consonants. Whizzfiddle tried to say a few in his head at first, but it was no use.

Gungren and Eloquen turned the corner at the far end of the hallway. Twenty steps later, so did Lucille.

When Whizzfiddle arrived at the turn, he found a small area that overlooked the gym. There were many people using various exercise devices. He couldn't fathom a solid reason for anyone to put themselves through such torture, but he assumed they had their reasons.

Gungren was punching a large bag with his bare hands as Eloquen attempted to hold it in place. The elf was failing miserably.

"Hello, Lucille," Whizzfiddle said as he stepped up beside the woman.

She jumped. "Oh! Uh…Whizzfiddle? My goodness, you startled me."

"Seems I have."

"I've not seen you in, what, ten years?" she said.

"Sounds about right."

"I hope you've been well?"

"I'm fine," he answered, and then decided to cut to the chase. "May I ask why you're following my apprentice?"

"Your apprentice?" she said, overacting. "I thought you swore off having an apprentice since that Treneth of Dahl fiasco?"

"Times change, Lucille."

"You can say that again. I remember my younger years like they were yesterday. Must be nice having perpetual life."

She was deflecting. This only served to solidify that she was up to no good.

When a person such as Lucille was innocent, they spoke freely, but when they were doing something wrong or they could not defend their position with logic, they sought to deflect. It was akin to the political arguments Whizzfiddle used to have when he was quested to aid a campaign in the Underworld. His job was to detect when people were lying. This wasn't a common practice for wizards on a daily basis… in fact, it was a punishable offense. But when there was a quest involved, rules were greatly relaxed. During that stint, he'd recognized that people generally tended to follow what they *wanted* to believe instead of what was factual. When logic seemed worthy of prevailing, those folks didn't want to budge, so they would instead deflect. It made no sense to Whizzfiddle. Why wouldn't a person want to know the facts of a situation instead of continuing to proliferate ignorance?

But in the instance of Lucille, she was deflecting *because* she was lying.

"Perpetual life isn't all that grand, especially when you accidentally take a drink of long-life elixir at the age of six hundred and fifty."

"I suppose that's true."

They stood silently for a moment. Clearly she knew that Whizzfiddle wasn't stupid, but she'd obviously hoped he would just let the matter of her following his apprentice go. He would not.

"Why were you following Gungren?"

"Who?"

"My apprentice. May I know why, please?"

"I…uh…" She spun towards him with a look of "eureka!" on her face. "I think he's cute?"

"Was that a question or a statement?"

"Both?"

"I see." That did nothing but prove she was full of hooey. "Are you working the event for someone this year?"

Her eyes darted about. "How do you mean?"

"Oh, come now, Lucille, I know the brand of wizardry you employ." He crossed his arms. "My guess is that you're here to either help one fighter or hinder another, and since I know you're not getting paid by me or Gungren, you must be intent on derailing my apprentice."

"I have no idea what you're talking about."

"I'm sure you don't." He wondered if maybe that damnable Fate was involved. "Did Heliok put you up to this? A little extra insurance, maybe?"

"Helly who?"

Whizzfiddle frowned at her. "The innocent act does not become you, Lucille."

"Honestly, I don't know any Helly guy."

"Heliok."

"Okay, Heliok." She shrugged. "Don't know him either."

She seemed genuine.

"You seriously don't know him?"

"Nope."

"Then, again, I ask why you are here?"

"I already told you, I think—"

"Gungren's cute," Whizzfiddle interrupted. "Yes, so you said."

She didn't reply.

Whizzfiddle doubted her assertion, but he had an idea to put her in a corner.

"Well, then go on in and talk to him," Whizzfiddle

suggested, pointing at the door. "I'm sure he'd like to know he has an admirer."

Lucille's eyes went wide. "Oh, I couldn't do that. I'm far too shy."

"Since when?"

Instead of answering, she just looked back at Gungren as he was punching the bag. Whizzfiddle couldn't help but feel bad for that bag, actually. It was getting quite dented up. And the look on Eloquen's face spelled that he was going to need a shot or two of that healing potion also.

Of course, that could explain why the elf was on this quest. He truly was Gungren's friend. It all started out with him being the camera guy, but when Corg moved to shooting everything from Fateland instead, that left Eloquen in a rut. Gungren, being himself, befriended the elf, who was now sticking by his side until the end.

"What *is* he, exactly?" Lucille asked.

"What do you mean?"

"Well, he's too big to be a halfling. I would guess dwarf but the lack of facial hair and the fact that his head is so big makes that unlikely. He's clearly not an elf or a human."

"He's a giant."

Lucille shook her head as if trying to clear the cobwebs. "How's that?"

"A giant."

"Him?" she said, pointing.

"Yep."

"There are dwarf giants?"

"Gungren is the first," Whizzfiddle replied. "He was transformed via a spell by Peapod Pecklesworthy some time ago."

"That's amazing."

"Believe me, I know."

Lucille began studying Gungren like he was some sort of

exhibit. This was only magnified by the fact that she was looking at him through a glass window.

"Does *he* know he's a giant?"

"Yes," Whizzfiddle answered. "He's also a wizard. A pretty decent one at that."

"Incredible! But wait…" She blinked a few times before looking at Whizzfiddle. "Why is he fighting at this event?"

"That's a piece of information I cannot share with you."

"Why not?"

"Because it's his business to share or not, as the case may be." He gave her a once-over. "Plus, I don't trust you, Lucille. You're too shifty." She seemed offended by this remark, but Whizzfiddle knew that, too, was naught but an act. "But, hey, seeing as how you claim to be sweet on him, why not just ask for yourself?"

"Oh my, look at the time," she said, glancing at a wrist that had no timepiece. "I have to run. Maybe I'll catch up with Gungren later."

Whizzfiddle nodded and gave her a warning look.

"I'm sure you will," he said. "Just remember that I'll be watching you."

WHIZZFIDDLE, EH?

*L*ucille was clearly on edge as they returned to the room. She was pacing and chewing her fingernails as she explained what had happened between her and Whizzfiddle.

Teggins wasn't worried about the old wizard. He wasn't worried about *any* wizard. Even if they got the better of him now, he'd get them back eventually.

"A giant, eh?" Teggins said, holding up the profile picture of Gungren that was delivered to his room, along with the profiles of all the rest of the warriors in the event. "Doesn't look like a giant."

"He was squished during a transformation spell."

"Ah, I see," Teggins said. "So he was one of those in that quest of undoing that Treneth of Dahl tried to have me stop."

Lucille stopped pacing. "What?"

"Nothing." He waved at her. "Old business. Everything has been resolved to my satisfaction and therefore it's in the past." He then remembered how Treneth had treated him during that time. "Unless, of course, I ever get my hands on either Treneth or Curlang. But that's not something to worry about for now."

"I see," said Lucille.

"No, you don't, and that's how I want it." He glanced back at Gungren's photo. "I'm thinking that a little giant playing around the ring without the ability to cast magic is interesting."

"What do you want to do about it?"

"Nothing yet," Teggins said, seeing that the little fellow had been listed as never having fought before. That must have meant this was a quest of some kind. Based on his size, the crossed eyes, and the kind face he wore, Teggins assumed that this Gungren fellow wouldn't even make it past the first round in his first fight. "Just keep an eye on him like you do everyone else. I can't see how he's going to make much of a fuss in the long run. He's too little."

"He seemed pretty strong when he was punching that bag."

"All the fighters are strong," Teggins countered. "Even Krag here."

"I will kill squish giant."

"See?" He flicked Gungren's picture across the room. "I'm not worried."

CLIMBING THE LADDER

*H*eliok had been summoned to Kilodiek's office.

While West could run interference for him when it came to Mooli, Lornkoo, and any other number of people beneath Heliok, he could do nothing to stop Kilodiek.

"I have been receiving complaints from your underlings, Heliok," Kilodiek said, sounding annoyed.

"Oh?"

"It seems as though you have brought in an Ononokinite to act as their superior?"

"Of course not, sir," Heliok replied strongly. "That would be preposterous."

Kilodiek glared. "Indeed, it would."

"I have merely brought him in to be my personal assistant, sir."

Kilodiek shot up from his chair. "Without my approval?"

"I don't recall there being a precept in the Fate management handbook regarding a manager requiring the approval of his manager in order to hire a new employee."

Heliok had him there.

Kilodiek slowly sat back down.

Managers were given autonomy when it came to filling their own ranks. Suggestions could be made by the higher-ups, actually, and sometimes following those suggestions was smart, politically speaking. But ultimately it was up to the hiring manager to decide who ended up working on their team.

"There isn't for standard protocol," agreed Kilodiek, "but you've not brought in a Fate, Heliok. You've brought in an outsider."

"Again, sir, I also know of no rule against that."

"And again, Heliok, there isn't one." He appeared flustered. "But...well, it's just not done, man!"

That much was true, and knowledge of this move on Heliok's part would undoubtedly rise up through the ranks of management. That would put him under scrutiny.

He had to play this carefully.

"I see no reason it shouldn't be allowed, sir," he said. "You must admit that we have done well with having Misty and Corg working on our team as of late."

"It *has* caused a lot more productivity, certainly, but it's just a temporary measure and you know that."

"But why? Think of how we've been pushed lately. Aniok was once one of the worst workers in our division. He improved over his time here, yes, but when Corg came along, Aniok became a dynamo of productivity."

"I can't argue against that."

"And were it not for Misty's involvement, I may still be hunting for a way to improve our numbers on Ononokin."

"Again, true, but that's your own fault. Twelve gods. I'll never understand it."

It was the wrong thing for Kilodiek to say. Managers could give you all the grief they wanted about most anything, but it was disallowed to chastise a Fate's creative outlets.

"Because it's my creativity," Heliok countered, "which is protected under the—"

"Yes, yes, I'm aware." Kilodiek had his hands up in surrender. "I'm not bashing your creativity, Heliok, but this entire mess was your fault to begin with and now you're bringing in people from Ononokin to solve it."

"What better way than to involve those who are most impacted by our decisions?"

It made tons of sense to Heliok. Who was most likely to fix a hole in a sinking ship? The people on it, or someone on a different boat watching it sink?

"That's actually a very good point."

"And imagine how good it will look on your report when you show that kind of foresight, sir."

"Yes, well, that's true." He was starting to nod now. "Fine, you may keep him aboard, but if I'm going to be seeing a non-Fate in our area, I will wish to meet him."

"Of course, sir." Heliok opened the door and called to West to join them. When he walked in, Heliok started his introductions. "Kilodiek, this is West. West, this is my superior, Kilodiek."

"Your superior?" West said appraisingly. "Meaning that he is higher up the ladder than you in the land of the Fates?"

"That's correct." Kilodiek's tone was suspicious. "What of it?"

"I only mean that I find it rather fitting, sir," West replied in his polished way. "You clearly have a nicer office, a more powerful desk, and your demeanor is one that displays strength and command."

Kilodiek's chest pushed out a little. "Well, that's true."

"And while I mean no offense to Mr. Heliok," West continued, "I must say that a Fate of your status is far more deserving of an assistant than a Fate of lower position."

Heliok was nodding happily at how West was playing

things. At least until he realized what the troll had just said.

"What?"

"You have a point there," Kilodiek said, ignoring Heliok's question. "I *don't* have an assistant."

"A travesty, in my humble opinion, sir," West stated.

"It truly is," agreed Kilodiek.

Heliok turned to the troll. "West, what are you doing?"

"Merely pointing out the obvious, sir," West replied effortlessly. "Would you find it acceptable if Mooli or Lornkoo had a personal assistant while you did not?"

"Absolutely not! They're beneath me—" Heliok's voice caught in his throat. "Oh."

"Exactly." West was nodding sadly. "Now, Mr. Kilodiek is above your station and therefore likely believes the same about you, Mr. Heliok."

"He's right," Kilodiek said to Heliok. "I do."

"I believe that a Fate at your level, Mr. Kilodiek, is far more deserving of my capabilities, no?"

Kilodiek was nodding so quickly that Heliok thought the Fate's head was going to pop off.

"Most definitely."

"But I just hired him to be my assistant," complained Heliok.

"And I've just given him a promotion."

"This isn't fair! I demand that—"

"I'm sorry to interrupt, sir," West said in a firm tone as he walked to the door and opened it, "but it appears that you're not on Mr. Kilodiek's calendar at the moment. If you would like to make an appointment to have this discussion with him at a more appropriate time, simply have your assistant contact me and we'll work out the details accordingly."

Heliok's voice was quiet. "But I don't have an assistant anymore."

"Such a pity," said West as Heliok walked out.

MEETING HIS CORNER

The time had come to check in.

Whizzfiddle led Gungren and Eloquen down a small corridor under the arena. It was where all of the fighters were put. It was also the place set aside for signups, rule changes, and so on.

They walked up to the main desk where a halfling was stationed.

"Name?" said the bushy-haired little man.

"Whizzfiddle. Xebdigon Whizzfiddle."

"I don't see anyone named Whippaddle on the card."

"No, not Whippaddle, I said—"

"I think him want my name, Master," Gungren interrupted. "I are Gungren."

"Good. I've got a Gungren here." The halfling glanced over the desk. "Who is in your corner?"

"My master and Eloquen," answered Gungren, pointing to each man in turn.

The halfling held out his hand. "I need your Corner Cards."

Whizzfiddle patted his robe. "Corner Cards?"

"You can't run in his corner unless you've got Corner Cards."

"Where do we get those?"

"You've got to go through training and pass an exam," answered the fellow.

Whizzfiddle rubbed his beard.

"How long does that take?"

"About a year, if you work hard."

"We don't have a year," Whizzfiddle stated.

"Then Gungren doesn't have a corner."

"So he just has to go at it alone?"

"That's right," the halfling answered. Then he tapped his pencil and looked up at Whizzfiddle. "Unless you want to hire a corner for him."

"Fine. How do I do that?"

"Third window on the left," the clerk replied, pointing. "Here's your access card, Gungren. Good luck."

They walked to the third window on the left. Inside was a troll with a wide nose and sparkling eyes. He even wore a smile in standard troll fashion.

"Hello, how may I help you?"

"I need a corner thing," Gungren answered.

"I see. So you have nobody in your corner?"

"Nope."

The troll pointed. "Who are these two?"

"That my master and that my friend."

"Ah, right, I see no Corner Cards." The troll nodded. "Well, all the corners were taken this morning except for one set. They come as a team."

The way the troll said it put Whizzfiddle on guard. First off, why would they be the only remaining ones left, and secondly, why did he specify that they were a team?

"Are they any good?" Whizzfiddle asked.

"They have their moments," came the honest reply. "If nothing else, they know their way around the event, and that is definitely worthwhile."

"Fine. How much?"

"One gold."

Whizzfiddle placed it on the table.

"Muriel and Barrie," the troll called to the back room, "you have a fighter!"

~

They were an older human couple with white hair. He had a beard and mustache; she did not.

"He's too old and scrawny," complained Barrie as he circled Whizzfiddle. "They'll rip his limbs off."

"I believe this fellow is the fighter, Barrie," Muriel said, pointing at Gungren.

"Oh, right." Barrie moved to circle Gungren instead. "He's too small. They'll rip his limbs off."

Whizzfiddle raised an eyebrow at Muriel.

"Don't worry," she said reassuringly. "He does this to every fighter. It's his way of getting them ready for action."

Barrie put his hands on his hips. "Well, it doesn't work if you tell them that, now does it?"

Whizzfiddle would be the first to admit that he was out of his comfort zone at this event, but these two weren't exactly giving off a great first impression.

"Are you sure you two know what you're doing here?"

"I've fought in three of these events, thank you very much." Barrie had said it with much gumption. "I know quite well how the process works."

"Oh, my apologies," Whizzfiddle replied, taking a step back. "Out of curiosity, how did you do?"

"He lost in the first round each time," Muriel replied before Barrie had the chance.

"Could you *please* not tell everyone that whenever they ask?"

"It's the truth, isn't it?" She smiled at Whizzfiddle. "He prefers to tell the story as though he nearly made it to the finals, but a twisted ankle forced him to bow out."

"That happened, though," argued Barrie.

"Technically, yes, it did," said Muriel. "But, dear, you were knocked out of the first round that year, like always." She turned again to Whizzfiddle. "He still wanted to watch the final fight, but when he was climbing the bleachers, his leg got caught and he twisted his ankle. The poor man ended up in the hospital, didn't you, dear?"

"I was there, woman," Barrie said in disbelief. "But if you keep telling it like that, nobody's ever going to hire us."

"We're hired every time there's a battle, big or small, dear." Another glance at Whizzfiddle. "This is just the main event. There are many of these fights every year, and we've never gone without a paycheck."

"I'm assuming you're always picked last, though?" Whizzfiddle asked, but suddenly felt bad about it.

"Better last place than never to show up," Muriel replied in a cheery voice. "That's our company motto."

Barrie was shaking his head. "I don't even know why I bother."

"It okay, mister and missus," Gungren piped up. "I know how to fight already, but I not know how to navergate stuff. That where I need help."

"I think you mean navigate," corrected Whizzfiddle.

"That the one."

Muriel patted Gungren on his head and gave him a warm smile.

"Well, we can certainly help you there."

"And with getting your gloves on and..." Barrie's eyes went wide. "Whoa, those are some big hands. We're gonna need extra tape, Muriel."

She nodded. "And gloves made for an ogre, I'd say."

INTERVIEWING THE CROWD

The arena was crowding in with spectators as Payne walked along with her cameraperson. Now that the event had started, she also had help from the control booth. They would point her in the right direction and provide names and information as needed.

She was specifically looking for the notable-people section. The famous, infamous, and well-to-do paid enormous sums of money, or were invited as VIPs, to frequent this section. It was good for publicity.

"The crowd is amassing for the tournament," she said while the camera scanned the rows of seats. "Thousands will be in attendance today, but we're going to focus in on those who have risen to the level of celebrity."

She shielded her eyes from the sun and pointed to the third row.

"I spot Gappy Whirligig of the famous Gappy's Gadgets, which everyone knows is a division of Contraptions, LLC." Actually, Payne *didn't* know that, but her control person fed the information and so she used it. "The parent company is owned by his wife, Tootz Gibdawdle-Whirligig, who is seated next to him. To her right is a rather attractive young man and there's also a large orc." She put her finger to her ear. "I've just received word that the young man is Merton Myron Wambles and the orc's name is…" She couldn't be sure, but it sounded as though something wrong occurred in the booth, because an expletive had been used. "What happened?" she said and then lifted her head and looked at the orc again. "Oh, that's his name? Huh." Turning back to the camera, she said, "Okay, so the orc's name is Sh…" She paused and covered her ear again. "Are you sure? Hmmm? Oh! Right." She smiled. "His name is *Shrit.*"

A flock of dragons flew overhead and everyone pulled out steel umbrellas. Considering what a mere bird could do to you as it flew over, Payne understood the need for the umbrellas to be made of a sturdy metal.

"Over here we have the royal families of Henroot and Nubbins." She was smiling at the camera. "The Henroot family owns a large soap empire in the Underworld, and all of their product comes by way of the Nubbins hemp farm."

There were many faces that she didn't recognize, so she just kept moving until she was told to stop.

"Ah," she said, pointing to a middle-aged, baldish man who was sitting with a fellow who was broad-shouldered and had long, princely hair. "I see the vampire Paulie Vergen and Prince Hughbarian Tessan." Information continued flowing in. "Rumor has it that the prince is a werewolf, but you'd never know it by looking at him. Also, insider information claims that Paulie Vergen has been in discussions about doing a travel series called *Around Ononokin in 90 Days*." She winked at the camera. "We can only hope that pans out!"

Just as she was about to continue her walking tour, a huge ogre stepped up to her. One look told her that he was the dumb type of ogre. Mean ones didn't smile.

"Excuse me, lady," he said.

"Yes?"

"I are named Kone." He patted his chest. "You seen my puppy?"

"No, I'm sorry, I haven't."

"Him not really a puppy no more, but we calls him that anyway."

"That's nice," said Payne in response.

"Selly poopy," a smaller man with a red beard said. He was clearly a wizard, if wearing a pointy hat was any indicator. "Gonin' ghat lahzed agern."

"Sorry?" said Payne, not understanding the dialect.

"That my friend, Redler," explained Kone. "Him say that the puppy keep getting lost."

This wasn't exactly the best time for an interruption, but she didn't want to come across as harsh while on live television.

"I'm sure he'll be okay," she said sweetly. "We're unfortunately in the middle of filming something here, but if I spot him, I'll let you know."

Redler squinted at the camera. "Foolmen?"

"Hmmm?" said Payne.

"Ye gorda cumrah der?" Redler went to tap at the lens, but the cameraperson pulled it away just in time.

"I'm…" Payne looked up at Kone. "What's he saying?"

"He asking if you got a camera."

Payne pointed. "That's a camera, yes."

"Or wee oonet?"

"Are we on dat camera?" Kone translated.

"Ah, right. Yes, we are."

Redler's eyes opened wide. He smoothed the sleeves on his robe and ran his fingers through his beard.

"Whooz my har look?"

"Can't see your hair, Redler," Kone replied. "It under your hat."

"Oooh yah," the odd little wizard said. "Whooz my haht look?"

"Your hat looks fine," Payne said, understanding the man for the first time that day.

Just as she was about to ask them to kindly move along, a hot dog vendor approached. As if things couldn't get much worse, now Payne and her cameraperson were going to be trapped between a nice ogre, a strange wizard, and a hot dog vendor.

"Excuse me," said the vendor, "but is this your dog?"

"Yay! Puppy!"

"Boob?" Redler said, rubbing his eyes and giving the vendor a second look. "Boob Emenemen?"

"What?" the vendor replied and then rubbed his own eyes. "Wait...Redler? Kone?"

"Yep," said Kone with a huge smile.

"Dat's oos!"

And that's when it hit Payne what was going on. The control booth caught on, too. They were nearly yelling in her ear.

"Hold on a second here," Payne said, interrupting the little reunion. "Are you Bob Mermenhermen? Better known from your famous books on zombieism as 'Bob the Zombie?'"

Bob sighed. "Yes, that's me."

"Why are you selling hot dogs?"

"Because the only way I was allowed to leave the Afterlife and watch the match was to work the event." He shrugged. Then he looked around as if to see if he were being watched. "Speaking of which, do any of you want to buy one?"

Kone ordered five of them. Three for him, one for the wizard, and one for his dog.

"Well, this is unbelievable," Payne said as her smile

returned. "We're seeing a lot of famous faces in the crowd today, folks. Dead and alive!" She shook her head at the camera. "It's clear that people are doing whatever it takes to watch the one hundredth Ultimate Dragon Fighting Championship!"

THE LOCKER ROOM

Gungren walked into the locker room and looked around at his competition. There were fighters of all shapes and sizes. Some were sharpening their swords, others were donning their armor, but all of them were preparing for battle.

"Hello," Gungren said, causing all heads to turn to him. "I are Gungren. I are a fighter, too."

A mean-looking ogre grunted at him. "You're a squished giant and I'm going to kill you in the ring."

"Okay," Gungren said with a shrug as he found a seat.

"Dinnae ye worry about him," said a dwarf who was putting a finishing edge on his axe. "He's just a grumbly type, that's all. It's in his blood."

"He's a creep is what he is," agreed a lithe elf who was looking down the edge of a long blade.

"Dinnae start goin' after agreein' with me, ye blasted elf."

"Oh, shut up, you tiny twit."

"Tiny twit, am I?" the dwarf said, standing up to his full height, which wasn't saying much.

"I'm glad we agree," the elf replied with a smirk.

"What?" The dwarf looked confused. "I dinnae agree to nothin'. I'll rip yer dainty arms from their sockets, I will!"

"You can't even reach my arms."

"Oh yeah, well—"

"Hey," said Gungren, causing the two men to stop their bickering, "how come you guys is so mad at each other?"

"'Cause Toross is after bein' an elf."

"And Emrek is a dwarf."

"So?"

"So that's why we're fightin'," stated Emrek. "Are ye daft or somethin'?"

"You am saying that you don't like each other because you were born a dwarf and you were born an elf?"

Emrek nudged Toross with an elbow. "This one's quick on the uptake, eh?"

"A real overachiever."

Gungren shook his head at both of them. "That dumb."

"What is?" asked Toross, lowering his weapon.

"Fighting just 'cause of where you am born."

"It's not after bein' dumb," Emrek argued. "It's tradition."

"It's dumb."

"Yer sayin' our cultures after bein' dumb?"

"Yeah," Toross said, "who are you to say such a thing?"

"I already told you that I are Gungren."

"Oh," Emrek said, jumping onto one of the benches and waving his hands around in grandiose fashion, "well then go ahead and make fun of our cultures all ye want, then. Seein' as you're after bein' Gungren and all."

Gungren knew that the dwarf was being flippant, but he didn't mind. His mocking only proved that he felt unsure about what Gungren was saying.

It bothered the little giant when people fought over silly reasons like this. He grew up a giant and it was drilled into him at a young age that dragons were bad and that humans were worse. To be fair, the dragons attacked their villages now and then, and the humans were also shooting little pointed sticks at the giants whenever they walked into the wrong spot of the woods.

Now that his mind had been altered, he saw that people were just people regardless where they came from. Different ideas and cultural elements? Sure. But underneath all of that, they were generally the same.

"What your favorite thing to do?" he asked the elf.

"Me?"

"Yep."

"I don't know. Kick my feet up and have a couple of ales, I suppose."

"Seriously?" Emrek said with a surprised look. "That's after bein' me favorite thing, too."

"No point in being obstinate, Emrek."

"I'm not after bein' abstinent, ye goofy elf," Emrek countered. "I've got me a wife and everythin'." Then he cleared his throat. "Now, it's true that we've been married a long time, so I'm basically abstinent now, but that's not after bein' me choice."

"No, I..." Toross shook his head. "Never mind."

"So you both like kicking up them feet and drinking ale?" Gungren sought to clarify.

"Yes."

"I suppose so." Emrek shrugged. "What's yer point?"

"Do you like puppies?" he asked the dwarf.

"Are ye kiddin'? I love 'em!"

"Me...too."

Emrek nearly fell over. "Say it ain't so, elf!"

"I'm feeling very confused right now," Toross said while frowning at Gungren.

He was hoping that his point was getting across, but he

still had to put in one more piece of information to really drive things home.

"Do you love your ma and pa?"

"Of course I do," answered Toross. "They're wonderful people."

"Aye," Emrek said next, his cheeks turning rosy, "me ma is the best breadmaker in the land, and me pa is a smithy with no equal."

And now Gungren had them both where he wanted them.

"So you both love your ma and pa, you also think puppies am cute, and your favorite thing is to kick up them feet and drink ale, right?"

"Aye."

"It sounds like it, yes."

Emrek looked up at the elf and began to nod. Toross was staring back down at him as well. They were clearly finding this quite difficult to process. All the years that they'd been fighting with each other merely because one was an elf and the other was a dwarf.

"So why them not friends?" Gungren asked finally. "Sound like you both like the same stuff."

"It does, doesn't it?"

"Aye, it does." Emrek chewed his lip. "If'n ye was a dwarf, we'd prolly be the best of pals."

"Same if you were an elf."

"But why that matter?" Gungren declared. "You am an elf and him am a dwarf. So what? You both Ononokernites! That all that matters."

"I daresay he's right," Toross stated with some trepidation.

Emrek's jaw was slack. "I'm not after feelin' comfy with it, but I got no choice but to agree."

And that's when the clerk came in the room, cracked open his pad of paper and yelled, "Toross and Emrek, you're the first two up. Get out on the field!"

They began picking up their weaponry and they didn't look all that happy about it. When Gungren had entered the room they were at each other's throats, ready to fight at the drop of a hat. Now it seemed like they were loathing the proposition.

"And now I gotta go out there and be after rippin' yer limbs off?" said Emrek after hopping down from the bench.

Toross nodded. "Business is business, I suppose. But whatever happens, assuming one or both of us doesn't end up dead, maybe we could grab an ale sometime?"

"Aye. Let's do that."

And with that, both men dragged themselves out of the room and towards the field of battle.

IT'S ABOUT TIME

*R*icky wisely stayed outside of the cave this time as he yelled for Crazell to get ready.

She already knew it was time for battle, but she wasn't interested. This day would mark the starting point for the real struggles the rest of her life would bring.

"I really would rather not," she said, sulking.

"It's the big game, baby," he yelled back in. "You know it. This is what we've been working for your entire career."

"Not for the same reasons you think, I'm afraid."

"Semantics."

"I don't want this, Ricky."

"Maybe it's just nerves, ya know?"

"It's really not. I've been putting a lot of thought to this and I genuinely don't want to win this tournament."

"How can you say that?" he said. "I mean, I get that you don't want to have to deal with the ramifications of winning. But to say you don't want to win at all? That's just baffling, Craz."

"Be that as it may, it's true."

"Look, Craz, we've been talking about this for years. This is the big one. The twenty-fifth title defense. Nobody'll ever eclipse that. You'll be a legend. Your name will be revered."

She eyed the cave mouth. "So?"

"So that's a big deal," he replied. "You're a dragon, for crying out loud. How can you not want this?"

"Like I said before, it won't end there."

"I've already told you that I'll stand at the microphone with you after the event while you announce that you're leaving the sport." Ricky was standing at the opening of the cave now. "That's not a problem at all."

"Right, and then we go our separate ways."

"Well, hopefully we'll stay friends, but that's the right of it."

"And for the rest of your life you'll be a sought-after coach?"

"My prospects are looking pretty good."

It *would* be good for him and the Schmicky family, too. How could it not be? Who else in the world could claim to coach as many victories as his lineage? Granted, it was all through a single dragon, but they wouldn't care about that.

"And what about me, Ricky?"

He squatted down and looked up at her.

"What about you, Craz?"

"Remember, I'll be the dragon that everyone will want to find and challenge." They'd *just* had this discussion, for crying out loud! "They'll all want to see if they can best me in a fight. I'll never be left alone. I'll never get any rest. I'll spend the remainder of my days taking on one challenger after another."

"Yeah, that's what you said before, but it's too late to do anything about that right now. This is the big show, Craz." He stood up and sighed. "I promise you, though, we *will* figure out everything afterwards."

"I hope so, Ricky," she said as she started to move. "I truly hope so."

THE FIRST BATTLE

*T*he announcers arrived at roughly the same time. They weren't exactly friends, but rather professional acquaintances. This was because the announcer business was quite cutthroat, especially in the Upperworld.

Optical was a jeans-and-T-shirt kind of guy. He was born in the Underworld to a halfling father and a troll mother. The halfling side of him made for a short stature, bushy hair, and oversized feet. The troll side gave him a rich-timbre voice and exacting dialect. He enjoyed public speaking, but he would be the first to admit that he had a face for radio.

His counterpart for this event was Homer Melvin Durfitz. Homer was a wizard—or used to be until he lost his wizarding license. The records were sealed on precisely what he'd done to lose his Guild membership, but Optical guessed it had something to do with a rigged betting scheme on some type of sporting event.

Optical had no issues with Homer, personally, though he did find it odd that the man dressed in fancy sport coats and pants so tight that they almost appeared to be painted on. To each his own, was Optical's motto.

"Optical," Homer Melvin Durfitz said with a nod as he donned his swim goggles.

This was another oddity that Optical recalled about Homer. It seemed that the human felt it best to protect his eyes at UDFC events because body parts and blood tended to hit the crowd during battles. Seeing that they were sitting near the top of the stadium, though, made the goggles rather pointless.

"Homer," Optical replied in turn.

He got to setting up the panel and microphones, putting on his headset and adjusting volumes. They both did sound checks to make sure all levels were set.

Optical had already familiarized himself with the various fighters, but only so he could run the play-by-play. It was Homer's job to do color commentary.

The green light flicked on, signaling that they were on the air.

"Welcome, everyone, to the Ultimate Dragon Fighting Championship," Optical said in his smooth voice. "This is event number one hundred in the UDFC and the cards show some pretty interesting warriors. My name is Optical and with me through this event is Homer Melvin Durfitz."

"It's a pleasure to be here, or anywhere for that matter."

"Indeed it is, and we should note that this year's event is being brought to you by Stackowiak's Pub. Located on Main Street in the town of Planoontik in the Underworld, Stackowiak's Pub carries beer, liquor, fine wine, and not-so-fine wine. They also offer plenty of fried yummies on the menu. If you want booze, Stackowiak's has it!"

"*Very* good booze," agreed Homer.

Optical cleared his throat. "Right. So, what do you see for the event, Homer?"

"There is a lot of talent on the cards this year," Homer

replied. "Fighters will fight and blood will be shed. There will be swordplay and fisticuffs and dragon flames."

Optical sighed. "Thank you for the deep insights."

Homer nodded, pulled out a bottle of whiskey, and poured a glass.

"The on-field announcer has just introduced our first contestants and the bout is underway." Optical adjusted in his chair for a better look at the field. "On the one side we have Emrek the dwarf and on the other we have Toross the elf. These two match well on the card, eh, Homer?"

"Oh, most definitely. I'd give the dwarf the edge, though, seeing as how his reach is easily half that of the elf."

Optical had to think twice about that.

The bell rang to signal the fighters to begin.

"And the two take the center of the ring," Optical said as the action began. "Emrek swings his axe outside the range of Toross, who turns, jumps forward, and stabs the ground."

"This is an odd start to the fight," noted Homer. "Must be nerves."

"They've gone to pacing around each other as if seeing who will make the first move."

Homer took a sip of whiskey. "It's the standard feeling-out phase of the fight, Optical."

"They seem to be having a conversation of some sort," Optical noted.

"Insider tip is to get under the skin of your opponent," explained Homer. "If his emotion gets the better of him, he'll make more mistakes."

"One would imagine," agreed Optical, "except that they've both thrown down their weapons."

Homer leaned forward, setting his glass down.

"Ah, they're going to go old school and fight hand-to-hand. That's something we've not seen in years."

"They've moved into a clinch. It looks like there is a

struggle to see who can get whom on the ground first and..."
He paused and did a double-take. "No, wait, that's not what's
happening at all."

"I count myself as being well-versed in the sport," Homer
said slowly, "but this is definitely a new style of mixed
martial arts."

"It appears that they're hugging each other."

"Well, that's a strategy you don't see every day."

"And they've both thrown in the white towel as well,"
Optical said as both men sat there dumbfounded.

"The crowd isn't going to like this."

"Indeed," agreed Optical. "In fact, they are launching
tomatoes and drinks at the two as they leave the arena."

FIGHT THE KNIGHT

*G*ungren heard his name announced after Barrie and Muriel got his gloves put on and set.

His stomach felt strange as he walked down the hallway and out onto the field. There were a lot of people in the stands and they were all cheering. That didn't make things any better.

A human with a powerful voice was introducing both fighters, but Gungren was having trouble focusing. Part of it was nerves, but there was also a flicker of something deep in his mind that made him desire to throw rocks. It had to be due to the impending battle.

It was just one more thing to worry about.

"You're fighting the toughest knight in the land here, kid," said Barrie. "But you've got the edge. Get him up against the ropes and keep jabbing him in the gut until he keels over."

"There aren't no ropes, mister," Gungren pointed out.

Barrie glanced around. "Oh, yeah. Well, get him up against the wall then."

"The wall is out of bounds."

"True." Barrie snapped his fingers. "Okay, so just punch him in the stomach a lot."

"But he got a sword."

"Nobody said this was gonna be easy, kid."

Muriel leaned in. "Just do your best, Gungren. There's no shame in losing, if that's what it comes to."

"Don't tell him that," Barrie said in shock. "He needs the eye of the dragon if he's to have any chance of surviving this fight!"

∾

"Chimsley has made it to the semi-finals at every event I've worked," Optical said into the microphone. "He's tall, muscular, and wears his full plate armor for these events."

"Some say that plate armor should be banned as it gives an unfair advantage," noted Homer. "I don't see a problem with it, personally. Why shouldn't a fighter be able to wear a suit of armor that makes him nearly impossible to defeat?"

"It's a solid point," said Optical, even though he knew quite well Homer had meant it sarcastically. "His challenger is a late entrant by the name of Gungren. He is a wizard's apprentice and a former giant."

Homer glanced at the field. "I have to say that the last giant I saw was much taller."

The bell rang.

"And the fight is on. Chimsley charges full on at Gungren, lunging his blade at the smaller man's midsection, only to miss as Gungren steps to the side."

"That little guy is faster than he looks," said Homer.

"Chimsley spins and lifts the blade high in the air for a downward arcing strike. Gungren steps in and punches the knight directly in the stomach."

"Punching steel plating?" Homer said with a laugh. "His brain must still retain that stereotypical giant intellect."

"Or does it?" countered Optical. "It seems that Chimsley has dropped the sword and is gripping at his stomach." Then both Optical and Homer stood up and stared down at the knight. "By The Twelve, look at that dent!"

"Maybe this Gungren fellow has lead weights in his gloves?" Homer said, sounding as baffled as Optical felt.

"I couldn't say, but Chimsley is having a whale of a time trying to breathe." Optical nearly had to rub his eyes at what happened next. "Wait a second. It looks like Gungren is rushing to Chimsley's aid."

"Now I've seen everything," Homer said and then took another drink.

"He's squeezing the sides of the knight's armor and the front has popped back out. Chimsley has fallen over, though. The referee is waving his hands, signaling that the match is done. Gungren has won it."

The two men sat back down.

"I must say that this is by far the strangest start to any tournament I've been privy to in all my years," Homer said.

"That it is," Optical agreed. "There was that one cage match a few years ago on the amateur circuit where the halfling went around using his massive feet to crush the toes of his competitors."

"Oh, yes, I remember that one. It was definitely outside of the norm."

"It was a shame to see that fellow get all the way to the semi-final only to face an ogre with steel spikes on his boots," Optical said, wincing as he recalled the visual.

Homer shuddered. "Dreadful memory, that."

"Indeed."

PREPARING TO SAVE GUNGREN

*H*eliok, Corg, Misty, and Aniok stood with their jaws hanging slack as Gungren's hand was raised in victory.

"Didn't see that comin'," stated Corg, unable to tear his eyes from the screen.

"It was definitely a step up from watching that dwarf and elf hugging each other in the first fight," Aniok agreed.

"Aye, that was right disturbing." He then quickly added, "I'm not one of them who hates elves, mind, but warriors are meant to be trying to cleave each other up. It's only right."

"Yep."

Heliok stood next to Misty, shaking his head. She looked just as perplexed as he did.

"So our Gungren has made it through his first fight," Heliok said. "This is rather impressive."

Misty nodded her agreement. "It's going to make for excellent ratings."

"For both of us, Ms. Trealo."

"Huh? Oh, yeah, sure, right." She then glanced around and said, "What happened to West?"

Heliok cleared his throat. "I'd rather not talk about it."

COLLECTING WINNINGS

*S*tillwell was all smiles as he saw the little giant's hand raised in the air. He had put a bet on the fellow after seeing him walk into the ring.

Typically Stillwell carefully studied numbers and sheets, looking over statistical data and running scenarios before he would put his money on an event. But that had never won him anything, unless you considered being forced into becoming Teggins' right-hand man as winning.

So this time he just went with his gut. Something told him that this Gungren fellow would win. Hopefulness for the underdog, maybe? Possibly, but seeing as it was the first time Stillwell had ever won anything, it made it all the sweeter.

"You won two hundred gold, temporary-boss," said Bank after doing a quick calculation.

"Did I?"

"Yep. I took it off what you owe the boss."

"That should put me far ahead," said Stillwell, thinking that maybe he was free of this world. "I had only borrowed one hundred gold originally."

"Yeah, but with interest you was in for five hundred."

"What?" choked Stillwell. "That's impossible. It's only been a year."

"Gotta read the fine print when you is filling out an agreement with the mob."

"Ridiculous." Stillwell knew that organized crime was built on shady dealings, but this was beyond cruel. It was time for his gut feelings to get him out of this mess. "Put me down for another ten on Gungren in his next fight."

"You got it, temporary-boss."

Bank then clapped his hands and a couple of goons dragged in a man who looked to be in his late thirties. He was wearing a tunic that was likely not as tattered and torn when he'd arrived to confess his inability to pay. The goons certainly roughed him up slightly before delivering him to Stillwell.

"This guy bet on the knight and lost," announced Bank, "and he can't pay up."

"It was supposed to be a sure thing," complained the man, shaking free from the gripping hands of the goons.

"Ain't no such thing as a sure thing," Bank explained, "unless you consider not paying up and therefore having your jaw busted as a sure thing."

The man looked utterly lost. "But there's no way that little guy could have beaten a knight." His eyes grew wide. "It's been rigged."

"Don't know nothin' about that," Bank replied without emotion. "I just know that you owe us money. Right, temporary-boss?"

"So it seems. How much does he owe?"

"Fifty gold."

"How much does he have?" Stillwell asked while staring at the debtor.

"Twenty-five silver."

"I see." That didn't bode well for this guy's ability to continue walking. "What kind of collateral does he have?"

"Fingers, toes, kneecaps, teeth, jaw, elbows, and his head," answered Bank.

Stillwell remembered his call with Teggins and knew that he had to work to get the money from this man, and he also recalled the feeling of power at sentencing others today, but there was something about this guy that gave Stillwell pause. And he knew exactly what that was. It was like Stillwell was looking into a mirror.

"What's your name, good sir?"

"Mooch," the fellow replied.

That was fitting. He looked more like a "Kirby" to Stillwell, though.

"Do you own a house, a vehicle, or property of any kind?"

"I've got a house, yeah."

"And how much is it worth?"

"Bought it for five thousand gold back in the day."

"Do you know its value on the market today?" Stillwell asked, his finger hovering over the calculator that Teggins had used the day that Stillwell was dragged into this room.

"Yeah, it's worth nine thousand gold now."

"Perfect," said Stillwell. "How much do you owe on the house?"

"Eight thousand nine hundred and ninety." Mooch coughed lightly. "We just refinanced."

"And got cash-out, I see." Stillwell sighed.

Didn't that always seem to be the case with people? They catch a financial break and immediately just jump right back into debt. It happened to Stillwell every time.

That gave him a thought.

"Did you purchase anything with the money you got out?"

Mooch looked around and his shoulders slumped.

"Bought my wife a new diamond ring. She loves it. Cost me seventy-five gold."

"Anything else?"

His shoulders slumped farther.

"A boat."

"Price?"

"Two hundred gold," he said with a faraway look. "It's a gem."

"And what are the return policies on this ring and this boat?" asked Stillwell.

"Thirty days, full refund."

"How long have you had them?"

The nearly inaudible reply was, "Just over a week."

Stillwell felt a small win at hearing this. It was obvious that Mooch loathed the idea of having to return either of these items, but something told Stillwell that he'd rather go down that road than suffer broken limbs.

"You just need to return one of the items if you're to pay off your debt to us."

"But I gotta keep them both," Mooch said, his face the picture of desperation. "My wife would lose her mind if I took back her ring, and my boat is...well, it's my boat!"

"And your legs are your legs too, pal," Bank pointed out. "If you don't fork over the money you'll be walking on crutches for the next six months."

"Fine, fine," Mooch said, putting his hands up in surrender. "I get it. It's completely unfair, though."

"Nobody forced you to place a bet," Stillwell said.

"Yeah, yeah, I know."

"Besides," he added reassuringly, "I'm sure there are less expensive boats that will still allow you to keep your dream alive."

"What? I ain't returning the boat." He said it as though Stillwell were insane. "The ring's going back."

This was confusing to Stillwell. He'd never been married, but even he knew the saying, "Happy wife, happy life."

"But didn't you just say that your wife will lose her mind if you return her ring?"

"Oh, most definitely," answered Mooch with a firm nod. "But she'll get over it after a while. Until then, I'll be out on my boat."

HE GOT LUCKY, IS ALL

*T*eggins couldn't help but feel impressed with the way Gungren had taken out Chimsley. A punch that powerful was something that he would never have expected. He could use a guy like that as one of his goons.

Still, Teggins wasn't worried. Yeah, he'd keep an eye on the little giant, but his guess was that Chimsley just assumed he'd roll through the guy. One thing Teggins learned when growing up on the streets is that you *never* underestimate anyone in a fight. The smallest ruffian could wipe out the biggest guy in the bunch by landing the right punch at the right time.

He scratched the back of his neck at that thought.

The fact was that this betting scheme he had going on *was* his fight. Not that he was physically in the ring, no, but he was pulling the strings to make sure that everything fell in his favor.

So he'd let himself worry a little.

He glanced down at the field to see Lucille bump into a scary-looking orc. A tiny flash of light bounced from her to him, signaling that she had just cast a small spell at him. The orc stopped and shook his head, looking as though something had just gone wrong.

This was the kind of fighting that Teggins excelled at. He was also deadly in standard fisticuffs, but that wasn't on the agenda today.

He looked over to see Gungren entering the tunnel, obviously returning back to the locker rooms.

Teggins decided in that instant that it would be unwise to underestimate the little giant.

GETTING READY FOR THE NEXT ONE

*W*hizzfiddle was thrilled that Gungren had won his bout. Even more impressive was the fact that the little giant hadn't been injured in the slightest.

They headed down the hallway and back to the fighter's area. Since Gungren had moved beyond the first battle, he'd be given a private room.

Up ahead of them was Knight Chimsley. The fellow was having a difficult time moving. He was holding the wall and walking quite gingerly.

Gungren rushed up to him and helped him the rest of the way.

"Sorry about your stomach, mister," Gungren said.

"Nothing to apologize for," Chimsley replied between grunts. "You have done well and you have a lot of power in your fists. I am honored to have fought such a worthy foe." He winced. "Besides, I've been considering upgrading to iron plating anyway. I shall need to become much stronger first, though, I'm afraid."

"Where am your corner?" asked Gungren.

Whizzfiddle had been thinking the same thing. It seemed

odd for a man of Sir Chimsley's caliber not to have help during an event like this.

"I tend not to use one," he answered. "I fear that was yet another misstep on this eventful day."

"Yep."

Gungren directed the knight into his own private dressing room. Then he and Muriel helped the man out of his outfit until they got to his pants. That's when Barrie shooed Muriel away.

"Master," Gungren said as he looked at the massive bruise on Knight Chimsley's belly, "you got my healing stuff?"

"I do," answered Whizzfiddle, patting his chest pocket. "Why?"

"Give it to this guy. Him need it more than me."

"*Now* maybe, but you still have many fights to go..." Whizzfiddle stopped as he saw the look on Gungren's face. "Oh, fine."

Chimsley drank the potion and the bruising began to dissipate. It was rather incredible to watch, though Chimsley did seem to be in some distress during the fast heal. There was even the sound of a rib fusing. That couldn't have felt great.

Still, Whizzfiddle made a mental note to stock up on these potions before his next quest.

He was never one to think witches were less than wizards. Different, certainly, but less? Never. In fact, he felt they brought an entirely different perspective to magic than wizards. They studied their craft, where wizards more fell into it. Some wizards scoffed at the notion of witches, but they were just magicists. Holding a negative attitude towards another simply because their elective way of practicing an art was silly in Whizzfiddle's estimation.

"That's so much better," Knight Chimsley said. "You, my friend, are an honorable fellow."

"I just do what is right."

"If that doesn't define the basis of honor, then I don't know what does." He stood up and grabbed his gear, looking like he felt much better. "Good luck to you, Mr. Gungren. If you ever are in the land of Dahl and are in need of assistance, I shall be at your service."

"Thank you, mister!"

Chimsley bowed and left the room.

Only Gungren could punch a fellow in the gut, take away his chances for winning a tournament that only happens once every ten years, and then turn the entire situation around to the point where he'd earned a lifelong friend. Whizzfiddle rather enjoyed that aspect of the little man's personality. It was charisma that was not ascribable to looks, height, or station.

"That was quite impressive, Gungren," Whizzfiddle said, speaking about the fight now. "Was that something that Bekner taught you to do?"

"Sort of, yep," Gungren answered. "But I couldn't reach that knight's head so I hit him in the belly."

"Right."

"The punishing of fisticuffs twists the underlying current of rationality," Eloquen said with a voice of dismay.

Barrie gave the elf a funny look. "What did he say?"

"Him don't like fighting stuff."

Most elves didn't. They were *very* good at fighting, but they preferred to use diplomatic means to resolve disputes. Some elves *did* enjoy battles, obviously, seeing there were a couple participating in this event, but most would rather just have a nice tea party, a few dainty finger cakes, and an underlying hum of flowery music while they discussed potential resolutions.

"You did a decent enough job in your first bout," Barrie

said as he massaged Gungren's shoulders, "but it's going to get tougher from here, I'd imagine."

"You'd imagine?" Whizzfiddle said loudly. "You mean you don't know?"

"Remember, Mr. Whizzfiddle," Muriel noted as she riffled through her bag, "he's never been beyond the first round of a fight."

"Damnable woman," grumbled Barrie.

KRAG VS DOMINO

"It looks like we have another interesting match underway, folks," Optical announced after the green light illuminated. "We have Krag the Destroyer—a mean ogre, versus Domino—an orc of some size." Without looking over, he asked, "What do you make of this one, Homer?"

"Honestly, I thought I knew everything there was to know about this sport," Homer replied, sounding a bit tipsy, "but taking a three-month hiatus to try and regain my wizarding license clearly put me behind the eight ball." The sound of whiskey filling a glass could be heard through the headphones. "Still, I'd say Domino has the edge here."

"Indeed," Optical replied in his usual way as the bell rang. "The fight has started and Domino is running away from Krag. He's not facing him either. Krag is literally chasing Domino around the ring."

"I've never seen an orc run away from a fight before," said Homer. "It *could* be that he's trying to tire Krag out, but it doesn't seem to be working."

"Hmmm," Optical said before Homer could continue.

"The referee has stepped in and is having a word with Domino. He's wagging his finger in the orc's face. I wonder what that was all about."

"Fighters are paid to fight," answered Homer, "not to run away."

"True. The referee has signaled them to resume and Domino is standing his ground so far." A cloud passed over, casting a shadow over the stadium. "Krag moves forward and swings, but Domino just yelps and runs away again."

"There are no words to describe this," Homer said in disbelief.

"You're paid to have words, Homer."

"Then I'll have to give a refund because I've got nothing."

"It seems that Krag feels similarly to you as he's pounding his fists against his own thighs in frustration." Optical leaned forward to get a better look. "Wait, wait, we have something here. Yes, the referee has called the match with a...huh. That's new." He searched his memories but couldn't place the term he'd just heard. "I know that a TKO is a technical knockout, Homer, but I've never heard of a TCO."

"That's because it hasn't been used in all the years this event has been running, Optical. It's an embarrassment is what it is."

"I see," Optical replied. "But what does TCO mean?"

"Technical chicken out."

ANOTHER WIN

*M*urray was watching the tournament at his computer as he ate popcorn and drank a fizzie. While fizzies were only available in the Underworld, Murray was now connected to the grandness known as the Undernet. He could order anything he wanted and the UUPS delivery person would bring it within a day or two.

He scanned his cave and found boxes and boxes of things that he really didn't need, though. But with all of the money that was pouring in due to the skills he had recently learned, he had gotten carried away.

"Maybe I could create a site on the Undernet where people could sell their old stuff?" he said aloud. "Yes, yes, that would be amazing. I could call it Murray's Auctions, or mBay!"

The screen flicked over and showed Gungren standing across from Haley the Horror.

Haley was a dark elf who was covered with white tattoos. She was wearing just enough to cover up her naughty bits, which allowed for her skin-art to shine. Her weapon of choice was the spear, and Murray knew she was very good at employing its use because they'd just finished showing a brief documentary on her skills.

The elf jabbed a few times at Gungren, but he stepped out of the way.

Murray cringed with each thrust and parry.

"No, no, no," he said, covering his eyes. "I can't watch. I can't watch!"

He slightly uncovered one eye, just enough so that he could peek through.

"Oooh...good move, Gungren," he yelped as the little giant stepped past the elf's spear and pulled her arm hard enough that she had to do a somersault. "Go, go, go!"

Haley spun around and swiped at the air. Had Gungren been a foot taller, he would have ended up being a foot shorter because he would be minus one head.

"Jab, Gungren, jab! Watch out for her spear. She's very good with..." Haley darted in. "Oh no! Jump away. No, don't reach out for the spear! You don't want to grab..."

Gungren snatched the spear out of the elf's hands and then he snapped it in two over his knee. He threw the pieces in opposite directions.

"Oh, I guess you *do* want to grab the spear."

Murray was still getting to know Gungren, but he was baffled to see such a gentle soul fighting so well. It was as if he had grown up as a giant or something.

Murray looked up and to the left. "I guess he *did* grow up as a giant. Hmmm."

Haley didn't seem all that pleased with losing her weapon of choice, but she was clearly not done. She reached behind her back and pulled out a blade. It flashed in the sunlight.

"Look out, Gungren," Murray yelled at the screen, "she's got a knife! Ack, I don't want to see this!"

Gungren wasn't flinching, though. He merely waited for Haley to launch her attack.

She complied within seconds, diving forward and driving the knife directly at his chest.

Just as the point was about to pierce his flesh, Gungren turned, grabbed Haley by the wrist, and began to rotate. The combination of his strength and her momentum brought her into a fast orbit around the little giant. Just as she was about to lose her footing completely, Gungren spun the opposite direction, twisting her wrist backwards.

The elf shrieked and flipped, landing directly on her stomach.

"Ouch, that looks painful."

Murray started clapping and bouncing around in his chair as Gungren sat on Haley's back and pulled on her arms until she gave up.

"He wins again! He wins again!"

WASN'T EXPECTING THIS

While Heliok was impressed that Gungren had made it past the first round, seeing him get through the second one also unscathed was nothing short of incredible.

"Are we sure he's not using magic?" he asked the room.

"It would be detected," Misty answered. "The judges you see there are in charge of catching any magic-use in the ring."

"So he's just seriously *that* good at fighting?"

"I'm not after believin' it either," Corg stated. "It takes years for a fighter to be seasoned enough to do what he's after doin'."

"He *is* strong," Aniok said as if that answered everything.

"Aye, Ani, that's obvious."

There was no denying that strength played a heavy role in events like this, but the speed that Gungren was moving was also downright impressive. Plus, he always seemed to jump in the right direction at the right time.

Heliok was not well-versed in these sorts of matches, though. To him it was just barbaric. Two beings stepping out in front of a crowd and tearing each other apart while thousands cheered them on was disturbing. He wasn't sure whom he felt more concern over, though—the fighters or the people cheering them on.

"You're sure you're not giving him additional powers or abilities, Heliok?" Misty asked dubiously. "If the people learn that he's been given an edge—"

"I just asked if he was using magic," Heliok said before she could finish. "If I was doing something that was making Gungren really good at this, why would I ask that?"

She raised an eyebrow. "A ruse, possibly?"

Just because dark elves played nefarious games all the time didn't mean that Fates did...not *all* the time anyway.

"Aye, lass. I'm after agreein' with ye." Corg's eyes narrowed as he turned to look at Heliok. "Yer not playin' games with the games, are ye?"

"No."

"If'n ye do, ye shifty Fate, it'll mean my career." His eyes grew even darker. "And that'll mean I'll be after givin' ye a swift kick to yer tender vittles."

Heliok rolled his eyes.

"I'll keep that in mind, little man."

DISCUSSION

*G*ungren had somehow managed to get to the semi-finals.

His first bout had been relatively easy, though Whizzfiddle had imagined it shouldn't have been. Taking down a knight was not a simple thing to do. The wizard had done it on numerous occasions, but he had used magic. Gungren had done it with a single punch to the stomach.

The second fight had been definitely more challenging for Gungren, seeing that there was a spear and a knife involved, and also because the dark elf wielding them was quite deadly. But, again, Gungren just went in and took care of business as though he were a seasoned professional.

"This are kinda fun," Gungren said, "but it am making me want to throw rocks."

"You consider pummeling people fun?" Whizzfiddle asked worriedly.

"I fix them up every time," Gungren replied with a shrug.

Whizzfiddle sniffed. "You have an odd way about you sometimes, Gungren."

"Yep."

"A maelstrom of angst and bone inspires discoloring of flesh," said Eloquen with a heavy dose of exasperation.

"Him said it just a bunch of people punching and bruising up each other."

That *was* rather the point of the event.

It wasn't exactly Whizzfiddle's cup of tea, but the number of people in the stands demonstrated that many found it to be okay with them. He was certain that at least a few of the celebrities in attendance would rather not witness such battles—the ambassador to Argan, Pauli Vergen, came to mind.

Eloquen's face turned wistful. "Albeit gleams of sunbeams ignite prominence and rounded countenance."

"Him say he like the outfits, though."

"Right," Whizzfiddle said. "Anyway, what were you saying about the rocks?"

"I think the fighting am making me want to throw them more."

"You have to stay away from that, Gungren."

"I know, but it hard."

This was one of Whizzfiddle's greatest concerns. It wasn't *the* greatest concern, of course—that would be Gungren being killed in the ring. A close second, though, was that Gungren would not be able to contain the giant living inside of him.

"Just keep your mind on the task at hand," he said, trying to lend strength to his apprentice. "You have been doing quite well...incredibly well, in fact." He thumbed his coin purse. "Honestly, I've been considering putting a few gold coins down on your next fight, but I fear that would not be the wisest of moves."

"Gambling am not good, Master."

Whizzfiddle sighed. "I suppose it isn't."

Barrie and Muriel had returned from the main desk.

"Your next fight is the semi-finals," Barrie said with excitement in his eyes. "You've got this in the bag. If you get through this guy, you'll be fighting the dragon!"

"Okay," said Gungren without emotion.

"That's the spirit," said Barrie. Then he turned to Whizzfiddle and whispered, "Is he always this calm?"

"Mostly."

"I've brought you a jam sandwich, Gungren," Muriel announced, handing over a package to the little giant. "I do hope you like strawberry?"

"It are fine. Thanks."

"You can't give him a meal like that before an important fight," Barrie said reaching for the sandwich. Muriel deftly pulled it away before he could get at it. "He needs to eat raw eggs, woman. That's what real fighters eat."

"Didn't you used to eat those, Barrie?" she countered with a raised eyebrow. "I don't recall them helping you very much."

"Blasted woman."

CONFRONTATION

$\mathcal{K}$rag was not happy. Of course, he was rarely ever happy, and even when he was happy it usually had to do with the fact that he had recently made someone else decidedly unhappy.

But this time he had to put his foot down. What was happening was wrong. His fights were being manipulated and Krag wanted it stopped.

Fighting was his life. He was good at it. Damn it, he was *great* at it.

So when Teggins walked in to his private locker room, Krag spoke up.

"I'm not happy about this and it's gotta stop," he said.

"You've won all your fights so far and you're in the semi-final," Teggins replied. "What aren't you happy about again?"

"Ain't it obvious?"

"Not really, Krag. You are incessantly grumpy."

Krag knew this, but he didn't know other people were aware of it. Maybe it was how he growled at people a lot? That probably had something to do with it. He'd once gone to a professional image consultant who had suggested that he work on his smile and also say "please" and "thank you" to people. He beat that guy to a pulp, paid him, smiled in his sinister way, and said, "Thank you."

"I'm not insensitively grumpy," Krag replied.

"*Incessantly*, you dope."

Krag didn't like being called names.

He also didn't like that Teggins was being uppity with him. Krag usually killed people for being uppity. Many times he'd wanted to punch Teggins in the head for being this way. There was something different about the crime boss, though. Something that gave Krag pause. It was as though Teggins harbored no fear at all regarding the mean ogre.

"Do you recall the last time you smiled?" asked Teggins.

"What's smiling got to do with being happy?"

"Forget it," Teggins said, rolling his eyes. Again, with the uppity! "Anyway, what's got you mad now?"

"You ain't letting me fight."

"What are you talking about?"

"I'm here to punch and kick and cut and bite," explained an exasperated Krag. "But every time I get into the ring, my opponent runs away, cries, or shrieks and throws in the towel. I haven't been able to hit one person yet. Not one!" He was beside himself with frustration. "If I can't hit 'em, how am I supposed to kill 'em?"

"I see." Teggins pinched the bridge of his nose and then cracked his neck from side to side. "You *do* recall the purpose of your being here, yes?"

"Kill things," Krag stated as fact. Then he added a derisive, "Duh."

"No," Teggins countered slowly. "Your purpose, which I shall state yet again, is to win me money."

"I can do that by killing stuff, making us both happy."

"And if you're killed instead?"

"Not gonna happen."

It was clear that Teggins was finding this conversation irritating, but so what? Krag was annoyed that he wasn't being allowed to battle.

This was *his* day.

He had worked hard for this.

"You gotta admit that there's at least a chance of it, Krag."

"Nope."

Teggins gritted his teeth. "So you're telling me that nobody's ever gotten the best of you in a fight?"

"Well, sure, but—"

"Then that means it can happen again, yeah?" Teggins asked without letting Krag finish his first response.

Back in Krag's youth he had lost a couple of fights. One was against a bully who was five years older than him, another came by way of three kids who had jumped him when he wasn't looking, and the last one was when a girl in his high school class punched him for staring at her thingums.

"Fine," Krag said, thinking that Gungren's thingums would not be appealing to him, "but it's not likely."

"I believe you, Krag," Teggins said as he cracked open the door. "I do. But the problem is that my pocketbook doesn't get fat by taking unnecessary risks. It gets filled up by smarts." He gave Krag an apologetic tilt of his head. "You don't have smarts. You got fists."

"Fists are better than smarts!"

"I think you've just proved my point."

Krag thought over what had just happened. "I did?"

"As far as you know, Krag," answered Teggins. "Now, is there anything else? I wanna get back to my chair before your next match starts."

The ogre wasn't sure what had just happened. Had he convinced Teggins to let him do his job or did the damn crime boss use words to twist things around like he always did?

"Does this mean I'm going to be allowed to actually fight and kill?"

"I'll make a deal with you, Krag. If you can get to your opponent before the ref stops the fight, you can hit him all you want."

PUT EVERYTHING ON GUNGREN

Stillwell's gut was right again and it felt great. All this time he could have been following his heart instead of his head and things would have been different, right?

"You paid everything back that ya owe, temporary-boss," Bank said as he looked over the documents again, "including the ten gold interest for today."

"Excellent." He was rubbing his hands together like a naughty scientist. "How much is left to me?"

Bank looked up at him. "Three hundred gold."

Three hundred was a lot of gold. A lot. Rumor had it he could buy a really nice boat with that kind of money.

But wait. Was that the right move?

His brain was screaming at him to put it into an account and get himself out of this lifestyle. He was free. There was nothing that Teggins could do about it if he just walked out and called it a day. Nothing.

His gut told a different story. It whispered to him with visions of wealth that he'd dreamed of since he was young. It spoke to him. It *spoke* to him.

"Put it all on Gungren," he said, barely over a whisper.

"But he's fighting Krag," Bank replied in a voice that almost sounded caring.

"So?"

"So the boss is fixing the…" Bank stopped, clearly realizing what he was about to say.

Stillwell understood and didn't fault the man. Bank was just like him, slaving under Teggins. But Stillwell had only been doing it for a short time. Bank had likely been here for years, and he had to know that he was never getting out. For him to try and protect Stillwell when it came to this much money could spell disaster if Teggins ever found out.

"I mean," he said softly, "you said you wanted all three hundred on that Gungren guy, right?"

"That's right," Stillwell replied, "and don't worry, Bank, I know that you're doing what you have to do. This is my decision, wholly."

"You got it, temporary-boss."

"Good."

He clapped his hands, feeling like a new man. No, he wasn't tough like Teggins, but that was okay. Stillwell had a different kind of tough, and it was starting to build inside of him. Each win brought him a little closer to it.

Still, he had to flex his sinisterness some or he feared that his confidence may wane.

"Now, about these people who owe us money," he said, putting on his business hat, "I want them to scrub the lower-level bathrooms with their own toothbrushes."

"No kiddin'?" Bank replied.

"I am absolutely serious. How can they be so irresponsible with my money?"

"*Your* money?" Bank really looked confused now. "You mean the boss's money, right?"

"Oh, yeah, that. That's what I meant." Stillwell's

confidence quickly declined. "I was...uh...just getting into character like the boss does."

"Ah, I see." Bank grimaced. "He wouldn't do nothing like the toothbrush thing, though. That's even too mean for him."

Stillwell's confidence dipped even lower.

"Is it? Well, what would you suggest then, Bank?"

Bank sat up straight, furrowed his brow, and stared at Stillwell. It wasn't a negative stare. It was more of an are-you-nuts? kind of stare.

"You want *my* opinion?" he asked, pointing at himself.

"Sure, why not?"

"Uh, just ain't used to it, I guess."

Maybe *this* is what Stillwell needed to do. Could it be that his confidence would come from doing things differently than Teggins? Not that he wanted to take over the joint or anything...though the thought *was* tempting.

No, that would be like signing his own death certificate. Gut feelings or not, he wasn't that dumb.

Regardless, he *could* push his own confidence by exercising his management muscles a bit until Teggins returned. No, this wasn't his place, but it *was* under his thumb through the night.

"You're a valued member of this team, aren't you, Bank?"

"I don't know," Bank answered. "I sorta get paid, and I do stuff for the money. The boss calls me a dummy a lot. That don't make me feel very valued."

"I'd imagine it doesn't," agreed Stillwell. "Well, he's not here and he left me in charge. And, Bank," Stillwell said with a nod, "I consider you valued."

"You do?"

"I do." Funny thing was that he actually meant it. Even funnier was that his confidence was on the rise again. "So what is your opinion regarding the punishment for these non-payers?"

"Well, if it was me, I'd maybe knock each of them on the big toe with a hammer." He scrunched his face like he was about to get thwacked on the head by a rolled-up newspaper. "Is that a bad idea?"

"I think it's a great idea, Bank," Stillwell said with two taps to the desk. "Let's go with that."

TAINTING THE WATER

*K*rag paced back and forth in his room. Something felt very wrong about the meeting that he'd had with Teggins. Very wrong, indeed.

He knew the crime boss only had one thing on his mind. Teggins wanted to bet his Diamond of Jaloof and collect massive winnings. Krag also knew that his own angst was probably making Teggins consider going a different way.

A double-cross.

Krag was no dummy, though. He understood that Lucille was a wizard who was there to do Teggins' bidding. She would do whatever it took to make sure the crime boss got what he wanted. Plus, Lucille didn't like Krag. That meant if Teggins *did* decide to double-cross him, Lucille would happily oblige.

Just as he finished that thought, a noise sounded outside his room.

He creeped to the door and peered out. Sure enough, there was Lucille hovering over one of the water jugs. She was chanting something odd and then a flash of light exited her hand and hit the water container. When she stepped away, Krag saw the name "Gungren" on the jug.

So Teggins *was* double-crossing him! Lucille was putting special powers into that little giant's water supply so that he'd be even stronger than he already was.

It was diabolical, but again, Krag was no dummy.

As soon as Lucille cleared the area, the mean ogre walked out, changed the name tags on the jugs of water, and—just for good measure—brought the magical one into his room.

Then he proceeded to drink down a number of gulps.

AND HE'S OUT!

Gungren stood on his side of the field as Krag the Destroyer faced him. The mean ogre was staring at him the entire time the announcer was speaking. Gungren assumed this was some kind of intimidation tactic, and it may have worked had it not been for the fact that Krag kept yawning.

"Ladies and gentlemen," the announcer said into the microphone, "it's gonna be a clash!"

The crowd went wild.

This ignited Gungren's inner giant again.

"In this corner is a mixed martial artist," said the announcer as he pointed at Krag. "He stands six-feet-eight-inches tall. Weighing in at three hundred and thirty pounds. He has a professional record of thirty-four and o, with twenty-seven of those wins coming by way of death or maiming. He is the Beast from the East. I give you Krag the Destroyer!"

Again, the crowd showed its appreciation.

The announcer then spun and pointed at Gungren.

"And in this corner, we have a wizard apprentice. He

stands around four feet tall, weighs in at one hundred and sixty pounds. He has a professional record of two and 0, all at today's event. He's a former giant and an all-around nice guy. I give you Gungren!"

The applause was easily ten decibels louder than when Krag was introduced.

"Your referee for this tournament is Benny Courtman."

The cheers died down.

"All right, come in here," commanded the referee. Gungren and Krag approached. "Keep it a clean fight. Obey my commands at all times. When I say break, you break."

"I can do that," Krag stated in a menacing voice.

"I don't mean breaking bones here, Krag," the ref pointed out. "I'm talking about breaking contact."

"Oh," Krag said while yawning. "Right."

"We keeping you awake?"

Krag gave Benny a look. "Huh?"

"Anyway, go to your own corners and wait for me to start the match. If you want to touch gloves, do it now."

Gungren smiled and said, "Good luck, Krag the Destroyer."

"I…" He yawned again. "I plan to kill you."

"Okay," Gungren replied.

≈

Teggins didn't like the looks of things.

His fighter was facing up against the little giant that wasn't supposed to have made it this far. This was acceptable because he had Lucille doing his dirty work, but something was amiss.

"Out of curiosity," Teggins said, "what did you do to impact Gungren's ability in this fight?"

"I cast a sleeping spell on his water."

"Do you see him looking tired at all?"

"No," she said with a gulp.

"Neither do I." Teggins then slowly moved his pointing finger across the ring until it rested on Krag, who was slumped over in his chair. "Now, let's take a look at Krag. What would you say he's doing?"

"I don't know."

"You don't?"

"Well, I mean I *do*, but it doesn't make any sense." She seemed to be pretty heated, which gave Teggins pause. "Contrary to what you may think, Teggins, I'm a professional. The name on Gungren's jug of water was very clear, and I cast the spell on it and it alone."

"Then what would you say to the fact that Krag is yawning and Gungren very clearly isn't yawning?"

"I don't know. Let me get down there and check it out."

He snaked out a hand and grabbed her by the shoulder. If she thought she was going to get away, she was mistaken.

She reached for her hair, and he said, "I'll snap your neck before you have the first words of the spell out of your mouth."

"I got the right jug."

"So you say," Teggins replied with a nod. "But if I lose my money on this, Lucille, it'll be your butt."

"Again, I did not screw up, Teggins."

"So you say."

"Well, this is the match that we've been waiting for," said Optical, having ordered up a bottle of brandy for himself. This day had just been too odd to continue on sober. "Whoever gets past this one will fight Crazell."

"It's been an interesting day so far," Homer said, echoing

Optical's thoughts. "Let's hope that these two really give us a show because up until now it's been just odd."

"It looks like Krag is shaking his head a lot," Optical said, and then poured another shot.

"Probably just psyching himself up," Homer said hopefully. "We see a lot of that in the sport. Of course, we've seen many things today that are quite new, so who knows what he's doing at this point?"

"True. He just let out a loud growl, so that's a good sign." Optical then focused in again. "No, wait, that was a yawn."

Homer was also leaning in. "Maybe he's playing a game of diversion?"

"What do you mean, Homer?"

"It's a ruse that gets the other fighter to lower their guard before an attack. Usually this is done by playing the game of being a slow guy. In other words you time your moves to be slower than normal. Not so much that it's obvious, but just enough to get your opponent in a rhythm. Then you jump to full speed and attack."

"Interesting."

"I've never seen the yawn tactic, specifically, though." He was nodding. "That one is novel, Optical."

The bell rang and both fighters stood up from their respective chairs as their corners cleared the area. The referee had his hands out, keeping the fighters at bay until everything was gone. Then he slashed his hand down the middle and yelled, "Get to it!"

"The warriors are walking to the center of the ring," Optical said into the microphone. "Krag is a bit wobbly, but Gungren is staying back."

"The little giant must be aware of the ruse."

"Krag has both hands in the air. It looks like he's going to go for his patented two-hand slam..." He then stood up and stared down at the field. "Or maybe not."

"Has he just fallen over?" said Homer in disbelief.

"You've clearly been gifted with top-notch eyes, Homer."

"I think he's asleep, Optical."

They were both standing slack-jawed as they looked down upon the body of the mean ogre. Not a single punch was landed. The fighters had never even touched each other.

Krag literally just passed out.

"Indeed he is," Optical said after realizing he'd not said a word in nearly twenty seconds. That was far too much time to pass for radio. "Uh, the ref has waved off the event without even a single punch thrown. This is astounding."

"More like ridiculous."

"The judges appear to agree with you, Homer," Optical said while pointing. "They're making their way out onto the field. Obviously, they think this may be a case of foul play."

"Good."

"Indeed."

SOMETHING ISN'T RIGHT

*G*ungren and the referee stood over Krag, who was snoring like he'd just passed out from an all-night bender.

The crowd was a mixture of boos, shouts, and murmurings. Considering how much money had been spent on attending this event, Whizzfiddle wasn't surprised at this.

He looked over to watch the judges heading out to the field. Seeing that he was certain they were searching for foul play, he strode out to help protect his apprentice.

"What is going on here?" said Teresa, since she was the first to arrive.

"I haven't the foggiest," the referee replied. "He sure is snoring a lot, though."

Stiermark knelt down and studied the fallen Krag. He lifted the ogre's arm and let it go, watching it drop like a stone. Finally, the wizard shrugged and stood back up.

"Looks like he's majorly wiped out, man. I could shroom it up and see what happened to him, if you want?"

"Every time you do that," said Sephnedra, "you end up

claiming there are purple horses flying around or some such."

Teresa raised an accusing eyebrow at Gungren. "Did you do something here?"

"What you mean?" asked Gungren.

"Excuse me," chimed in Whizzfiddle, who was standing behind the judges, "but I'll not have any of you casting judgment against Gungren for any wrongdoing. He's a fine lad."

Teresa spun around, shielded her eyes from the sun, and said, "Xebdigon Whizzfiddle?"

"Hello, Peg," Whizzfiddle replied.

"It's Teresa, thank you very much."

"Oh, right. Forgot. Sorry."

"You don't have a Corner Card," the ref said, pointing at Whizzfiddle. "You can't be out here!"

"He's right, dude," agreed Stiermark. "You gotta bolt."

"Gungren is my apprentice. Therefore, I have jurisdictional rights."

The referee's head shake was firm. "That doesn't make any difference."

"Yep, it does," Gungren corrected him. "It in the rule book. Page ten."

"You can read?" said the ref as he gave Gungren a surprised look.

"You can't?" Whizzfiddle shot back in his apprentice's defense.

"Watch yourself, wizard." The ref flipped open the rule book and began mumbling as his eyes scanned the page. "Well, I'll be. It seems he *can* be out here."

"Yep."

Whizzfiddle had never met Sephnedra or Stiermark before, but he had seen their names in the event pamphlet. He knew Teresa from a long time back when he had helped her to get permission to move to the Upperworld in order to get away from technology and pursue witchcraft.

"Why is Sephnedra doing ballet and looking like she's figure skating on the dirt?" the elderly wizard asked.

"It's her power source, dude," replied Stiermark.

Sephnedra finished her little dance, said a chant, and touched the fallen ogre. A hint of light left her hand and Krag roused. He shook his head a few times and grunted.

"What happened?" he said finally.

"You lost," answered the ref.

Krag clearly couldn't believe this, as his face was contorted into a mass of confusion.

"Did he knock me out?"

"No," replied the ref. "You...well, fell asleep."

"I what?"

"You fell asleep. You went for a two-hand slam and you passed out."

"Damn." Krag punched the ground, causing everyone to take a step back. Everyone except Gungren, anyway. "I thought they were double-crossing me, but they weren't."

Teresa tilted her head. "Who are you talking about?"

"Teggins and Lucille," Krag replied and then glanced up quickly.

"Teggins, eh?" Whizzfiddle said as he started scanning the crowd. "That explains why Lucille was following Gungren around."

"Are you talking about the crime boss from the Underworld?" asked Sephnedra.

"There he is," said Whizzfiddle, pointing.

Teggins was pushing through the crowd, obviously trying to make his exit. Lucille was going in the opposite direction.

Whizzfiddle pulled out his flask and took a heavy swig. He then cast a spell that lifted up Teggins and Lucille, bringing them both down to the field. Teggins was wriggling at first, but eventually he just started flexing his hands. Lucille undoubtedly wanted to pull out strands of her hair. Fortunately, Whizzfiddle already knew about her particular power source and so he had been sure to lock her arms in place.

"What's all this about?" said Teggins while looking from face to face. "I was just going to get some popcorn."

"I'm sure you were," Whizzfiddle replied, shaking his head.

"You were a friend of my old ma, Whizzfiddle," Teggins said with a grunt. "How could you?"

"Last I recall, you sold your old ma for ten gold to work at a hotel."

Teggins winced. "You heard about that, eh?"

"I'm gonna rip you in two, Teggins," Krag said as he stood up and lunged at the crime boss.

As if the ogre were naught but a fly, Teggins reached out and slapped Krag hard. The ogre flew a good five feet before landing in a heap.

The crowd cheered.

"Who's next?" said Teggins, giving them all the stink-eye.

"Me," Gungren said, stepping forward.

Teggins swung at the little giant, who ducked under it and then came up with a punch right to the crime boss's chin. It didn't knock the man out, but he was wobbly.

"Shouldn't have underestimated that guy," Teggins said while shaking his noggin as if trying to clear his brain from fog.

Whizzfiddle refueled and quickly cast a spell of binding against Teggins. It linked his wrists behind his back as iron chains hooked his ankles to each other.

Krag got back up, rubbing his head. Obviously he'd not known how powerful Teggins really was.

The ogre went to go after Teggins again, but Stiermark stepped in his way.

"Chill, dude. It's all good. We'll let the cops deal, dig?" He then handed the ogre something. "Here, have a shroom, it'll cool your bones."

"I *am* kind of hungry," Krag replied, taking the item from the wizard.

"Don't eat that," Sephnedra shouted as she grabbed it. "You'll see cosmic bunny rabbits and eight-headed field mice for hours."

"She's right, dig? It's pretty rad though."

Everyone eyed Stiermark for a moment before shrugging. *To each his own*, thought Whizzfiddle. He wasn't exactly in a position to judge the man anyway, considering what his own magical power source consisted of.

"Looks like you've been caught cheating, Mr. Teggins," Teresa said. "Would you like to save us all some time and just confess?"

"You'd like that, wouldn't you?" Teggins replied.

"Did you say, 'wooden shoe' just then?" Teresa asked darkly.

"What?" Teggins frowned. "I ain't confessing to nothing."

"Fine." Teresa pulled out some herbs and crumpled them up in her hands. She then cackled and yelled, "You will say what's right and true or for the rest of your days you'll be a fool!"

Whizzfiddle noted that she didn't need to speak her spells in all capital letters. That was one benefit to being a witch, for sure.

Teresa blew the mixture in her hand at the crime boss's face. His eyes turned red and he sneezed a few times.

"What in the blazes was that?" he asked while coughing.

Teresa squared her shoulders. "Did you try to rig this event or not?"

"I...I..."

"If you don't answer honestly," the witch warned him, "you'll get dumber and dumber."

"That's a very useful spell," Whizzfiddle stated.

"Witchcraft is so much better than wizardry."

The three wizards scoffed at this.

Whizzfiddle knew there were some *very* useful aspects to witchcraft—healing potions came to mind, but to claim it was better than wizardry was farcical. It was like claiming that one type of sport was better than another. Those who enjoyed sport A would say it's better than sport B every time.

"Well, Teggins?" Teresa asked again.

"All right, all right. I did it." He then sneered at her. "I entered Krag into the contest and I cheated to get him all the way to the finals. Doesn't matter anyway. I'll be out of the slammer in three days, tops."

Sephnedra did a quick dance as everyone stared at her. She then stopped and said a few words that caused Teggins' eyes to droop significantly.

"He won't give you any trouble now," she said to the arena guards. "Take him away and bring him to the Underworld authorities for immediate processing."

"This one, too," Whizzfiddle said, pointing at Lucille. "Her arms are bound. Make sure you keep them that way. If she's able to pull even a single hair from her head, she'll be able to do magic."

As the two were dragged away, Whizzfiddle noted something sparkling in the sand by his feet. He knelt down and picked it up while the judges conferred with the ref. It only took a moment to realize what he was looking at.

He shoved it quickly into his pocket and glanced around in shock.

"That was a steaming spell, Seph," Stiermark was saying. "Yours too, Teresa. Anyone else got the munchies?"

The ref gave the stoner wizard the onceover.

"Right," he said finally. "So seeing that Krag's manager was responsible for this debacle, does that mean that Gungren is the winner?"

"I judge that he is," ruled Teresa.

"Most definitely," agreed Sephnedra.

Stiermark smacked Gungren on the shoulder. "Little dude's got my vote."

NO WAY

"*I* can't believe it," said Corg with a gasp. "The dinky giant is after goin' to the big show."

"And you said he never had a chance," Heliok chided the dwarf.

"He didn't."

"But there he is."

"I can see that, ye flashy monkey," Corg retaliated, "but it shouldn't be possible."

"And yet it's obvious that he..." Heliok paused as his brow creased. "Did you call me a flashy monkey?"

"Aye, that I did." Corg started wagging his finger at Heliok. "Ye are absolutely sure ye didn't use any of your fancy Fate sprinkles to make him be after gettin' this far, right?"

"Fate sprinkles?"

"Yer wily magic, ye wispy cloud of—"

"Corg," Misty intervened, "let's not lose our temper just yet, okay?"

"Ye mean you're losing yours, too?" Corg asked.

"Heliok," she said without replying to Corg, "when this all

began, you said you wouldn't interfere unless it was absolutely necessary."

"That's correct."

"And Gungren winning this event is not an absolute necessity." She took a couple of steps away and then spun back. "In fact, your rules stated that he only needed to participate fully, which he could have done in the first battle."

Heliok gave her a dull look. "I know this already, and I've already told you before that I've had nothing to do with this."

"But you have to admit that the way in which he has climbed through to the final round is a bit incredible."

"I couldn't agree more," he said firmly.

Gungren had no business making it to the finals. He had won his first two fights fair and square, and though the last one turned out to have been a win due to unfortunate circumstances, the real culprits behind that were found and were now going to face justice...supposedly.

"I will say it one last time," he stated with resolve. "I've done nothing to influence this outcome aside from paying off the original competitor that Gungren replaced. I am as amazed about this as you are."

"Yer sure about this?" said Corg.

"Oh, for crying..." He pointed at the other Fate in the room. "Ask Aniok. He'd know."

"Well, Ani?" said Corg. "Is what he's sayin' after being true or do I need to give him a swift kick in his nethers?"

"He's telling the truth. There's been no interference by the Fates in Gungren's battles thus far."

It was nice to know that Aniok hadn't gone so far under the wing of Corg that he'd forgotten who his *real* boss was. Not that it would have mattered anyway, seeing that Heliok had done nothing wrong.

"Then the lad has really whooped up on the competition?" Corg said as his jaw slackened.

"If you want to call it that, sure," Aniok replied with a shrug. "The last guy kind of just fell asleep."

"Aye."

Now that this accusation was proved to be false, Heliok felt he was owed an apology. If anyone else had been so wrongfully accused, they'd get one, so why shouldn't he?

"Uh-hem."

"Well, we'll just get back to filmin' then," said Corg.

"UH-Hem," Heliok repeated, a little louder.

"No point in wasting time," Corg said, patently avoiding even looking in Heliok's direction. "Could be plenty of B-roll we can get."

"UH-HEM!"

Corg spun on the Fate. "Are ye after need some water or somethin', ye hackin' imbecile?"

"No, I do not need water. I would—" He jolted. "Hacking imbecile?"

"What's wrong with that?"

Heliok was nearly in a fit of rage. "How can you even dare to call me such a thing?"

"Well," Corg replied matter-of-factly, "ye was just hacking, right?"

"Yes," admitted Heliok.

"And ye *are* an imbecile, if'n ye remember?"

"Of course, but—" He jolted again. "What? No! I do not remember any such thing."

"You dinnae remember that yer after bein' an imbecile?"

"Absolutely not."

Corg scratched his beard. "Memory's goin', it seems."

"My memory is fine, thank you very much."

The dwarf studied Heliok for a moment. All it would take was a snap of the Fate's fingers and he could send the dwarf off to live inside the core of the nearest sun in an instant. Corg wouldn't live long, but that wasn't the point.

"Ye *do* seem to have your wits about ye at the moment," Corg said curiously.

"I *always* have my wits about me, Mr. Sawsblade."

"If that's true," countered Corg, "ye'd have to agree that while ye've got no memory of bein' an imbecile in the past, you know that you're after bein' one in the present, right?"

"Of course, but—" He nearly burst with frustration this time. "This conversation is over!"

GLORY IS UPON YOU

*R*icky and Crazell were at the arena in her dressing room. The rooms for dragons were obviously much larger than standard rooms. It was so big, in fact, that Crazell was doing her stretches.

"I've been thinking about what you said, Craz," Ricky said as he milled around in front of her, "and you gotta do what you gotta do."

She lowered herself. "Honestly?"

"I don't own you, baby. You're your own dragon."

"But your family has—"

"Has what?" Ricky said with his hands out. "Exploited your talent for many years? That's all we've done, when you get right down to it."

She wanted to agree with him, but the fact was she couldn't. It wouldn't be fair to place all the blame on the Schmicky family while taking none on her own shoulders. It would be the easiest way, sure, but it wouldn't be right.

"No, Ricky," she said as she gently stuck a talon under his chin and lifted his face to hers. "You have given me a purpose all these years. Yes, I have grown tired of it, but that's not your fault."

"And now you'll pay for it every day from this day on." He pulled away from her and plopped down in one of the chairs. "You were right, Craz. You're never going to get any rest after this. Unless you continue fighting in the UDFC, of course."

Crazell sensed the hopefulness in his voice during his last sentence.

"I can't do that anymore."

He gave a solemn nod. "The only other options are to be killed in battle or to lose."

"Even if I merely lose, there will still be challengers."

"Fewer," he said, "but yeah."

There was more at stake than Crazell's future, and she felt obligated to make sure that Ricky and his family would be okay.

"And if I lose, your family…"

"Will be fine," Ricky finished for her. "We took a dragon through twenty-four straight bouts in the biggest dragon championship in the world. Plus, we've got a lot of up-and-coming fighters who are doing great." He motioned to her. "None of them are you, Craz, but it only takes one to be good enough."

Crazell nodded. That much was true. Sure, she'd be a legend in the sport, but her record would stand for a long time, and the Schmickys were a part of that legacy.

Still…

"There is another option, Ricky."

"What?"

"I could go into hiding."

He looked even sadder than before.

"We could win this last one for you and your family," she pressed on. "I would then find a remote place to call home, have my jewels shipped there, and hire a bunch of sentries and bodyguards to keep me from being disturbed."

"Some would still get through, Craz."

"Yes, but it would be infrequent and they would have to get past many obstacles first."

"So what are you saying?"

She looked away from him, scanning the room that had served as hers for nearly 250 years. After today, it would be nothing but a memory. A good one, mostly, but a memory nonetheless.

"Just that I see no other way around this but to win, aside from actually dying," she answered with a whisper, "and I honestly don't think that a former giant can manage that feat."

UDFC 99 RUNNER UP

*P*ayne was in a room with her cameraperson and the runner-up from UDFC 99. The interview was being filmed live, showing all over the Underworld, on the Undernet, and on the big screens in the arena.

The man she was interviewing was named Sir Yalky Trulane. He was a former knight from the land of Metrian.

Sir Trulane was still wearing the outfit that he'd worn during his battle against Crazell ten years ago. It appeared quite burnt.

At least he had taken the helmet off.

"I'm talking with Sir Yalky Trulane," Payne said to the camera. "He's been allowed out of the Afterlife's agnostics area for this interview. Good day to you, Sir Trulane."

"Hello."

"First off, I notice that you are still wearing the outfit that you fought Crazell in ten years ago."

He adjusted in his chair. "It's a constant reminder of what happened, yes."

"Yet, you are in the Afterlife now. You clearly no longer

have to think about things such as this." She then raised a finger. "In fact, you're in the agnostic's area, which means you can essentially do whatever you want."

"I can't help it," he said, licking his lips. "I have been in therapy sessions ever since that fateful day." His eyes glazed over. "I have dreams. Terrible dreams."

"Oh. Well, we wouldn't want—"

"It's the same every time," he said in a voice laced with dread. "I'm at a campsite. I'm very tiny and I'm in a plastic bag along with a bunch of other knights." His breathing was erratic. "Some snot-nosed little brat reaches into the bag and takes me out. He then shoves me onto a stick and puts me over the fire."

Payne gave the camera a look that she assumed would resonate with everyone watching. Chances were that they were all thinking the same thing she was.

"That's...uh...strange."

"Can't you see what it means?"

"Uh..."

"I'm a marshmallow," he blurted. "I'm a blasted marshmallow!"

"Yes, I get that," Payne replied in a calm voice. "What I don't understand is the correlation to UDFC 99?"

"Because Crazell shot fire at me," Sir Trulane shrieked. He was pouring with sweat. "I was trapped in this suit. This damnable suit." He wiped his brow. "One instant I was seeking glory, demonstrating my ability on the field of battle..." He looked away. "The next instant, I was turned into a marshmallow by that infernal dragon."

Payne never quite understood why knights wore their armor when fighting dragons. It wasn't like it would help. If anything, based on the evidence seated in front of her, it'd do just the opposite.

"Right." She had to recover from this, somehow. "Well, I, uh…. Do you have any advice for Crazell's challenger?"

He nodded, though his eyes were unfocused.

"Throw in the towel before the fight and *don't* wear metal armor. It does nothing against a dragon but turn you into a portable stove."

YOU CAN DO IT!

W hizzfiddle was proud and frightened at knowing that his apprentice was about to go toe to toe with Crazell.

How did this even happen?

Gungren wasn't supposed to get this far. Actually, he should never have been involved with this at all. If Whizzfiddle could have just kept his big mouth shut, they would be going after the Diamond of Jaloof instead.

He thumbed the stone that he'd put into his pocket.

The fact was that they would have ended up following Teggins to the event anyway. But even that would be better than Gungren having to actually *compete*.

"How are you doing, Gungren?" he asked in a caring tone.

"I are okay."

"I *am* okay," he corrected halfheartedly.

"Of course you am okay," Gungren said. "You ain't got to fight no dragon."

"Right." Whizzfiddle sighed. "Look, I want to tell you something before you go out there."

"All right."

"Eloquen, may we have a moment alone, please?"

The elf began saying, "The cranium moves…" but he stopped when he clearly noticed that Whizzfiddle was not in the mood for his floweriness. "I'll be outside."

"Thank you."

As soon as the elf left, Whizzfiddle took a deep breath. This wasn't the kind of conversation he was comfortable with, but he felt that it needed to happen.

"Gungren, I'm not one to get all mushy, so know that this is not something I say lightly."

"Okay."

"When we first met, I thought you were the biggest pain in the rump I'd ever met," he said seriously. "You were belligerent, obstinate, nagging, and just downright difficult."

"I are feeling better already, Master. Thanks."

Whizzfiddle pushed forward. "Over the course of our time together, you have become like the son I never had. You've got the kindest heart I've ever come to know, especially for a wizard, and that's saying something."

"That nice to hear," Gungren said as he wiped his nose.

"The point of this is that I don't wish to lose you today, Gungren," Whizzfiddle said as he folded his arms. "You are too good of a person to be extinguished over something this silly. You have more than proved yourself worthy of being a full-fledged wizard. Doing this battle is not only foolish, it's unnecessary."

Gungren sat there nodding. He wasn't looking at Whizzfiddle, but rather at the floor. His face was drawn and he was obviously very tired.

"Master, you know me better than anyone," he said finally. "I know that I can get my wizard thing without finishing this, but I made a committing thing."

"Commitment."

"That the one." He cleared his throat. "If I give up now,

then I not keeping my commitment to finish the Fate Quest. If I not keep that, then I go back on my word."

Whizzfiddle's master would have said, "Word schmerd!" or something to that effect, but Whizzfiddle was not like his master. He agreed with Gungren's stance on this. Money was not what made a person, it was their word that mattered.

"Now *that* I understand, Gungren," he admitted. "A person is nothing if they don't uphold that which they have agreed to doing, as long as new information does not arise that counters what they had originally agreed to, of course."

"What?"

"Never mind. It doesn't matter." He sat down and hung his head. "I guess there is no use trying to talk you out of this?"

"Sorry, Master."

"Better to die as the man you are than to live as the one you are not."

"It a hard fight, too," Gungren said after a few moments of silence.

"Yes, that dragon is fierce."

"Yeah, that too, but I were talking about fighting from letting the giant come back." He looked at Whizzfiddle with strained eyes. "I want to pick up rocks so bad, Master."

"If Crazell gets the better of you, it may not matter anyway."

"That true, but I gonna try not to die." Gungren started stretching. "Also, I try not to kill that dragon, too."

"I know, Gungren." And he did. Gungren was just too kind of a person to ever want to permanently injure anyone. "I just hope she feels the same way about you."

SORRY, WHO IS THIS AGAIN?

*B*ank rushed into the office while holding a piece of paper. He shoved it into Stillwell's hands and began pacing.

Stillwell opened the paper and read it. A thin smile crept across his face. He fought to keep it in check.

"So Teggins was arrested, was he?"

"That's what it says," answered Bank. "Got caught cheating."

"Well, that's a shame."

"He's gonna be calling you soon to get his lawyer, temporary-boss."

"Yes, I would imagine so."

Bank was clearly finding this news very upsetting. Stillwell probably should have as well, but his gut was telling him it was a good thing, and so far his gut had been doing quite well with predictions.

It was time to start flexing those muscles again.

"Do you feel I've treated you fairly over the last couple of days, Bank?"

"Huh?" He stopped pacing, looked around, and then nodded. "Sure, I guess. Better than the boss does."

"And do you think the other fellas feel the same way?"

"They're already saying so," Bank replied. "You've been treating everybody decently."

Stillwell didn't want to ask this next question, but he did anyway.

"Even the ladies?"

"Yep. They're happy 'cause you said you was gonna talk to the boss about equal pay and all that." Bank pointed at him. "The ogres are happy about that equal pay stuff too, by the way."

"That's good to hear." He clasped his fingers together and rested his chin on them. "What would happen if we refused to help Teggins, Bank?"

"We?"

"Okay, me."

"He'd kill you."

"Right, right, I know about that. But wouldn't he be away for a long time?"

"Ahhhh, I see," Bank said cautiously. "He'd likely get twenty years for what he's done. But when he got out, he'd kill you."

That was a long time for Teggins to be in the slammer. If Stillwell played his cards correctly, he could make it so that Teggins had no ammunition when he was released.

He'd be nothing.

One thing that Stillwell had learned over these last couple of days was that money talks.

"I'm sure over the course of twenty years that we, as a team, could determine a way to stop that eventuality, no?"

It took a few seconds, but Bank finally began to smile.

"Yeah, we could."

"Especially if there was the promised continuance of

better treatment, more pay, and possibly even profit-sharing?"

"What about dental and vision?" Bank said, moving into negotiation mode.

"I'm sure that can be arranged."

"And maybe a retirement account?"

Stillwell flicked a dismissive hand. "If we work together to properly manage things, that too can be ironed out."

"Then, yeah, I'd say we could figure out something to stop Teggins from killing you..." Bank paused before adding, "boss."

So he'd transitioned from the "temporary-boss" moniker. That was a good sign.

He would have to be constantly on his toes in this job, but something told him that if he kept treating the people beneath him with fairness and respect, they'd weed out dissenters in a hurry. There was no evidence to back this up, seeing that the very point of a crime syndicate was *not* to treat people with dignity and respect. Intimidation, yes, but not respect.

The phone began to ring.

It was Teggins.

Stillwell didn't feel worried this time, though. If anything, he felt empowered.

"That's him," he announced. "Could I have a little privacy, please?"

"Good luck, boss," Bank said as he left the room.

Just to be irritating, Stillwell let it ring once more before picking it up.

"This is Stillwell," he said.

"We got a problem here, Stillwell, and you gotta help us out of it."

"Who is this?" Stillwell said, trying not to laugh.

"It's Teggins, you boob. Now listen, I only got one call and

263

it's to you, so don't screw this up. Me and Lucille got busted for cheating and we've been extradited down to Dakmenhem for sentencing. You need to contact my lawyers and get them down here pronto. They all owe me a lot of money, so they'll play ball or they'll be in trouble."

"I'm sorry, Mr. Teggins," Stillwell said in a haughty tone of voice, "but that won't be possible. You see, the lawyers that you speak of are being forgiven their debt so they no longer have an interest in being under your thumb."

The phone went silent for a few seconds. Well, not completely silent. Stillwell could hear breathing on the other end. It did not sound like happy breathing, either.

"What are you trying to pull, Stillwell?"

"Also," Stillwell continued without answering the question directly, "note that the goons have collectively decided that they wish me to remain in charge."

"This had better be a joke, Stillwell. 'Cause if it ain't, I'll rip your head from your body."

"You'll have twenty years to dream of that day, Mr. Teggins. I, on the other hand, will have a massive army of nefarious people who will be rather interested in my staying alive." Stillwell breathed in through his nose. "You see, I treat people with respect, Mr. Teggins. You do not."

The breathing stopped. It was replaced with the sound of controlled rage. Stillwell could not describe the sound, but it was definitely emanating from the other side of the TalkyThingy.

"Let me give you some advice, Stillwell," growled Teggins. "When I get out of here, you'd better be far away, living in a little cave in the middle of nowhere so that I can't find you."

"And I shall provide you some advice as well, Mr. Teggins," Stillwell countered calmly. "When you get set free from prison, you may wish to duck so you can at least get ten feet out of the gate before you breathe your last."

"You lousy, double-crossing, piece of dragon dung. You call them lawyers right now or you'll regret the day you were born!"

Stillwell had covered the mouthpiece as he chuckled.

Then, he thought about those lawyers, and he had to admit that Teggins was right. They *did* need to be called. Immediately.

"Fine, Mr. Teggins," Stillwell said, trying to sound a bit worried. "I promise you that I will call your lawyers as soon as we disconnect this call."

"You will?"

"Absolutely."

"Well, that's better, then."

"You see, Mr. Teggins, they work for me now, and I'll make certain they are on the side of the prosecution." He giggled maniacally. "Don't worry, though, I'm sure you'll get a nice public defender to state your case."

PLAYING TO THE CROWD

$\mathcal{P}$ayne Sawsblade stood at the entrance to the field, waiting for the contestants to come out. She had purposefully stood off to one side while her cameraperson stood on the other. This was because Crazell would be out first and she was one huge dragon.

The sound of claws striking concrete reverberated down the hallway.

As soon as Crazell turned the corner, Payne understood the meaning of the word "fear." The dragon's face was so deathly serious that it threatened to make Payne clam up. This was *not* the same dragon she'd interviewed earlier. This was a dragon who was ready to kill.

But Payne was a professional, so when Crazell approached, she forced herself calm.

"Crazell is about to enter the ring to defend her title for an amazing twenty-fifth time," she said in a strong voice before sticking the microphone in front of Crazell. "How are you feeling right now?"

"I have a job to do and I will do it," the dragon answered without inflection.

"You can see she has a very business-like attitude towards this match," Payne said to the camera. "Crazell, have you seen the challenger before today?"

"No."

"Have you watched his previous matches today?"

"Yes."

"And your thoughts?"

"He is clearly strong and fights intelligently, but he has nothing to offer in the face of my wrath."

Ricky Schmicky yelled out, "All right, we're moving!"

Payne wisely jumped out of the way as Crazell exited the tunnel and lifted up into the sky.

The crowd's cheer was deafening. It was so loud that Payne and the cameraperson moved into the tunnel a bit in order to interview the challenger before he entered the field.

"Strong words from a dragon who can absolutely back it up," Payne said to the camera as Gungren came walking up. "And here we have Gungren, the challenger. Hello, Gungren."

"Hello."

"Are you ready for this challenge?"

"Yep."

Payne was surprised at the lack of concern on the little giant's face.

"You seem rather relaxed."

"No point to worry," he replied with a shrug. "It won't help."

"You could take the advice of the knight who fought in UDFC 99 and throw in the towel before the fight starts," suggested Payne.

Gungren shook his head. "I not gonna do that."

"What's your strategy, then?" she asked, hoping to glean some intel for the audience.

"I got a couple of idea things," he answered, "but I not

JOHN P. LOGSDON & CHRISTOPHER P. YOUNG

gonna say them. I learned that sometimes people don't play fair. Not sure about dragons, but better safe than sorry."

Payne smiled at him. "Wise words."

"All right," yelled his corner, "let's get out there!"

Gungren headed into the arena with four people in his wake. Payne waited for the camera to follow them out. The crowd was cheering even louder for Gungren than they had been for Crazell.

Everyone loved an underdog.

"There goes a very brave little man," she said as the camera panned back to her. "He'll be in the Afterlife soon, unfortunately. One can only hope he's agnostic."

IN THIS CORNER...

The orchestra stopped, the dragon landed, and Gungren stood on his side of the field, looking at her. It reminded him of the days when he was a giant, except that dragons hadn't looked quite as large back then.

The memory of standing across a field while throwing rocks against a mountainside came to mind. It was peaceful. No, he hadn't been very smart in those days, but he also hadn't had any real responsibilities. Every day was a weekend, as it were. It hadn't been boring because he hadn't known any better, but to go back to that life now would be terrible.

"Ladies and gentlemen," said the announcer from the center of the field, "this is the moment you've all been waiting for. This is the UDFC 100 championship fight, and it's gonna be a clash!"

The eruption of cheers was so loud that it hurt Gungren's head.

"In this corner, we have the shock of the day. The wizard apprentice you've learned to love. He stands around four feet tall, weighs in at one hundred and sixty pounds. He has a professional record of three and 0. He's dented armor, twisted arms, put Krag the Destroyer to sleep, and won our hearts. It's Gungren!"

The crowd was on their feet, clapping, whistling, and yelling his name.

"And in this corner," continued the announcer, "we have the reigning champion, the top of the heap, the unstoppable, unfathomable, unflappable dragon who has struck fear in the hearts of humans, ogres, orcs, trolls, dwarves, halflings, and even other dragons. Her weight goes beyond the capability of our scales and nobody has been brave enough to measure her height. She has owned the title of Ultimate Dragon Fighting Championship champion for the last two hundred and forty-nine years. She has never lost a bout. She is the undisputed UDFC champion of the world. I give you Crazell!"

As if the cheering weren't loud enough before, they were now making Gungren cover his ears. He couldn't blame them. Crazell was the favorite and she was going for a legendary record.

"Your referee for this tournament is Benny Courtman."

The cheering stopped abruptly.

The ref frowned and waved at the fighters.

"Bring it in," he yelled. Then he called up to the dragon. "You need to bring your head down here, Crazell." She did. The ref gulped. "Okay, uh...I want a clean fight. When I say break, you break. If I send you to your corner, you go to your corner." He looked at Gungren. "You sure you want to do this, pal? I've got a white towel right here?"

Gungren kept looking at the dragon. "I are ready."

"You will die," Crazell said sinisterly.

"If that happens, it happens."

Crazell blinked a few times. "Hmmm."

"Okay," the ref said, shrugging, "go to your corners and wait for the sound of the bell."

"Good luck, dragon lady," Gungren said before turning around. "I try not to hurt you too much."

"You hurt me?" she bellowed in response and then began laughing. "Well, I thank you for your generosity, little man."

"That okay," Gungren said with a genuine smile.

Crazell stopped laughing, glancing at the ref. "Is this guy for real?"

"I don't know, lady," the ref replied with his hand up, "but I've seen him take out some pretty advanced fighters today."

"No one of my stature, though." She then dipped down and moved her head right up to Gungren's face. "Listen, little man, I will burn you to a crisp. Do you hear me?"

"Yep," Gungren said with a nod.

"Doesn't that strike fear into your heart?"

"Not really." He then looked around before saying, "Can I tell you something and you not get mad?"

"Huh?" She peered over at the ref, who just shrugged in response. "Uh...sure. What?"

"I know you am a dragon and stuff, but you need a breath mint."

Her eyes went wide as she brought a claw to her mouth. "I do?"

"Sorry, but it true."

"Oh, well, thank you. I didn't know."

"That no problem. Good luck."

"Thanks. You too..." Then she shook her head, realizing what had just happened. "What am I saying? I don't wish you good luck! I'm Crazell! I will destroy you!"

"Okay," said Gungren before turning around and heading back to his corner.

YOU'VE GOT TO SEE THIS

Zel, Bekner, and Orophin were seated in the basement under the Inn of Sargan, watching the event. There were a few others sitting at different tables as well, all of them either soldiers or people from the Underworld who were on travel visas.

Everyone was excited to see that the little giant had made it to the final show.

"I do worry that this time he has bitten off more than he can chew," said Zel.

"Aye," agreed Bekner, "but he's been quite impressive thus far, he has."

"How is your head?" Orophin asked.

"Aching like the devil, but I'm on the mend. Never been hit like that before, and I've had a hammer knock me noggin more than once. Gungren's definitely got the fists for the job."

"His skill with grappling was excellent, too." Zel glanced back at the screen. "Unfortunately, I don't think it'll work on a dragon. She is simply too large for him."

"Aye."

Orophin shook his head and snapped up some more popcorn.

"The one thing I've learned since meeting Gungren is that it's unwise to underestimate him."

Zel couldn't argue that point. Ever since Gungren was changed from a giant into a wizard, he'd been quite headstrong and very capable. Zel still remembered the tenacious nature of the little guy as he'd pressed Whizzfiddle to take him on as an apprentice.

"The aching in me brain can attest to your words, elf," Bekner admitted.

Zel pointed at the screen. "I wonder what he and the dragon are talking about."

"She looks confused."

"Exactly, Orophin," Zel agreed. "I never thought Gungren was the type to play mind games."

"He wouldn't know where to start," said Bekner.

"Now she looks angry." Orophin was really digging into the popcorn now. "She's all up in his face. That would be the perfect picture for the Elfstretchy line, don't you think?"

"The what?"

"That's what I'm calling the line of clothing that Eloquen and I designed, Bekner. It's what Gungren is wearing."

"Ah, right."

"Looks like the fight is about to start," said Zel with a measure of excitement he'd not felt in years.

YOU ARE GETTING THIS, RIGHT?

"*Y*ou *are* getting all of this, right?" Misty asked as her heart raced. Everything was riding on this. Everything.

"Are ye talkin' to me, lass?"

"Of course I'm talking to you, Corg," she snipped. "This is gold we're watching here. We can't miss a beat."

"Since when have ye known me to miss anything on film?"

Corg looked hurt by her words. She hadn't meant it that way, though.

That wasn't true.

She meant it *precisely* that way. But what she hadn't done was think about the fact that it was Corg Sawsblade she was talking to.

Misty was currently in her own world. Her future was in the balance. It was exhilarating, but also gut-wrenching.

"Sorry, Corg," she said with a weak smile.

"Yer after gettin' on me nerves with questions like that, ye blue devil," he said, obviously trying to hide his hurt feelings.

Her eye twitched. "Blue devil?"

"It's what me people call yer people."

"Is that right?"

"Aye."

"Well," she said with her ire on the rise, "my people call your people a bunch of little sh—"

"Shaping up to be a great video from where I sit," Aniok interrupted with excellent timing.

"Good, good," said Corg. "Keep your eye on the target, Ani. We can't afford to miss a beat." Then he turned and gave Misty a nasty look. "We'll get back to what yer mangy mob calls my mangy mob later."

She forced herself to calm down. The fact was that she needed Corg as much as he needed her. Yes, they were an odd combination to pair up in a working environment, but sometimes antagonism made for better productions.

"Look, Corg," she said, trying again to bury the hatchet, "I guess I'm just very wound up about this because my career is on the line here. But if we nail this, we'll be able to write our own tickets."

"I can write me own ticket now," Corg replied with a look that said, "Ye wonky Fate!" Then he pointed at the desk and added, "Ye get yerself a pen and a piece of paper and ye write down what yer after wantin'. It ain't that hard, lass."

"No, that's not what I mean. I'm talking about…" She looked into his squinting eyes and sighed. "Oh, just forget it."

ROUND 1

$\mathcal{R}$ ound one was about to begin and Gungren had done all of the stretching he could manage. What he had planned would require a lot of focus and stamina. With the constant thoughts of throwing rocks running through his head, this wouldn't be easy, but he had to stick with it.

"Now this fight's like nothing you've seen before," Barrie was yelling at him, barely audible above the crowd. "You have to weave and jab and jump and roll. You can't just stand still. It'll never work."

"Just go out and have fun, dear," called Muriel over her husband's shoulder. "You'll do fine."

"Have fun fighting against a dragon?" Barrie replied, looking back. "What kind of advice is that?"

"The boy may as well have a good time in his last minutes on Ononokin, love."

Barrie nodded. "Okay, you've got me there."

"I'll be all right," Gungren said. "I got a plan."

"I know you do," Barrie yelled. "It's called weave and jab and jump and roll, like I said."

"Nope. Different plan, but it will work."

Barrie threw his hands up. Then he looked at Gungren in frustration. Then he threw up his hands again.

"Fine. Don't take my advice. It was nice knowing you, kid."

~

"The bell has rung and the fighters are moving out into the ring," Optical said, moving to drinking coffee so that he would be at the top of his game during the final bout. "Any insights on what's about to happen here, Homer?"

"It's hard to say," Homer replied in his trademarked sarcastic edge, "but I'm going to go with Gungren suffering a flame-induced death."

"Likely to be just that," Optical replied, finding it difficult to argue the point. "Wait a second. Folks, I know I'm starting to sound like a broken gnomeDisc here, but I can't believe my eyes."

"That's it," exclaimed Homer. "I'm going to have to take some refresher classes on the latest Dragon Martial Art techniques. Things just aren't what they used to be."

Optical was having a hell of a time rationalizing what he was witnessing. In fact, if he weren't certain that he'd been on his third cup of coffee, he might have believed that he was still greatly under the influence of brandy. A couple of small glasses of the booze was all he'd had, too, and that wasn't enough to cause hallucinations.

"Ladies and gentlemen," he said, nearly laughing, "if you're only hearing this on the radio, you are seriously missing out. Gungren has just run over and latched himself to Crazell's leg. She's shaking it like mad, but he is on her like a tick."

"You think he's bitten into her and is sucking out her blood?" Homer asked with wide eyes.

"No," said Optical. "Why would you think that?"

"Is that not what ticks do?"

"Ah, yes, I see. I was being metaphorical."

"Oh." Homer coughed. "Well, it feels like I've been saying this the entire day, especially where Gungren is involved, but grabbing hold of a dragon's leg and not letting go for anything is definitely a tactic I've never seen."

"Indeed," agreed Optical. "Crazell has just moved into a quick roll, but Gungren remains latched on. She's now lifting off and is flying around the arena. Gungren just won't let go, though."

"It doesn't look like it, no." Homer was laughing out loud at this point. "He's got to have incredible strength to be able to manage that, especially with her barrel rolls. And she's not likely to try to flame him because she'll have to hit her own leg in order to do that."

"No argument there, Homer. She's coming back down and landing. There's definitely a look of frustration on her face."

"Can you blame her?"

"Not really."

The bell sounded the end of the round.

"And the bell has rung, making Gungren the first challenger to get out of round one against Crazell!"

"I have to hand it to the little guy," Homer said, his voice still full of joviality, "that was the most fitting technique he could have employed."

"Do you expect we'll see more of that in the second?"

"If we do, Optical, I'll be amazed. Crazell knows to get in the air quick now." Homer opened the bottle again, but then closed it back up and pushed it away. "Besides, Gungren isn't going to win by grabbing her leg. So unless he wants to go down in history as being the only warrior to go the distance with Crazell, he'll have to try a different strategy."

"Looks like we'll see," said Optical. "We'll be back for round two shortly."

COACHING

Barrie was doing his best to coach Gungren.

"I'll admit that it was a solid tactic to use in order to protect yourself from being killed," said the man, "but you're not going to win a fight like that."

"Better he lives as a loser than dies trying to be a winner, dear," Muriel stated as fact.

"Do you even hear the things you're saying to the boy?"

Whizzfiddle pushed past them as they continued their bickering. The truth was they didn't know Gungren like Whizzfiddle did. Whatever he had on his mind was what he was going to do. By the time his corner figured that out, the event would be over.

"Gungren?"

"Yes, Master?"

"Remember the protection spell you built up?"

"Yep."

He pointed across the way at the dragon who appeared to be fuming. She had smoke pouring from her nostrils and her eyes were smoldering.

"Now might be the perfect time to use it."

"I think I gonna throw rocks at her instead," Gungren said, speaking in monotone.

"What?"

"Rocks," he droned. "I wanna throw rocks."

"Did something shake loose in your head when you were flying around up there?" Whizzfiddle asked while knocking on his apprentice's noggin.

"Huh?" Gungren said, blinking.

"You've been fighting this like mad, Gungren," Whizzfiddle stated, shaking the little giant by his shoulders. "You can't give in now."

"Actually," interjected Barrie, "that rocks idea ain't half bad."

Whizzfiddle glared at Barrie. "Keep your mind off rocks, Gungren. Use that protection spell instead." He then reached into Gungren's backpack and pulled out a large, leather-bound book of magic. "And once you're under that spell, start reading this. It'll keep you focused."

"You know casting spells ain't allowed in the UDFC, right?" Barrie asked.

"He won't be casting any spells," Whizzfiddle answered back. "Will you, Gungren?"

"Nope. I gonna throw rocks."

"Gungren, listen to me. You have to fight this throwing-rocks thing!"

"What's wrong with throwing rocks?" asked Barrie.

Whizzfiddle turned on the man. "Will you stay out of this?"

"I'm his corner," Barrie fought back, puffing out his chest. "You stay out of this."

Whizzfiddle didn't have time to bicker with Barrie. His apprentice's life was hanging in the balance.

"If you don't back away from me, by The Twelve, I'll turn you into a goat."

Barrie's face went pale. "What?"

"Come along, Barrie," Muriel said while pulling her husband by the arm. "Let the man have his words with his apprentice. The last thing I need is a husband who chews up all my furniture."

Whizzfiddle waited until they were out of earshot before turning back to Gungren.

"No rocks," he said, kneeling down and looking into his apprentice's eyes. "You have to stay strong."

"But it tough, Master."

"I know it is, but you can do it." A moment of inspiration struck. "Besides, you have to remember that if you touch a rock it will sting because of that spell I cast on you back before we left on this journey." Gungren didn't seem to care. "Look, just use the spell you made before and concentrate on staying a wizard by reading your book."

"Okay, Master."

"Promise me," Whizzfiddle said, knowing how much keeping his word meant to Gungren.

"I promise."

ROUND 2

*T*he moment the bell rang, Crazell flapped her wings and launched straight up into the air, obviously making sure that Gungren had no chance of grabbing her leg again.

But that worked in his favor because he just walked to the middle of the ring, took the box out of his pocket, set it on the ground, and pressed the button on its side. Then he took a seat and started reading about magic.

His master was right, it *did* help him take his mind off rocks. This was because it reminded him that to go back to being a giant would mean losing his ability to comprehend the things he was currently reading. That would be such a shame because Gungren really loved magic. It was intricate, complex, and yet so simple and smooth at the same time. Each spell was like a little puzzle to him. He loved magic so much that he'd even considered attempting to learn the elements of witchcraft. Their spells wouldn't work by eating dirt. They required deep study and practice.

That was an exciting thought.

A screeching sound came from off to his right and he glanced over to see the huge red dragon diving at him.

He casually turned to the next page as a ball of flame erupted all around the area, deflecting off the dome of protection that the little box afforded him.

The referee blew his whistle and waved his hands as Crazell landed beside Gungren and snaked her head out to look over his shoulder. He knew she was there because she bumped her nose on his shield.

The judges ran out onto the field, as did Crazell's manager, and Whizzfiddle.

"He can't cast a spell in the ring," Ricky Schmicky yelled. "That's a disqualification."

"I agree," the ref said, "but it's up to the judges. Now just go back to your corner and let us handle this."

"He hasn't done anything—"

The ref pointed at Whizzfiddle. "Look, pal, rule book or not, you don't belong out here. Go back to your corner and let the judges handle things, yeah?"

"But..."

"It okay, Master," said Gungren as he pressed the button on the box to shut the shield down. "I got this. The book are helping."

"Are you sure?"

"Yep."

Whizzfiddle nodded, gave one more glance at the judges, and then walked back to the corner. Gungren was glad he had found such a good teacher. While he learned more about magic from books than he did from Whizzfiddle, he had learned more about himself than any book could teach.

"You realize you're not allowed to cast magic during a fight, right?" the witch named Teresa said to Gungren.

"Yep."

"But you just decided to wing it and do so anyway?" asked Sephnedra.

"Nope."

"Then I would say he has clearly broken one of the—" She stopped and looked at him. "Sorry, what did you say?"

"I not wing nothing," he answered her. "I plan it."

"Speak out, little pal," Stiermark said as he squatted down near Gungren. "What are ya talkin' about?"

"The rule book say that you can't cast spells in the fight," Gungren explained.

Teresa pointed at him. "Exactly, so…"

"But I not cast a spell during the fight."

"There was a magical shield surrounding you, young man," Sephnedra noted. "We all saw it."

"Yep, but it wasn't 'cause I cast a spell during the fight," Gungren argued. "I cast the spell for this at the hotel and put it in a box. That one." He pointed at the box. "I opened the box here and the spell happened."

The ref sighed and pulled out his rule book. Then he rolled his eyes and looked at Gungren.

"What page?" he asked.

"Fifty-eight."

"Damn it, he's right," the ref said with his finger on the text. "He found a loophole. It specifically states he can't *cast* a spell, but it doesn't mention anything about *enacting* a previously cast one."

"Yep."

"Ah-ha, wait! It also states that an opponent may not be imbued with the magic of another wizard."

"I not inbred," Gungren said swiftly. "I just look that way."

"Imbued," the ref said again, this time more distinctly.

"Oh."

"I'll check it out, dudes," Stiermark said as he popped a shroom in his mouth. "Just a sec."

"Oh boy," said Teresa, "now he'll be running around and screaming about a big yellow dot with a chomping mouth chasing him."

"Nah, gonna use it up when I cast the spell." He picked up the box that Gungren had made and said, "WHO-CRAFTED-UP-THE-SHIELD-THIS-DUDE-HAS-SPINNIN?"

A flash of colors surrounded the cube. It was dancing in various hues until finally forming the word "Gungren."

"Says this dude did it," Stiermark stated, pointing at the little giant.

"Then I would say that there is nothing more to discuss," Teresa commented.

Sephnedra looked at Gungren thoughtfully. "It does seem like it's on the up and up."

"At least as far as the rules are written," agreed Teresa.

"Correct," said Sephnedra.

"Stickin' it to the man, Gungren," Stiermark said while slapping the little giant on the back. "Rock and roll, dude."

"Thanks," Gungren replied. "I think."

For the rest of the round, Crazell blew flames at the shield, scraped it, bit it and even jumped up and down on it, but it wouldn't budge. Gungren was as safe as could be.

Finally, she stopped trying and spoke to Gungren instead.

"What kind of warrior sticks a shield around himself and just sits there reading a book?" Crazell said in accusation as the crowd looked on.

"I gotta read this or I'm gonna want to throw rocks at you," Gungren replied.

"So throw rocks at me," she growled. "This is just

embarrassing. I have been the champion for years. I don't want to go out like this."

"What do you mean?" Gungren said, closing his book and looking up at her.

"I mean that I'm going to retire after this tournament. It's my twenty-fifth win in UDFC 100, and you're making me look like a fool."

"I are sorry about that," Gungren said, feeling bad. "I didn't know. But I'm afraid to pick up the rocks."

"I don't care if you're afraid," she said as the bell rang to signal the end of the second round. "Just do it and let's end this thing already."

HE IS A CLEVER ONE

*C*org shook his head in fascination at how Gungren was getting through this event. He knew that the fellow had gumption and was able to stand strong in the face of adversity—that much was proved over his last two quests. But this was beyond fathomable.

"This is going to be the absolute bestselling show to ever hit the Underworld," Misty said in that way only a business mogul could manage. "I'm going to be the most sought-after producer in the history of television."

"You have to give it to this Gungren fellow *I* selected," Heliok said with heavy inflection. "He is quite a miracle worker."

Misty clearly hadn't cared what Heliok had stated. She just kept looking off into the distance. Her dreams had obviously overtaken rationality.

"Companies will be lining up and begging for me to lead their teams."

"It's these kinds of selections that mark *me* as being the one who should have an assistant, too, when you really think about it. I mean, what does Kilodiek do all day but sit there?"

Corg eyed them both with contempt.

"What are you two on about?" he said in a harsh voice, interrupting their thoughts. He pointed at Misty. "Yer over there making like ye suddenly poop gold, and it's gettin' on me last nerve."

"I'd treat me respectfully, if I were you, Corg," she said. "You're looking at the soon-to-be most important person in all of the film industry here."

"And yer lookin' at the dwarf who can take yer precious little plans and twist them about during post-production," he countered.

Her breath caught. "You wouldn't."

"Not if I'm after bein' treated fairly," he stated. "Remember, lass, that I ain't like these Fates we're after working for. I can't be snapping me fingers and havin' gold coins linin' me pockets."

She was about to reply, but Corg spun on his heel and pointed at Heliok.

"And yer off whinin' about not bein' after havin' an assistant. What do ye need an assistant for? Anything ye want, ye can have at the clap of yer hands." He grunted. "Yer just bein' a dopey Fate."

"Hey, you're right," Heliok said after a few moments.

"About which part?" Corg sought to clarify. "I'm guessin' both."

"The clapping of my hands part, thank you very much."

"Ah."

Corg honestly hadn't expected the daft Fate would have agreed with the other part.

"In fact," Heliok continued while strolling around the little room, "I'd argue it's a sign of weakness for a Fate to have need of an assistant." He stopped walking and started nodding. "Yes. Thank you, Corg. I feel much better now."

"Aye, okay," Corg said heavily. "Definitely wasn't after what I was shootin' for."

CONFRONTING STILLWELL

*S*tillwell had finished going over the books and calculating how much money would be left if he forgave everyone's debt. There was still enough to live one hundred lifetimes. Teggins definitely knew how to pack money away.

Bank opened the door and stuck his head inside.

"You got company, boss-for-not-much-longer."

"Why are you calling me that?"

A bunch of mobster types suddenly pushed past Bank. They were carrying baseball bats, brass knuckles, and chains, and they didn't look happy.

"Oh, I see." Stillwell's bladder threatened to loosen again, but he had to act strong. He pointed at the guy who was front and center. "Who are you?"

"The name is Ruffins," said the man.

He wasn't big, but he looked mean. Now, this was obviously a stereotype, and Stillwell felt bad about that, but the fellow was unshaven, had a scar running down the side of his face, was wearing an eyepatch, had gold teeth and, again, he was carrying a baseball bat that had undoubtedly been used to dent a few heads in its day.

"I got a phone call from Teggins sayin' that you was trying to muscle in on his territory," the guy said.

Stillwell blanched. "I thought he only had one phone call?"

"Some of the guards owe him money," replied Ruffins.

"Ah." Stillwell fought to calm himself as he remembered how loudly money spoke. "Do all of you also owe him money?"

"Of course," Ruffins replied as if it were a stupid question. "Everybody owes Teggins money." The rest of the mob nodded their heads. "And by taking you to the cleaners, we get ten percent off what we owe forgiven."

It was time to start playing the game. This crew had just tipped their hand. They weren't interested in putting the hurt on Stillwell just because Teggins had told them to do it. Their goal was to alleviate some of the financial pressure the crime boss had them under.

"That's not very much," Stillwell said.

Ruffins tapped the bat on his hand. "It helps, pal."

"Not really." Stillwell held up the ledger he'd just completed working on. "You see, I've been looking over the books and it seems that Mr. Teggins has inflated his interest percentages and rules to the point where you'd have to pay him off, in full, with an additional thirty days interest to get out of your debt."

"Huh?" said Ruffins.

Bank spoke up. "He's sayin' that you ain't gettin' out of debt. Ever."

"But I've been making payments," Ruffins said, confused. "We's all been making payments."

There were more nods.

"I'm sorry to be the bearer of bad news, gentlemen,"

Stillwell said sadly, "but for every payment you make, you are further and further behind. You'll never catch up." He slowly looked up at their faces. "You'll never be free from the leash of Mr. Teggins."

These guys obviously hadn't placed in the top ten percent of their classes in school. Honestly, Stillwell imagined they had problems spelling their own names.

"I don't get it," Ruffins said eventually.

He decided to just get straight to the point.

"Do you even know what you owe, Mr. Ruffins?"

"I borrowed twenty-five gold, and I know there's some interest and stuff, but I gotta be down to like five gold by now."

"Sorry, no." He held up the book again. "It shows here that you currently owe ninety-seven gold."

"What?" The bat fell to the floor with a thud. "I've been paying that back for two years. Three gold a month!"

Stillwell couldn't help but feel pity for the man. Hell, even Stillwell himself had fallen into the same pit and he *was* in the top ten percent of his class back in school.

"That just means you should have thirty-six gold paid down on a twenty-five gold loan." He let that sink in for a moment. "Even at advanced interest, Mr. Ruffins, that is robbery. But again, your new balance is nearly four times what you originally borrowed, and that's only after two years."

He let the book fall on the desk for dramatic effect. It reverberated throughout the room before leaving nothing but silence.

The goons were staring at the floor in shock.

"You'll never get out, unless you win the lottery," Stillwell said finally.

"I'll kill him," Ruffins said as the angst built on his face. It was soon shared by the rest of the mob. "We'll all kill him."

"Yes," Stillwell agreed. "I would imagine you may want to, indeed." He then held up a finger and added, "Out of curiosity, how would all of you like to win the lottery?"

Ruffins blinked. "Huh?"

"I'm taking over Teggins' business, as you know," Stillwell reminded them. "Clearly, he doesn't like that, which is why you're all here." He leaned forward and put his elbows on the desk. "However, if I were to forgive all of your debts, and pay each of you fifty gold for a single favor, how would you feel about that?"

They were all nodding with such vigor that Stillwell felt a breeze. He wasn't surprised. If he had been in their shoes at the moment, he would be accepting the offer as well.

"Bank, please give each of these men fifty gold and have them sign a paper that states they will aid me in the physical demise of Mr. Teggins upon his release from prison."

Then he glanced back at the goons.

"I'm assuming all of you are okay with these terms?"

Their nods continued.

"Excellent."

The TalkyThingy rang. It was, of course, Teggins. Stillwell had fully expected this. Now he was relishing in it.

"Want us to go, boss?" Bank asked.

"No, I don't," he replied, feeling stronger than ever, "but I do expect you to remain silent. Understood?"

Again, nods.

Stillwell pressed the speaker option on the TalkyThingy and said, "Hello, Mr. Teggins. How is prison treating you?"

"Did my guys show up?"

"They have, yes," Stillwell replied, "and it has genuinely made me rethink things."

"I'll bet it has," Teggins said with a menacing chuckle. "But you ain't out of the water yet, Stillwell. I'm still gonna pummel you to a pulp and then when you heal up, I'm gonna pummel you again. Five times of that and I'll let you live to work cleaning toilets in the lower levels for the rest of your pathetic days."

"It *does* seem fair," Stillwell said as he winked at the mob.

They were all wearing greasy grins. The kind of grins you saw on people who knew well that one day they would be exacting revenge.

"Yeah, it does," Teggins said. "I'm glad you're starting to see things my way, Stillwell. Who knows, maybe one day I'll actually forgive you for this stupid attempt on your part?"

"That would be a dream come true, Mr. Teggins."

"I'll bet it would be."

"Sir, if I may speak to the guard who let you make the call, I'm sure I can work something out straightaway."

"You do that and I'll knock off one of your beatings."

"You're far too kind, Mr. Teggins," Stillwell said as he rolled his eyes.

"Yeah, I know." Teggins called out a second later. "Hey, guard, come here. This guy wants to talk to you."

Stillwell was loving every minute of this. He knew if Teggins ever *did* get to him, that would spell the end of days, but something told him this plan was going to make that an impossibility for the former crime boss.

"Hello?" said the guard.

"Hello, friend," Stillwell said while grinning evilly. "How would you like to have all of your debt forgiven?"

ROUND 3

*T*he bell rang on round three and Gungren walked out to the center.

He had no magic box to use and he knew quite well that Crazell wasn't going to let him grab hold of her leg again.

His thoughts were foggy anyway. All he could think about was throwing rocks. To the outsider, the incessant desire to throw rocks sounded silly, but it was a way of life for giants. It was how they hunted, how they played catch, and how they built rock mounds—they used these in case they went to war, which had only happened once in his lifetime, and it had been against the dragons.

"So what are you going to do this round, Gungren?" Crazell chirped from a spot just far enough away that he couldn't reach her. "In the first one you grabbed my leg and wouldn't let go, and in the second you figured out a loophole in the rules and used magic." She swung her head around, motioning towards the crowd. "Curious minds can't help but wonder what you have in store for us now."

Gungren felt a protruding bump under his sandal. He knew what it was immediately, and his mind dulled even further. Without rational thought, the little giant stepped backwards and crouched down.

He grabbed the rock.

"Owww," he yelped instantly as his body manufactured a crack of electricity, signifying that Whizzfiddle's spell had indeed worked. He dropped the rock and shook his hand. "That stings!"

Then something odd happened.

He began to grow.

Fast.

His robe was the first to lose the battle against the strain. The seams ripped and the buttons popped. Within seconds it was lying on the ground in tatters. Next were his sandals. Their leather straps shredded. Fortunately, the Elfstretchy outfit that Orophin had built him was doing just fine keeping intact. Yes, it was riding up on Gungren again, but it didn't rip. Even his pointy hat had fallen off and bounced off the ground below.

The crowd was silenced as Gungren now stood face to face with the red dragon.

"Okay, that's actually a good one," Crazell said with a look of concern. "I honestly didn't see that coming."

~

"Notice that his Elfstretchy still fits?" Orophin pointed out while jumping up and down.

"Aye," Bekner said, lowering his mug of ale, "though it is after makin' his naughty bits look somewhat mountainy."

Orophin was quite proud of that fact. "Exactly."

"Regardless of that," Zel said, "he'll now be able to employ those grappling techniques against the dragon." He looked at the other two. "Not because of the suit, but because he's big again. This is rather exciting."

"Can't even imagine the power he's got in that fist now." Bekner rubbed his head again. "If he punches that poor dragon, its head will explode."

"That's true."

"And he'll look wonderful doing it," exclaimed Orophin, feeling immeasurable pride over his creation.

~

"Blast," said Whizzfiddle. "He's turned back into a giant. After all the work we've done."

"What's the problem?" Barrie asked, glowing. "He could win this thing like that."

"The problem is that he's going to go dumb again, and I may never get him back."

"There, there, Master Whizzfiddle," Muriel said, patting the elderly wizard on his hand, "things have a way of turning out as they should."

He sighed and nodded. "That is true. I've got more years than anyone in all of Ononokin to know it, too."

"Besides, at least now he's able to have a good time," she added.

Barrie clearly felt differently. "He can have a good time once he wins this blasted tournament."

~

"Honestly," Homer said from the radio booth, "I don't even see a point on commenting anymore. This day has been full of surprises, twists and turns, and excitement like I've never seen in all my years doing this sport."

"It has been something, that's for sure," Optical agreed. "Ladies and gentlemen, Gungren is standing toe to toe with Crazell now. She looks worried, but she seems to be gearing up for a round of fire." He jumped to his feet, unable to contain himself. "Oh, boy! Gungren has stepped in and knocked her to the ground. They're wrestling."

"Are you sure they're not hugging?" Homer asked, peeking through a set of fingers. "Happened in the first fight, after all. Why not the last one, too?"

"No, I'd say he's trying to get her in a wing-bar."

"Another new fun item showing up this year at the UDFC." Homer was shaking his head now. "A wing-bar? Who's ever heard of such a thing?"

"Crazell broke free and is using her talons to keep Gungren at bay. Wait, he's grabbed her by the tail and is starting to drag her in circles. Pretty soon he'll have her in the air if he keeps up this rotation."

"What'll he do with her?" said Homer. "Throw her? That won't work. She'll just flip over and her wings will catch air."

"It looks like Crazell is opening her wings all right," exclaimed Optical. "Looks like she is trying to slow the spinning."

Homer nodded. "Yep, but now Gungren is bouncing her off the ground during each revolution. Not sure how much of that Crazell can take."

"I think Gungren is getting ready to let her fly, Homer."

"You don't think she could end up in the bleachers, do you?" Homer asked as they both turned to look at each other and then ducked down and peered over the edge.

The bell rang and Gungren slowly decreased the spinning, bringing Crazell to a gentle landing on the ground. The dragon appeared to be seriously disoriented as she stumbled her way back to her corner, clearly trying not to fall over.

"I can't believe I'm going to say this," Homer said, "but the judges must have Gungren winning that round."

"Indeed," agreed Optical.

WHAT IN THE BLAZES?

*R*icky wanted to rush out and help his fighter get back in the corner, but she was wavering pretty badly and he didn't want to get stepped on.

Fortunately, she made it back and sat down.

"You okay, Crazell?" he called out.

"Not really. That's never happened to me before."

"Definitely surprised me with the turning-into-a-giant thing," Ricky admitted.

"Just a bit."

"That's okay, though," Ricky said, thinking fast. "We know now. We got this. You've fought giants before."

"Not ones as strong as Gungren," Crazell replied after releasing a heavy breath.

"It just means you're going to need to dig down deep."

"I don't know if I have anything to dig down into, Ricky." She grunted. "I've been trying to fight this guy and he's been making a fool out of me." Crazell was staring across at the giant. "You'd think that would rile me up, but it doesn't. The fire just isn't there."

"You're out of fire?"

"I mean passion, Ricky. There is none."

Ricky wasn't sure what to do here. He *wanted* his fighter to win, obviously. He didn't care about himself and his family, they'd survive, but it'd be good for Crazell. She would have to move, yes, but she would ever-harbor that feeling of being the best.

"Look, I believe in you, Crazell. I know you can do this. You can win for the twenty-fifth time, but only if you want it."

"How many times do I need to say I don't want it?" she asked, looking at him. Then her eyes softened. "I'm sorry, Ricky. You're right. I'll do this for you."

"No, no, no," Ricky said, waving his hands around frantically. "I won't have that on my conscience. You need to do it for you, Craz. You're the queen of this tournament. For the rest of your life this day is going to be playing in your head" He pointed at the field. "If you lose fighting another dragon, fine. If you go out fighting an orc, an ogre, or even a knight...fine." He then raised his eyes to meet hers. "But do you want to lose to a giant?"

It was probably a bit of a dirty trick, seeing as how the giants and the dragons had fought in a war against each other many years ago. They mostly got along now, but there was that ever-burning angst that still remained between their two peoples.

"I didn't think so," Ricky said finally. "You attacked and tried to battle in the first two rounds. He just grabbed your leg in one and sat down behind a shield in the other. That's not fighting. They's just surviving. So I'm positive you've still got him two rounds to one, but you need to take this next round decisively."

WHAT'S HAPPENED?

hizzfiddle had never spoken to the large giant version of Gungren, so he wasn't sure what to expect, but he had to try.

"Gungren," he called up, "bring your head down here."

"Sorry, Master," Gungren said in his normal way.

His voice had a touch more boom to it, but Whizzfiddle still recognized it as belonging to his apprentice.

"Oh, good, you're still able to understand and speak normally. Well, normally for you anyway."

"Yep, but it hard. I just want to play with rocks and sit in a cave and knock my head on the wall."

Whizzfiddle frowned at this admission. "Why would you knock your head on a cave wall?"

"That how giants make music."

"Oh." He searched his memory, trying to recall if he'd ever heard anything about giants and music. Nothing came to mind. "Anyway, you have to keep fighting."

"I know. I can win this."

"I don't mean the match," Whizzfiddle explained. "I mean you have to fight your brain from wanting to return to being a full giant. Obviously your body has already lost this fight, but you still have your mind, Gungren. For now, anyway." He then got an idea and went to reach for the white rag sitting by his corner. "In fact, I'm going to throw in the towel and get you some proper help."

Gungren leaned in ominously. "You do that and I'll pick you up and throw you like a rock."

"Right, right," Whizzfiddle replied with his hands up in surrender as a sense of dread filled his being. "No need to get rude about it."

"Sorry, Master," Gungren said, blinking and shaking his head. "I not meaned that. It hard to control fings." Gungren's eyes widened. "Oh no, I'm saying 'fings' again instead of 'fings.'"

"It's all right, Gungren. You just have to stay strong."

"I know, but I also gotta finish this fight."

"You really don't," Whizzfiddle implored.

"Yep, I does."

ROUND 4

*T*he bell rang to signal the start of the next round. Optical had gone back to drinking, as did Homer. Both of the announcers agreed that there was little sense in trying to maintain levelheadedness at this point in the game.

"Gungren jumped across the ring and grabbed Crazell before she could get in the air," he said, just tipsy enough to find things fascinating while still sober enough not to slur his words. "He's got her on the ground again and they seem to be fighting tooth and nail."

"Definitely seems to...*hic*...finally be some ser...ser... serious intentions again."

Homer was obviously a fair bit more inebriated.

"Crazell is slapping him in the head with a wing," said Optical. "It doesn't seem to be having much effect, though."

"Ah," said Homer as his eyes fought to stay open, "remember that giants ban...ban...ng theirs heads on cave walls to make music."

"That's a tidbit I was unaware of," Optical said, assuming that the wizard was making that up. "Oh, he's finally gotten hold of that wing and has pushed it behind her. They're rolling around again, but Gungren seems to be gaining the upper hand."

"Honestly, Optimum…Optipupil…Optipotato…" He frowned and then shrugged. "Well, whatever your name is, I'd say…*hic*…they're doing that hugging crap like the first fight."

"Except that these two are on the ground," Optical pointed out.

"That just makes it worse."

"By The Twelve," Optical said, pushing his own drink away in the hopes that he wouldn't end up sounding like Homer, "I daresay that Crazell is weeping."

Homer was snoring.

"That giant must really be working her over," Optical said after reaching out and flipping off Homer's microphone.

~

Gungren was shocked at what was happening. He had taken down the dragon and was winning the fight, but she just seemed to give up at one point and began sobbing. Feeling bad, he began to hug her, telling her that everything was going to be all right.

That's when she opened up and told him everything that was really going on.

"So you not want to be doing this?" Gungren asked as they stayed on the ground, pretending to fight.

"Not even remotely," she replied between sniffs.

"Did you ever?"

"Oh sure, at first. The fame and fortune was amazing, and the cooked knights tasted like eating marshmallows around a campfire. But after a hundred years I amassed so much wealth that I no longer needed to do this." She started to sob again. "And now I'm stuck."

This was definitely a strange turn of events. When they'd started this bout, Crazell had stated repeatedly that she was going to destroy him. Now she was very sad, and Gungren understood why. He wouldn't want to spend the rest of his days being constantly challenged to duels either.

"It okay. It okay." He patted her back. "There got to be some way out of this."

"Not unless I'm killed."

"Well, I not gonna do that," Gungren said. "That not in my gernetic things."

"Genetics."

"That the one." He pursed his lips for a moment. "I not sure if I remember right, but I thought I read that dragons can play dead."

"We can actually stop our hearts for a brief time, yes."

"Well, then I got an idea, but you have to play along."

YOU GOTTA WIN THIS ROUND

"*Y*ou have to win this round, Craz," Ricky was saying when she came back.

She felt somewhat upbeat. There was a positiveness that she hadn't experienced in many years.

"No, I don't," she replied, almost giddy.

"Oh, come on, baby. You have this. It's just a giant, remember?"

"Actually, he's not *just* a giant." Her response was wistful. "He's smart, sweet, and adorable."

"What?" Ricky moved in front of her and looked up. "Oh, boy. Craz, are you in love with the guy now?"

"Of course not, you idiot," she answered as if slapped. "I'm just saying that he's a genuinely good person. I'm also saying that I don't have anything left to prove."

"I know, I know." He then squared his shoulders. "Are you sure, Craz? I mean *really* sure?"

She was at peace. "I am."

"Fine," Ricky said, shrugging. "I'll throw in the towel."

"No, don't," Crazell said, stopping him. "I've been talking

with Gungren while we were rolling around pretending to fight."

Ricky laughed. "So you *were* hugging. That's kind of what it looked like from here."

"We have a plan, Ricky," she said. "I think it'll work, but you have to play along."

"I'm listening."

YOU COULD WIN THIS THING

Whizzfiddle knew something was up, but he couldn't quite tell what it was. There didn't seem to be any actual fighting going on after Gungren had wrestled the dragon to the ground. He could hear their voices. Not distinctly, of course, the crowd was too loud for that. But they'd obviously been discussing something.

"You got her right where you want her, Gungren," Barrie was saying. "Now it's time for the brass ring. You just gotta want it, my boy!"

"I have to agree with Barrie this time, Gungren," Muriel said in support of her husband.

Barrie was clearly taken aback by this statement, because he glanced away and murmured, "Maybe I should reexamine my position on this, then."

Whizzfiddle moved between them and stepped up to Gungren. It was quite a different thing talking to his apprentice while looking up.

"How are you feeling, Gungren? Are you okay?"

"I are fine."

"I *am* fine." Old habits die hard.

"I glad for you, Master," Gungren said as he patted Whizzfiddle on his head, flattening his hat.

GET MORE CAMERAS IN HERE

"More cameras," yelled Corg as he raced from position to position. Up until now, it had just been him and Aniok doing all the filming, but with more Fates helping, Corg had to make sure they were all following his rules. "This is the big show. I want ten cameras from all angles. Anyone who misses a shot will be after havin' me shoe permanently attached to your bottom." He wagged a finger at the various Fates who had been brought in to assist. "If more than two of ye goof up, I'll buy more shoes!"

Aniok stood up and grabbed Corg by the shoulders.

"We're all good here, boss," he said, obviously trying to help the dwarf get control of himself. "It's a full panoramic view, crowd and everything."

"Right, right," he said with a nod. Then he glanced up. "And you're not after just filmin' the tops of their heads, right?"

"Damn," replied Aniok. "All right, everyone, make sure we're filming faces." They all looked at him askance. "Don't question it, just do it!"

ROUND 5

*G*ungren and Crazell stood in the center of the arena. The bell hadn't rung yet and the referee kept yelling at them to get back to their corners, but they stood their ground.

"Am you ready?" asked Gungren.

"I am," Crazell replied.

They nodded at each other and backed away until the ref was appeased.

The bell rang and they ran out at each other, but stopped before engaging.

Crazell had her wings up and Gungren had his hands out. They both looked ready to pounce as they circled around while the crowd cheered.

"You sure you am going to be okay?" Gungren said.

"As long as you get me back to my lair in time, I'll be fine."

"I will," said Gungren. "I promise."

"I trust you," Crazell said. "Now, lunge forward and punch me on the chest for effect, but try not to hit me too hard."

"Don't worry. I won't."

"Okay," she said with a nod. "Three...two...one...now."

Gungren lunged forward with his right fist straight out. It connected with Crazell's sternum solidly. He held back, but he needed to make sure that it wouldn't look fake to anyone.

Crazell looked at him for a moment, winked once, and then her eyes rolled up into her head and she fell over, crashing to the ground in a heap.

It was so silent in the stadium the moment after she fell, you could almost hear the waves crashing off in the distance.

The ref walked over and put his hand in front of Crazell's nostrils. He slowly turned and looked up at Gungren with disbelieving eyes. Then he stood up and swung his arms in a gesture that said, "The fight is over."

Gungren had to cover his ears at the deafening roar of the crowd.

AMAZING

*E*veryone in Fateland was dancing and cheering and jumping around. They were all beside themselves at how well Gungren had done.

"I cannae believe it," Corg said, smiling.

Heliok was not used to seeing this look on the dwarf. It was a welcome reprieve from the constant angst, certainly.

"We're going to rule the world," Misty yelled as she cracked open a bottle of bubbly and started gulping it down without even using a glass.

She was right, too. Misty Trealo and Corg Sawsblade were about to become two very powerful people in the Underworld.

Sir Zelbaldian Riddenhaur stood and saluted the thing that Whizzfiddle called a television.

"Well done, Gungren," he said with a massive dose of pride. "Well done."

Bekner grabbed his frothy mug of ale and tipped it back

so far that it began pouring down his beard. This was a very big compliment coming from the dwarf. Wasting ale was quite a big no-no to the Diamondcrusher king.

"Couldn't have happened to a better lad," he stated as he slammed the mug back down.

Orophin jumped from his chair and did a pirouette.

"My Elfstretchy designs are going to sell like hotcakes," he bellowed.

≈

"I can't believe it," said Bank as his jaw hung slack. "Gungren won. That means you won again, boss."

"*We* won, Bank," Stillwell corrected his second-in-command. "All of us."

Bank blinked at him. "Really?"

"For today, yes. Tomorrow we plan the future of our particular enterprise. But today, we all win."

≈

Murray was so excited that he couldn't possibly stay seated.

In fact, he flipped on his speakers and cranked them up.

Then he put on his favorite tune and started dancing around while singing at the top of his lungs.

"You should be dancin'...yeaaaaah!"

≈

Optical was too shocked to be happy. Sure, he felt glad for Gungren, seeing that the giant seemed like a genuinely nice fellow, but the day had just been too odd to comprehend.

"I can tell you one thing, fans," he said after rousing

Homer from his slumber, "you got your money's worth today."

"Hard to argue that, Optometrist...OBGYN...Obiwan..." He waved again. "Anyhoo...this has been the strangest...*hic*... UDFC event by far." He burped. "I can't even explain half of what happened, but I have a feeling that won't ma...ma... matter at this point."

"It sure won't," agreed Optical. "Crazell the dragon has finally been bested, and by a newcomer to the sport who seemed like a genuinely nice...well, giant, I guess."

Homer held up his glass in salute. "Indeed."

"Hey," replied Optical, "that's my line!"

ANNOUNCING THE WINNER

*G*ungren's heart was racing because he knew there wasn't much time left for Crazell. He wanted to just pick her up now and start running, but if he didn't first accept the belt and all that, it would look far too suspicious.

The announcer was in full voice as he yelled into the microphone.

"Your winner and *new* champion of the world,"—he dramatically pointed at the giant—"Gungren!"

The ref handed him the belt. It was only big enough to fit around his wrist though. That was fine. He didn't care. There were things to do.

He saw a group of people running out onto the field towards him that he recognized. It was the Wizards' Guild folks. There was Muppy, Zotrinder, Ibork, and the Croomplatt twins.

"I'm so happy for you, Gungren," Muppy called up as she cooled herself with her hand fan. "You have done wonderfully."

"Thanks."

"I must admit that your prowess against the dragon was admirable," Zotrinder said, looking like it took some effort to admit that.

"Thanks."

"That was unfathomable," yelled Ibork. His voice was so loud that Gungren stood back to full height. "I've never watched such a thing before, of course, but you were incredible, Gungren."

"Thanks."

The Croomplatt twins stood proudly, nodding to each other.

"Ha!" they yelled, stating the only word they'd mastered. It was used to mean many things, and now and then they were able to take a brief departure to the word "huh?" when needed.

"Thanks."

Gungren then studied them all, seeing that Barrie, Muriel, Eloquen, and Whizzfiddle had joined them.

"Thanks, everybody," he said with one eye on Crazell. "I got to go now."

"Gungren," Muppy said, either not hearing him or choosing to ignore him, "I know you have been working hard, and so as the…" She paused and looked over at Ibork. "Did he say he has to go?"

"I believe he said he thinks real slow," Ibork replied.

"He said nothing of the kind," argued Zotrinder. "Clearly he said that he has a stubbed toe."

Ibork scoffed. "Oh, please!"

"Ha?" queried the Croomplatt twins.

Nobody replied.

"Right," Muppy said after a moment. "Gungren, the council hereby awards you the title of 'Full Wizard' with all rights and privileges therein."

"Thanks," he said, taking the little piece of paper from her. "This am great. I gotta go now."

The council wizards were all staring at him in disbelief. They all knew how important it had been for Gungren to become an actual wizard. He felt bad about not telling them what was going on, but he couldn't risk that the word would get out. Crazell desperately wanted to disappear, and Gungren had promised to help her do just that.

"Sorry," he said with a smile. "I really does appreciate this, but I gotta go."

Just when he turned to head back to Crazell, Heliok arrived with Corg, Misty, and Aniok. They were ready for their interview.

"Just a minute, my boy," Heliok called out as Aniok and Corg worked on getting things set up. "You've done so incredibly well, and there is much to do."

"Thanks," Gungren replied, "but I gotta go."

"Are we rolling yet?" Misty said in her pushy way.

Corg scowled. "Aye, ye blue pigeon!"

"What?"

"I'm stressed," he replied. "Be after givin' me a break on me lack of creativity at the moment."

She sighed and looked at the camera while grabbing Gungren by the finger.

"We are here with Gungren, the new champion of the Ultimate Dragon Fighting Championship."

"Excuse me," said the voice of Payne Sawsblade, who had run up to the scene with her cameraperson on her heels, "but this is *my* interview."

"I think not," countered Misty.

"Oh, yes it is," Payne declared.

"Out of the way, sister," Corg said. "We've got filmin' going on here."

"That *is* true," Misty said, obviously not happy with the

way Corg had spoken to Payne, "but you shouldn't just call a woman 'sister' like that, Corg. It's not polite."

"What are ye talkin' about? She's after bein' me sister!"

"What?" Misty said, looking back at Payne. "She sounds nothing like you."

"I'm Payne Sawsblade," Payne stated, "and this is *my* interview."

Misty gave her the onceover. "Right, well, you can have him when we're done."

"I don't think so," Payne said, moving to stand directly in front of Misty.

Gungren pulled his hand away. "I gotta go."

"Freeze," stated Heliok in a sharp voice. Everyone stopped. "I am a Fate and I say that *we* go first."

Payne turned and gave him a stern stare. "And I'm a dwarf and I say that if you yell at me one more time, I'll put a boot in your nethers."

"Definitely Corg's sister," Aniok said to Whizzfiddle.

Gungren didn't care who wanted to do what first. That wasn't his problem. He just wanted it all done because he had to help Crazell.

"I'll tell ye what," said Corg to his sister, "if ye let us finish what we're doin' here, I'll handle your post-production for ye."

This seemed to impress Payne, because she said, "You promise?"

"Aye," he answered, shaking her hand.

"Fine."

Gungren was really feeling anxious now.

"Now, Gungren," Misty said, "you have just won the UDFC 100 event. What are you gonna do now?"

"I gonna go."

Misty just nodded and looked at the camera. "We have

taken this fellow from nothing to something in just a few quests."

"Fate Quests," Heliok said, moving his head into the view of the camera.

"Of course." Misty scooted over to him slightly. "Here is Heliok, the Fate who implemented my brainchild."

"That's right and... What?"

"Show the commercial on the big screen," Misty directed before Heliok could reply.

"Already called it in," Corg replied. "Should be showin' any second..."

The huge screens flipped over and fancy graphics and camera-work filled in. Then a deep voice began booming through the speakers.

For the last few months, The Learning Something Channel has been working with the Fates—yes, the creators of The Twelve. They have followed around this unfortunate-looking fellow as he works to complete three separate quests, with each increasing in difficulty. After finishing each quest he's been fixed in some way. New teeth, a new body, and soon...a new head. In three days, we will show the first of his amazing adventures. And we'll also show that when a Fate does a makeover, it never fades away. Watch the event that people will be talking about for hundreds of years. This weekend, tune into The Learning Something Channel for Unreal Makeover: Gift of the Fates*!*

The crowd went absolutely bonkers.

"Look, guys," Gungren said desperately, "I really gotta go!"

But Whizzfiddle was obviously feeling somewhat differently all of a sudden. He had a look on his face that Gungren had seen before. A look that conveyed something fishy was going on.

"Wait a second here," he said evenly.

"Not now, Whizzfiddle," chided Heliok.

Whizzfiddle stepped right up to the Fate and stared at him. "You have set this entire thing up since the beginning to be a television show?"

"Uh...well..."

"And you never got Gungren's consent either, did you?"

Heliok pulled his collar. "He agreed to take on these quests."

"And was there mention of him being on a television show whereby he would receive *none* of the proceeds?"

"I...uh..."

"I believe we have a very serious problem on our hands," Whizzfiddle stated with dark intentions.

"No, we don't," Heliok replied, standing his ground. "I'm a Fate and I may do as I wish."

Whizzfiddle nodded at Heliok with an impressed look. Actually, Gungren knew his master wasn't really impressed. He was pretending because he was about to put Heliok in his place. This was one of those things that Gungren had never mastered, and likely never would.

"Is that so?" said Whizzfiddle. "Well, I am a wizard. And Gungren, *too*, is a wizard. And I believe I speak for the entire Wizards' Guild when I say that we do not appreciate being manipulated in such a way." He let that sink in and added, "Note that we have no problem making countless calls to the Fates customer service department with complaints, either." He motioned to the members of the Guild. "Do we, gang?"

"I've got nothing better to do," said Muppy.

"I'll call day and night," agreed Ibork.

Zotrinder was looking at his nails, but obviously caught on that the wizards weren't going to stop staring at him until he supported the cause.

"Fine, I'll jingle the line as well," he said.

The Croomplatt twins said, "Ha," while giving a firm nod.

Gungren didn't have time for this, and Crazell *really* didn't have time for this.

"What do you want?" said Heliok.

"Get Peapod Pecklesworthy here right now," Whizzfiddle demanded.

"Who?"

～

Master Wizard Peapod Pecklesworthy was walking around in his garden.

There were butterflies fluttering around as a cool breeze caressed the top of the grass, bending the blades ever so slightly. The flowers were open and accepting the love of the sunlight. Birds sang their beautiful melodies as they sat in the leafy trees.

It was peaceful.

This was the type of day where nothing could possibly break through his calm frame of mind.

He felt a tingling sensation.

～

"What happened?" Peapod said, glancing around rapidly. "Where am I? Oh, hello, Whizzfiddle, Muppy, Ibork, Zo…" He shook himself. "What's going on?"

Whizzfiddle wasted no time. "Do you remember Gungren?"

Peapod glanced up.

"Yes," the wizard said with a gulp. "You're not looking for revenge, I hope? I was just doing my job. But it looks like he's back to being a giant anyway, so no harm done, right?"

"Except for the fact that he didn't want to go back to

being a giant," Whizzfiddle replied. "He wants to stay small and remain a wizard."

"Oh yes, I *do* recall the wizard thing now." Peapod did not look comfortable at all. "But if he's back to being a giant, he couldn't have made it to full wizard."

"Actually," Muppy said, "he was just indoctrinated."

Peapod frowned. "Then why is he big again?"

"It happened before he was given the full credentials," answered Whizzfiddle.

"It's too late then, I'm afraid."

"I got to go now," Gungren said again.

"He speaks decently," Peapod said as if finding that completely out of the ordinary.

"Just a minute, Gungren."

"Master," Gungren said, "come here a second."

"I'm in the middle of something, Gungren, so you'll just have to—"

Gungren picked him up and walked away from the group.

"Okay, then," Whizzfiddle said with a glare as Gungren set him back down, "what is it?"

"If we doesn't get her back to her lair fast," Gungren whispered while looking at Crazell, "she going to be dead for good."

Whizzfiddle seemed taken aback. "What are you talking about?"

"Gungren?" Ricky yelled as he rushed over. "I believe you have a deal to uphold, yes?"

"I are trying, mister."

"Wait," said Whizzfiddle, "are you saying that all of this was a setup?"

"Keep your voice down," Ricky said. "We don't want anyone to find out. But we have to hurry."

Whizzfiddle looked at them both. "Fine. Give me two minutes."

"We not got that much time."

"One, then," Whizzfiddle said, holding up his finger.

"Well, that was rude," said Ricky.

"Him just held up the wrong finger," explained Gungren. "Him does that all the time."

"Ah."

Whizzfiddle had darted back to the group with Gungren in tow.

"Peapod," he said by way of introduction, "this is Heliok. He's a Fate. He's going to give you whatever you want so that you'll turn Gungren back into what he was before."

"I am?" said Heliok.

"Calls to customer service, Heliok," Whizzfiddle reminded him.

Heliok coughed. "Name your price, Mr. Peapod."

"Gee, I don't know."

"How about all the peapods you can shuck and also the ability to control yourself when around them?" Whizzfiddle suggested. "You'll still be limited in power, of course. Heliok will make certain of that."

"That'd be a dream come true," Peapod said with awe.

"You heard him, Heliok."

"Fine, fine. It's a deal!"

Whizzfiddle grabbed Peapod by the shoulders and turned him until he faced Gungren.

"Do it!"

"Uh... I don't have any unshucked peapods!"

"Heliok?"

"Okay, okay," said the Fate an instant before a bushel of unshucked peapods showed up.

Peapod started shucking as fast as he could. After he got through a good many, he turned to Gungren.

"TAKE-THAT-GIANT-OVER-THERE-AND-MAKE-HIM-FIT-IN-TINY-UNDERWEAR!"

Gungren looked down at all the expectant faces. He didn't feel any different, and he was definitely still a lot taller than everyone around him.

"Nothing happened," Whizzfiddle exclaimed.

"Wait…" Peapod snapped his fingers. "Did he ever talk to his ma?"

"Oh," Whizzfiddle said with a gulp. "No."

Gungren furrowed his brow. "What him talking about?"

"I'll explain later," Whizzfiddle answered. "Peapod, does he have to do that first?"

"Only for it to stick," Peapod replied. "It would have changed him back immediately if he already had, though, which is why I asked. Since he didn't already speak with her, his size will return to small in about fifteen minutes. But it'll only last for a few days, then he goes back permanently."

"Fine," Whizzfiddle said, rushing away. "We have to go now!"

"What?" Misty called out. "You can't leave yet, we have to film the rest of the makeover."

"Aye, we ain't done yet," hollered Corg.

Payne chimed in with, "And I still have to interview him too."

"I'll be back, everyone," Gungren said, kneeling down and looking them all in the eye, one by one. "I promise."

"And that's a promise you all know you can count on," Whizzfiddle called over his shoulder as he ran towards Crazell.

～

"Well, now I can definitely say that I've seen everything," Optical said just before flicking off his microphone. "Gungren the giant has just picked up Crazell, threw her over his shoulder, and is running out of the ring with her. The crowd is stunned."

"That's the first...*hic*...time I've ever seen a contestant take the corpse of another contestant as a trophy." He put the cap back on the bottle. "That is ser...ser...seriously warped."

DIDN'T MAKE IT

Gungren ran with all his might as Crazell was slung over his shoulder. He was carrying Ricky Schmicky in his left hand, too, since the man was the only one who knew where the dragon lived. Whizzfiddle was using something called "speedy feet" to keep up with them. Eloquen had stayed back at the stadium to promote the outfit that Gungren had been wearing.

They arrived at Crazell's lair and Gungren laid the dragon down after setting Ricky on the ground.

She didn't rouse.

Gungren pushed her and then shook her lightly, but she was like a limp rag.

"Why she not coming back?" he said, looking at Ricky.

"I don't know, Gungren. I've never done this either."

Whizzfiddle was scanning the area. "Are you sure we're close enough to the lair?"

"This am the spot," Gungren replied, pointing at the ground. "You can see the glow."

"True."

"Ouch," yelled Gungren as the feeling of a massive weight

crushed in on him. He hit the grass and groaned for a second. Then his equilibrium returned. "That hurt."

"You're small again," Whizzfiddle said, helping the little giant get back to his feet.

"Yep," he said as the fog lifted from his thoughts. "My brain clear up too. No more interest in throwing rocks."

"What about Crazell?" Ricky asked, walking around her like a worried father.

Whizzfiddle sighed. "It looks as though we are too late."

Gungren started thinking about all the things he'd read over the years. He wasn't just into reading magic books, after all. In fact, he was widely read. Mostly non-fiction, too, which included textbooks and journals.

One of those periodicals had to do with health and anatomy. There was nothing specifically written about dragons, but he could only hope that one of the studies he read might be applicable anyway.

"I got an idea," he said.

Whizzfiddle glanced up. "Okay, what is it?"

Gungren pointed. "You get on that side, Master."

"I'm no longer your master, Gungren," Whizzfiddle pointed out as he moved to where Gungren had told him to go. "You're a full wizard now."

"Okay," Gungren said, thinking it would take a while for him to stop considering himself as an apprentice.

"Is this where you want me to be?" the elderly wizard asked.

"Yep. Now drink some alcerhol stuff."

"Right."

"Here am my plan," Gungren said. "When I eat dirt, we am gonna cast a spell of electric on her chest at the same time."

"Why?"

"No time to explain." He shoved a handful of dirt into his mouth and said, "CAPHSTUM-ELECTRICALUM."

"CASTUM-ELECTRICALUM," Whizzfiddle said at the same time, but without the dirt-induced mumbling sound.

An arc of electricity flew from them, striking Crazell on both sides of her chest. Her back arched for a moment and then she collapsed back down again.

She remained still.

"Do it again," commanded Gungren, "but real strong this time." He shoved a bunch of dirt into his mouth. "CAPHSTUM-ELECTRICALUM!"

"CASTUM-ELECTRICALUM!"

The energy transference was so strong this time that it launched both Gungren and Whizzfiddle up into the air with a popping sound. Gungren's Elfstretchy outfit was smoking as he sat up, shaking his head.

He looked over to make sure that Whizzfiddle was okay.

"Your hair is pure white, Master," he said, forgetting again that he was no longer an apprentice.

"It is?" Whizzfiddle said, looking somewhat dazed. "It's not been white since I drank my long-life elixir."

Crazell groaned and then began to cough.

"Craz, baby," Ricky yelled as he rushed to her side. "You're alive!"

"What happened?" she said, sounding hoarse.

"Gungren saved your life, that's what happened," Whizzfiddle said. Then he turned around. "You really are quite something, Gungren. Quite something, indeed."

"I just doing what right," Gungren said, feeling self-conscious.

Gungren helped Crazell to sit up.

She looked at him with sincere admiration.

"I don't know how to thank you, Gungren," she said. Then she turned to her manager. "And thank you, too, Ricky...for everything. I'm sorry to have let you down."

"Bah! You didn't let me down, baby," he said with his

trademarked smile. "You're golden. Nobody's gonna bug you now. They all think you're in the Afterlife."

"Dragons don't have a place in the Afterlife," she pointed out.

"They do in the Ascendant area," Whizzfiddle corrected her, "and I'm certain you'll make it there one day. You've done great things, after all."

"Maybe. For now, I'll be happy just living my days out in slumber with my jewels, after I find a new place to live, of course."

"Now *that* I understand entirely," Whizzfiddle stated with a chuckle.

Gungren felt a lot of relief at seeing that Crazell was okay now. She was correct that she'd have to leave the area. Thieves would undoubtedly be along to claim her jewels within days, and when she defended her cave, everyone would learn the truth of what had happened.

That gave him an idea.

"Crazell," he said, "I not allowed to do big magic stuff without a quest, but if you want to hire me to change the way you look, I can do that."

"Really?" she and Whizzfiddle said at the same time.

"Remember that I read a lot of spell books and stuff," he said to Whizzfiddle.

"That's true."

Ten minutes later, Crazell had been transformed from a red dragon to a green one. She also had a few scars on her face and her eyes were changed to bright blue, per her request. Nobody would know it was her, except for those standing here.

"That's perfect, Craz," Ricky said. "You look scary enough to keep away the riffraff, for sure."

"Thanks, I think," she replied. "And thank you too, Gungren. How much do I owe you?"

"Your thanks is good," he replied with a smile. Then he looked over at Whizzfiddle. "Master? Erm, sorry...Whizzfiddle?" He shook his head. "Nope. I gonna stick with Master for now, if that okay?"

"It's fine, Gungren. What do you need?"

"Peapod said something about my ma?"

"Oh, right." The elderly wizard cleared his throat. "Well, remember that day you asked me to cast a spell on you to see what was required to keep Peapod's spell from being undone?"

"Yep."

"One of those things was that you had to say goodbye to your ma."

"For good?" he asked, feeling suddenly worried.

It wasn't like he spent a lot of time with his mother, especially since they no longer had much in common, but he still wanted to see her from time to time.

"It didn't specify," Whizzfiddle answered, "so I would say that it's not for good."

"And that's it?"

"Yes, but you have to do it within a couple of days or your transition back to being a giant will be permanent."

"I not sure if I can walk there in two days," Gungren said.

"You have the ability within you to transport there now, Gungren, remember?" He took the little man by the shoulders. "There are no more limitations on your abilities. You're not supposed to do magic of that level without a quest, as you've just pointed out here, but I would argue that a personal quest is still a quest!"

"That true, I guess."

Crazell started to get up. "I'd be happy to fly you there, Gungren."

"No, no," he said. "You am needing rest and my master am right. I can do it anyway."

She breathed out heavily. "Phew," she said. "Dying really takes it out of you."

They laughed.

"When you're done," Whizzfiddle said, "come back to the house in Rangmoon. We need to finish up a few more things."

"I will," answered Gungren, "but first I gotta do them interview things and stuff. So I go do that now, then see my ma, and then I come back home."

Whizzfiddle nodded. "I'll be waiting for you."

"Say, Gungren," Ricky said after giving Crazell a hug, "could you take me to the arena with you? It's kind of a far walk."

"Yep."

"Thanks again, Gungren," Crazell said, reaching out a wing and putting it around him. "If you ever have need of anything, I'll be there for you."

"Thanks," the little giant replied. "Same for you."

SUCCESS

Unreal Makeover: Gift of the Fates hit #1 in the ratings and broke so many records that Misty Trealo was the talk of the town.

"And so it seems that you are now my boss," Mr. Grutch said without malice, though he did seem to be somewhat beside himself. "I'm sorry if I seem a little flummoxed, but I've never promoted someone *over* me before."

"Excellent," Misty said, relishing in the fact that the tables had turned. "And well-deserved, too, wouldn't you say?"

"Oh, by all means," came his enthusiastic reply. "You've done a wonderful job, Ms. Trealo. I couldn't have done as good myself."

"I know."

"Right, well, I have taken the liberty of having your office set up down the hall." He was smiling, which looked odd to Misty. "I have made certain that you have only the highest quality of furnishings."

"Thank you, Mr. Grutch," she replied, deciding to twist the screws a little, "but I think I'd prefer a corner office with a view."

"But there's only one of those and we're sitting in it." Their eyes met as realization set in. "Ah, I see. I'll have it taken care of."

~

Corg Sawsblade had been fielding offers left and right. It had gotten to the point where he'd run out of clever ways to call people names as he told them, "No!"

"We'll be able to make the best films ever now, Corg," Misty said as they sat in her new corner office.

"Yeah…about that," Corg replied at length. "It seems as though them Fates is wantin' me to head up their film crew." He shrugged. "They're after askin' me to teach their daft camera folks which end to point the lens and such."

Misty seemed taken aback by this.

"That's an incredible opportunity."

"Aye."

"I'm assuming you're going to take them up on it?"

"Kinda have to, if ye know what I mean?"

"You mean they're forcing—"

"What?" Corg interrupted with a frown. "Nobody forces Corg Sawsblade to do nothin' he's not wantin' to do, ye flippity elf."

"You're speaking of yourself in the third person," Misty pointed out.

"Aye, so?" She didn't reply. "Anyhoo, it's just that coming back to the old style of filmin' here after bein' up there is like eatin' nothin' but bread after ye've had puddin'."

"I understand," Misty said, and she looked genuine about it, "but if you ever decide to come back, there will always be a place for you here."

"Thanks, ye blue devil," he said with a wink.

She grinned. "Don't mention it, you little sh—"

"Show's on in the conference room, Ms. Trealo," Mr. Grutch called out as he walked by.

"Right. Thank you, Mr. Grutch."

Corg could see the elation on her face. This was a rare thing with dark elves. Of course, she *was* smashing her ex-boss under her thumb, so it sort of made sense.

"That's got to be after feelin' good," Corg said.

Misty grinned even bigger. "It's definitely not horrible."

Just as they were about to get up to check out the show, Eloquen stepped into the office. He was shifting back and forth, looking uncomfortable.

"Is something wrong?" asked Misty.

"Yeah," agreed Corg, "ye look like somebody just stole yer favorite doll, ye shifty elf."

"Sorrow expands to the extent of the soul as the cravings of unrestraint summon my sentience towards profligacy. Hence, my individuality is impelled to vacate."

Corg looked at Misty and she looked back at him. It was obvious that neither of them had any idea what the elf had said.

As one, they turned back and said, "Huh?"

Eloquen sighed, obviously recognizing that there was nobody around to translate for him.

He rolled his eyes. "I said, 'I'm sorry, but I've got a shot at making a stupid amount of money. Therefore, I quit.'"

Heliok had gotten the numbers in. They were pretty incredible, too. Well beyond what he'd expected them to be.

He headed up to Kilodiek's office to share the news, when that damnable West stepped in his way.

"Do you have an appointment with Kilodiek?" the troll asked, moving to open his little book.

"As far as you know," Heliok said, flicking his wrist and causing West to immediately transport back to his chair. "Kilodiek, the numbers are in."

"Sorry, sir," West said, rushing into the office an instant later, "but he just barged past me."

"It's fine, West. Leave us alone." Then Kilodiek mumbled something under his breath that Heliok could not hear. "What are the numbers, Heliok?"

"We're in the mid-twenties."

"No kidding?"

Kilodiek's eyes grew larger than any human's could have managed, and seeing that he had currently arranged himself to look human, it was somewhat grotesque.

He snatched the paper from Heliok and began studying it.

"Well, it looks like The Twelves' numbers are down, but that's not my problem." Kilodiek glanced up, his eyes still out of proportion. "It's *your* problem, Heliok, but it's not mine."

"I'll handle it."

"I'm sure you will," he said more kindly than usual. Then he glanced out his office and leaned in. "Say, listen, I was wondering if you wanted West back?"

Heliok found this odd. "Is he not working out?"

"He's too pushy for me."

"I see," Heliok replied. "Honestly, after how he did his little power play, I'm not sure I would be able to trust him again."

"He's tried to go over my head and work for Rimbodiek, you know?"

Heliok cracked a smile. "I had a feeling he might. He seems very enterprising."

"That's an understatement," Kilodiek said, taking another glance at the troll. "I sense that he will one day run everything in Fateland if we don't do something about it."

"I have an idea," said Heliok. "We could always just grant his original wish and send him back to Ononokin."

"What wish?"

"To be young again, have eternal youth, and unlimited money."

≈

Everything went dark for West for a moment, but then he awoke to find he was no longer in Fateland. He sensed he was back in Hazpen, in fact.

A voice that sounded like Heliok said, "We're sorry that the position you had as an assistant didn't work out, but we have decided to grant your original wish for a younger body, eternal youth, and loads of money. We promise you'll always have money and that you won't age even a single day."

West had all his memories and faculties and learning, but when he tried to move, he found he could only wiggle his arms and legs uncontrollably.

He also felt a bit damp in his under region.

"Oooh," said the huge face of an elderly troll. "It looks like our little snuggle bunny has done a poopie."

She lifted him up and he saw a room full of gold and diamonds and countless other things that spelled wealth.

The woman carried him over to a table that housed a mirror.

He looked to be roughly six months old.

Recalling Heliok's words that said, "You won't age even a single day," made West scream out in the only way he'd ever be able to.

"Waaaaaaaaaaaaaaaaaaaaaa!"

BACK HOME

*W*hizzfiddle was having tea when Gungren arrived. This was both a happy and sad day for the elderly wizard. He'd never expected he'd work with another apprentice after Treneth of Dahl, but Gungren had made up for all that Treneth had sullied.

"Did everything go well with your ma?" he asked as the little giant entered the kitchen. That's when he noticed Gungren was back to being the same old Gungren. "Oh, wow…your teeth, your body…"

"Yep, I know," Gungren said with the same gap-toothed smile he used to wear. "I let that Heliok guy change me for the show but made him change me back after. I promised I would let him change me again at the follow-up thing."

"Didn't like your new look, then?"

"Nope. Plus, people will try to find me like what they did with Crazell. I not want that."

"Good point," Whizzfiddle agreed, "but don't you have to fight again in ten years?"

"Nope. I retired." He shrugged. "They kept the belt thing and I had them donate that winning money to poor families."

"Good man, Gungren."

"Thanks."

"And your ma?"

"It weren't easy to talk with her," he admitted, "but I speak giant pretty good still."

"And Peapod's spell, did you..."

"I heard a 'ding' sound when I told ma goodbye. It all done now. I not gonna change back."

"Excellent. Excellent."

He felt very proud of his *former* apprentice. The little fellow would undoubtedly go on to do wonderfully. It was inevitable.

But now was when things became somewhat difficult.

"Well," Whizzfiddle said in a heavy voice, "we have the problem now that you are no longer my apprentice."

Gungren frowned. "Yep."

"And I honestly don't need a roommate," Whizzfiddle stated. "It kind of gets in the way of my encounters with the fairer sex."

"Uh-huh." It was nice that Gungren didn't judge Whizzfiddle's capability to secure a partner for the evening. "Wait, am you kicking me out?"

"Don't think of it that way, Gungren. Think of it as me pushing you on your way." He took a sip of his tea. "If you stay here, you'll forever see yourself as my apprentice. You need to have your own space where you can grow and learn and hopefully lay around doing nothing like any good wizard should." Whizzfiddle then shrugged. "Besides, someday you may have your own apprentice."

"That would be fun."

"Don't count on it."

Gungren was looking around the room, stopping and studying each area. He appeared almost more nervous than he had when he'd been about to face Crazell in the arena.

"But I got no place to go," he said finally.

"You've got tons of money, Gungren. You may go wherever you want."

"I not has money." Gungren pulled out his pockets to show they were empty. "I gave it to them poor people, remember?"

And that's when Whizzfiddle pulled out a bag of diamonds and set it on the table. He pushed it over towards the little giant.

"After you left to finish your interviews and to see your ma, I contacted Misty Trealo and told her of my desire to bring charges against The Learning Something Channel for using our names and faces in their show without our permission. They decided to settle out of court immediately."

"Wow."

"Indeed," Whizzfiddle said, and then he reached into another pocket. "There's something else."

"What?"

"When Teggins was caught cheating, he dropped something and I picked it up. It turned out to be the Diamond of Jaloof."

"That diamond Heliok wanted me to find before you told him about the dragon fight thing?"

"The very same," Whizzfiddle answered with a nod. "Well, I took a quick portal trip to the Museum of Finer Things and returned it to them. They gave me a sizable reward." He pushed that bag at Gungren, too. "Since I would never have spotted it had you not done your quest, I am splitting the coins with you."

"This am a lot of money, Master!"

"It sure is," agreed Whizzfiddle, "and remember that I'm not your master anymore."

"Oh, yeah."

"Anyway, if you spend it carefully, you'll never have to

work again." He then giggled. "Of course, knowing you, you'll probably just give it all away."

"Yep, but so do you. You always help the poor."

"That's true, Gungren," Whizzfiddle was happy to admit, "but I keep a lot as well because I can't continue helping them if I have nothing. You have to trickle the help, if you wish to help forever."

"That make sense."

"Yes, I suppose it does," Whizzfiddle said, smiling to himself. The he rapped his knuckles on the table twice and stood up. "Anyway, there is one more thing, if you have a moment?"

～

They walked outside and down a path that led behind a thick set of trees. From this spot, Whizzfiddle's house was completely blocked from view.

In front of them was a quaint home with fresh paint and a nice garden. The colors on the shingles were lively and multifaceted. It was a happy-looking house.

"Who lives here?" asked Gungren.

"You do, Gungren," Whizzfiddle said. "If you choose to, that is."

Gungren's face lit up. "You made this for me?"

"I called in a number of favors with the local builders and they put it together while we were away." He then winked at the little man and added, "There may have been a little magic used to help speed things along as well. The entire Wizards' Guild chipped in on that."

"Wow," Gungren said as his eyes welled up. "I love it."

"Now don't go getting all emotional. It's not becoming of a man my age to shed tears, happy or not." He wiped his nose. "Anyway, you'll find that it's all built for your particular measurements, too. Including the kitchen and such."

"Thank you, Master," Gungren said, nearly crushing Whizzfiddle with a hug.

"Call me Xeb."

"Nobody calls you that, though," Gungren replied, stepping back.

"That's true, but that's only because I've never met anyone I'd allow to do it."

"Okay, Xeb it are, then."

"Nope," Whizzfiddle said with a sudden sour look. "That's terrible. Whizzfiddle will have to do."

"Okidoki." Gungren was beaming as he was scanning over his new home. "This am great. I can finally ask Agnitine out on a date thing."

"Hadn't considered that," mumbled Whizzfiddle.

"What?"

"Hmmm. Oh, nothing, nothing." Whizzfiddle would have to remember that Gungren was now his peer. He could no longer push his personal judgments on the little man. This wasn't going to be easy. With some effort, he said, "It's *your* house, Gungren, so you may invite over whomever you wish."

Gungren smiled in his good old gap-toothed way. At least the little giant looked like himself again. Whizzfiddle found the physical changes that Heliok had done during the quests to be naught more than disturbing, truth be told.

"One more question before you go?" asked Gungren, keeping his eyes on the house.

"I have to go?"

"Well, I want to get settled in and stuff."

"Oh, right. Go on."

Gungren moved his foot around in the dirt.

"Am it okay if I still come over and make you sandwiches? I like to do that."

"Truly?"

"Yeah. Maybe sometimes you can come over here and I make you a sandwich, too."

"I'd be a fool to turn down such an offer, Gungren," he said, patting the little giant on his head. "A downright fool!"

A LETTER FROM INNKEEPER SARGAN

*D*ear Reader,
     I just wanted to take a moment to thank you for reading this book.

Ever since the story of Gungren and his training for the Ultimate Dragon Fighting Championship event, and because the new material known as Elfstretchy was invented in my building, the Inn of Sargan has flourished.

In fact, the entire town has seen a marked increase in revenue.

I have converted the entire basement into a media room with multiple televisions and such. Only those who are in-the-know about the Underworld are able to get in, but they pay a pretty penny to do so.

Before this newfound pool of funds, it looked as if I was moving towards bankruptcy.

Now, though, I always have a packed house, the inn has been completely paid for, and I'm planning to go on my first holiday in nearly ten years!

None of this would have been possible without your help.

So I thank you from the bottom of my heart, and I offer you 50% off your stay in any one of our suites.

Sincerely,

-Alvin Sargan

THE ULTIMATE DRAGON FIGHTING
CHAMPIONSHIP WALL OF FIGHTERS

*O*n the outside of the arena there is a giant wall that contains the names of all the fighters who have lost their lives during a UDFC battle. Each has a little epitaph that describes how they were ended.

Here are some of the most notable ones.

~

Bessie
UDFC 9

Bessie, an elven wizard and the first female contestant allowed in a UDFC tournament, was fried to a crisp during a magical battle with Ebinsleezer Noodlington during UDFC 9. Though it was never proved, due to a blindness spell that'd been used to cover the entire crowd and all the cameras, there was evidence of dragon flame on the remains of Bessie and the area surrounding her. This, and the fact that Bessie was heard yelling "You can't summon a dragon, you cheating bastard!", suggested that Noodlington, an old-school wizard who felt that the rightful place for the fairer sex was in the kitchen, had summoned a dragon to do his bidding. The tournament was halted and a UDFC rule was added to the books that disallowed casting of magic within the arena. It was made immediately effective. Noodlington, who was no longer allowed the use of his magic, was subsequently beaten to death by a gnome in the 1st round of his next bout. Due to her determined spirit, Bessie opened the door for women to participate in the UDFC while simultaneously, and inadvertently, closing the door on the allowance of magic being cast during an event.

~

Lelah
UDFC 11

Lelah, a young dark elf with the prowess of a panther, was the first contestant to win the UDFC without leaving the ring alive. She'd beaten every contender with ease until the final bout when she came face to face with Traxor Rufflezang, the werewolf who had held the championship title for thirty years. After a ferocious four rounds of mayhem, Lelah knew she was in trouble, but she had a plan. At the start of round five, barely able to stand from the wounds given to her by Rufflezang, Lelah raised her blade. Rufflezang went to attack but Lelah took out a doggie treat and threw it, catching the werewolf's attention long enough to side-step his attack and drive her blade home. The two lay side by side, exhausted and unable to move, until Rufflezang finally closed his eyes and was gone. Lelah followed him to the Afterlife moments later, but only after being crowned the champion of UDFC 11. As a side note, Lelah and Rufflezang became the best of friends in the Afterlife, and to this day she still takes him to the doggie park at least once a week.

~

Rachel "Dark Bane" Pegrum
UDFC 19

Rachel "Dark Bane" Pegrum was a dark elf who was known to be somewhat cocky...even more so than your average dark elf. During UDFC 19, she got matched up against the dwarf known as Gikrir Speedbarrow, known for his fast-moving legs. The bout was promised to be one for the ages, though Rachel seemed to think Gikrir was beneath her. Being that he was a dwarf and she was a dark elf, there was a lot of truth to her thoughts on the subject. What she didn't expect was that the dwarf would be even faster than he was touted to be. Rachel spun around at the sound of the bell, closed her eyes and flipped her hair back, and then yawned to let the dwarf know she was not planning to waste too much effort on killing him. Then, she took two arrogant steps forward and tripped over her opponent. It turned out that he had crossed the expanse almost instantly. She cracked open her skull upon hitting the ground and Gikrir spun around to finish the job with his hammer.

~

Mindya Hed
UDFC 22

Mindya Hed, a giant with an enterprising mind (one of the

first in his community), lost in round three at UDFC 22 to Yonogood Anvilsmasher, a pious dwarf with a mean temper. Mindya, knowing the biggest weak point of any giant is his shins, took a bunch of sport swimsuit catalogs and taped them to his legs for protection. It got him through the first few bouts because his opponents kept staring at the pictures of orcs, ogres, and elves who were wearing bikinis. But when he met up with Anvilsmasher, things got messy. The dwarf was annoyed by Mindya's hedonistic images and began using his hammer's nailpuller side to strip the magazines away, exposing the giant's tender shins. Anvilsmasher claimed a spiritual victory after crushing Mindya Hed's...well...head. It should be noted that Anvilsmasher went on to win the tournament but was later expelled from his church after they found copies of the swimsuit catalogs in his footlocker.

~

Dennis "BS" Vergen
UDFC 23

Dennis "BS" Vergen was a vampire who perished in UDFC 23. His challenger, a short, cloak-wearing fellow with greenish-brown arms who went by the name of Grends, stuck the rotted end of a spear into Vergen's chest at only 27 seconds into round one. It was noted that Vergen had kept trying to see what the creature looked like, and it seemed he ventured just a bit too close. As an aside, Grends left the tournament immediately following the slaying. It was reported that a cloaked creature was overheard saying, "I got him... I finally got him" in a hissing voice, though nobody has unraveled what he may have been talking about.

~

G. Val. Hart
UDFC 24

G. Val. Hart was a giant who felt his height was an unfair advantage in the ring. He wanted to win his fights fair and circle (he didn't use the word "square" because he wasn't sure what it meant, precisely). At the start of round one in his first fight in UDFC 24, G. Val. Hart asked his opponent, Quinn Zaxprin, a vampire who was known for having a deadly bite, to give him a moment to get down on his knees so they would be the same height. Quinn took a step back and waited for the giant to finish. Then the vampire got down on *his* knees, making himself again smaller than the giant. Hart frowned at this and moved to being on all fours to try and even the playing field. Quinn got down on all fours as well. The giant grimaced and then lay flat on his belly, feeling it was only fair. Quinn took this opportunity to launch himself at G. Val. Hart, biting him repeatedly on the neck until the giant found that he was no longer lying face down on the arena floor…he was now on the floor in the Afterlife.

∿

Kathleen "The Slicer" Portig
UDFC 26

Kathleen "The Slicer" Portig was a dark elf who had a thing for halflings. She found them incredibly cute, especially their overly large and hairy feet. In UDFC 26, her worst nightmare became a reality when she was pitted against Welly Hummins, a halfling with bright blue eyes, bushy brown hair, and a pleasant smile. Her heart was filled with dread when the bell rang as she didn't want to hurt the sweet-looking little fellow. They met in the center of the ring and smiled at each other. Welly held up his arms like a small child asking to be picked up. Kathleen found this irresistibly adorable, so she put away her blade and reached down for him. Just as she neared to pick him up, Welly pulled out a very long—very sharp—knife and swung it at her. She jumped back and soon found herself running around the ring, trying to get away from the little monster. Using his overly large and hairy feet, he tripped the dark elf and then jumped on her back and sent her to the Afterlife. Once she arrived, the person who was helping her noted that she was listed as a follower of the halfling god. With a grunt, Kathleen decided it was time to switch affiliations back to dark elves because she now considered them the safer option.

~

Haon "Da Rock Guy" Tnavedruts
UDFC 28

Haon "Da Rock Guy" Tnavedruts was sent to the Afterlife during a match against the dark dwarf known as Thurnaer Armbender. Tnavedruts was said to have contracted Boulderrhea, a giant-specific STD that resulted from "playing" with rocks. Because of this, Tnavedruts had worn extra protection on his abdomen since one of the side effects of Boulderrhea was the likelihood of exploding if hit too hard in the stomach. In round two of the bout, Armbender landed a shin-crushing blow, causing Tnavedruts to howl in pain, jump in the air, and fall face-first on the ground, dropping the entirety of his massive weight directly on his stomach. It's been said that the audience in the first eleven rows will never forget the effects of UDFC 28. (Anyone sharing a history with Tnavedruts and/or the slightly promiscuous boulder patch two fields in Restain are advised to get tested. They should also avoid sumo wrestling, serving as target practice for cannons, and other similar activities until the results come back.)

~

Jan Mummy-Sir
UDFC 30

Jan Mummy-Sir was an elf who suffered from the disease known as narcolepsy. She had it mostly under control, assuming she had her medicines with her, that is. Unfortunately, due to nerves regarding being accepted into UDFC 30, Jan had forgotten to bring her pills with her to the event. During round one of the first battle, against Rex "The Biter" Preston—a werewolf who was known for ripping the limbs off his opponents, Jan fell asleep at the sound of the opening bell. This would have meant an easy attack for Rex, but the werewolf never got the chance. The reason for this was because Jan had fallen forward, impaling herself on her own spear, giving her the distinction of being the only warrior in the history of the UDFC to bring about her own demise.

~

Carowatt
UDFC 33

Mean ogres tended to do well in the UDFC fights, but

Carowatt was not a mean ogre. She wasn't a dumb one either. In fact, she was one of the rare relatively-smart-and-kind-of-nice ogres. But she loved to fight, and she'd use anything as a weapon, often daring her opponent to specify an object for her to use during battle. In UDFC 33, Soilan, a vampire known to fight dirty, dared her to use knitting needles during their bout. Carowatt found this request odd since knitting needles were known to be pointy, meaning they should cause Soilan all sorts of pain by using them. But Soilan had learned some insider information about Carowatt: She couldn't stand seeing a shirt that was missing a button. During the first round of the fight, Soilen walked out and dropped such a shirt on the ground, followed by a nice silvery button that was just dying to be sewn back on. Carowatt's eye twitched as she looked back and forth between the smug vampire and the shirt in need of repair. The ramification of her decision was literally a life-and-death situation. Carowatt snapped up the shirt and began running around the arena as Soilen chased her with blade in hand. While Carowatt breathed her last on that day, she *did* succeed at reattaching the button.

~

Flatulent "Flat" Butts
UDFC 34

Flatulent "Flat" Butts, an ogre with Fatal Bowel Disease (FBD), was bested in the second round of the semi-finals at UDFC 34 by Fried Bakonz, a dragon who also suffered from FBD. The crowd nearest the fighters at the end of the bout claimed to have heard Butts yelping "Oh, crap!" moments before his pants exploded. This, it turned out, had nothing to do with the flames being released by Bakonz. The crowd, though, was rather pleased that the dragon flamed the area soon afterward, as Butts had made quite the mess. Of course, the effort expelled in flaming the area resulted in a similar explosion from Bakonz, and he was hovering over the crowd at the time. It should be noted that Bakonz felt so bad about the way Butts had gone out that he created a charity in the ogre's memory called the Urectumso Home for Dragon Riders. Donations are greatly appreciated.

~

Lynette "Fierce Fangs" Wood
UDFC 36

Lynette "Fierce Fangs" Wood was a vampire who had competed in UDFC 34 and 35, losing both times in the semi-final due to knockout. In UDFC 36, though, she faced the dragon known as Muddles. Though not particularly dire in the realm of physicality, Muddles was excellent at targeting his flames. During round three of the bout, Lynette had launched herself through the air, diving directly at the dragon with her sword extended. The dragon jumped to the side and Lynette's blade stuck directly into the wood-paneled wall he'd been standing in front of. Thinking quickly, the dragon held her legs up with his claw and cast flame at her while spinning her around. This gave Lynette the notoriety of being the first rotisserie-style death in UDFC history.

~

Enoch of Halsey
UDFC 39

Enoch of Halsey was a giant who was known for being

relatively intelligent, as far as giants go. In the semi-finals of UDFC 39, he squared off against the irritable Goozbee Shincracker, a female dwarf who sported a beard that male dwarves envied, and whose last name spoke of her particular desire to crack shins in battle. Two minutes into the first round, Enoch picked up Goozbee and prepared to throw her across the ring, but the dwarf asked him if he was able to count to twenty. Wanting to prove his intellect, he started rattling off the numbers, getting most of them correct, until he reached ten. Then he had to put Goozbee on the ground so he could continue counting on his toes. The dwarf took advantage of this lapse in Enoch's judgment, smacked his shins with her hammer, and dropped the poor creature to the ground. To Goozbee's credit, she did allow him to reach twenty before finishing him.

~

Tily
UDFC 42

Tily was a dark elf who despised ogres, especially the nice ones, so when she faced off against Yurb—who was one of the kindest ogres to ever participate in the Ultimate Dragon Fighting Championship—she had destruction on her mind. Yurb wasn't known for killing his opponents, but rather just making them submit and then buying them a drink later to apologize. But during their fight, a fan in the crowd threw a banana peel onto the arena floor just as Tily went to move in for the kill. Three things happened at that moment: The first was that Tily slipped on the banana peel and landed flat on her back; the second thing was that a small spider that had been running across the field scurried up and sat itself on Tily's helm; and the third thing to happen was that Yurb, being absolutely terrified of spiders, began stomping on Tily's head in an effort to kill the spider. It should be noted that the kind ogre succeeded in bringing about the demise of both the spider and the dark elf once known as Tily.

≈

K S'Myth
UDFC 43

K S'Myth was a dark elf who had risen through the ranks of the Ultimate Dragon Fighting Championship until finally being selected to battle in UDFC 43. She had worked for two years straight to prepare for the tournament, never taking even a single day off to relax. Hers was a mind of purpose and strength. Every angle had been considered, every potential challenger fully researched. She was the first called fighter that day and she strode onto the field and stood with her back to her opponent's side. She had no need to see him come in, after all. Her mind was focused on the task at hand and there would be nothing to distract her. Unfortunately, her opponent—a giant named Zirve—had taken a wrong turn when he was summoned to the field. He tried to get on the field through a side door, but it was locked. In his frustration, he ripped the door from its hinges, walked out onto the field, and threw the door with all of his might. K S'Myth noted only a shadow an instant before being crushed, making her the only competitor to lose in the UDFC before the opening bell.

≈

Natalia Fallonherwand
UDFC 47

Natalia Fallonherwand had an innate dislike for standard elves because she was a dark elf. Worse, those elves who employed flowery speech were enough to drive her to madness. So when she faced off against Melooraquen in UDFC 47, she was ready to punish the elf. What she hadn't expected was that Melooraquen was the type of warrior who loved speaking throughout the entirety of the match. His incessant rococo oration had driven her to the edge, until Natalia pleaded with him to just shut the hell up. His eyes glittered and he stood tall, pointing his sword directly out as he released a volley of euphemistic discourse. It caused Natalia to cast her blade aside, cover her ears, scream, and run into his outstretched saber, ending her ability to hear him ever again. It should be noted that she is now in the Afterlife, living a life of chosen solitude in the agnostic area.

~

Mark Brown
UDFC 48

Mark Brown was a vampire who preferred battling against people smaller than him. If they were weaker, too, that was a bonus. The best challenger for him, though, was one who was weaker, smaller, and not very good at fighting. In UDFC 48, Mark thought he found the perfect opponent in Zupper Boltspinner. Zupper was a gnome with a chipper disposition who appeared to be absent-minded and rather clumsy. But Mark soon learned that it's not wise to underestimate anyone in the UDFC. It was in the first minute of the first round of the first fight when Mark casually walked across the field toward Zupper. The gnome had his back turned, giving Mark the perfect opportunity to literally stab the fellow in the back. There were little lights glowing around the gnome, and a few whirring sounds came through as well, but that only made skewering the little fellow more enjoyable seeing that Mark was not a fan of gnomes. Just as he was about to put a point of finality to the tiny Zupper, the gnome cheered and ran away, leaving Mark to stare into the face of an oncoming rocket. The crowd "ewww"ed and "awwww"ed at first, but the second explosion was more colorful, causing them to change their expressions to "oooh"s and "ahhh"s instead.

∼

Tracitia "The Tooth" Burr
UDFC 50

Tracitia "The Tooth" Burr was not one of your standard double-toothed vampires. She had only one fang, and it was the left one. The right one had never grown in, and this had meant she was teased a lot. So much so that she learned the art of Dragon Martial Arts and began cracking heads. In UDFC 50, she met an orc by the name of Levkore in the second round. She'd never bitten an orc before and so that's how she planned to take him out. They battled, punching, kicking, and slicing until the orc made a deadly mistake. He lunged forward, exposing his neck long enough for Tracitia to chomp his jugular with her single, sharpened tooth. Immediately afterward, she learned why vampires went out of their way *not* to bite orcs. It turned out that their blood tasted like rotting cheese. Tracitia began to gag as she pushed herself away from the grunting beast she'd just bitten. That's when she remembered that orcs don't just instantly fall over when bitten by a vampire. She spun back to find a very irritated orc holding his neck in one hand and a gigantic, spike-covered club in the other. The rest, as they say, is history.

~

Teninch Mustdodadeed
UDFC 51

Teninch Mustdodadeed was a dwarf who had been known to illegally smuggle explosives into the fights. During UDFC 51, he went up against the pink dragon known as Oonakwe Kwanookwa. With nobody the wiser, Teninch had put a sunburst clusterbomb in his shorts. It was placed in the back since the security personnel knew better than to get near a dwarf's rear end. But during the fight, Teninch was unable to get the bomb out. It had somehow gotten stuck. After rolling around and dodging the flames that were being thrown at him by Oonakwe, he finally was able to get the fuse exposed. It wasn't much, but it was a start. Unfortunately, the pink dragon saw this also and so she sent a very directed flame to ignite the wick that was attached to the bomb. Teninch started to run at the dragon, knowing that she would snuff the flame if he was near her, but she leapt into the air and flew up well above the stadium. Teninch rolled on the ground and did all that he could to stop the flame from getting to the sunburst clusterbomb, but it was all for naught as the explosive detonated and sent a rainbow of colors through the air along with the pieces of one obliterated dwarf.

~

Lalin
UDFC 55

Lalin was a werewolf who had mastered the art of turning into her wolf form whenever she desired. This had allowed her to rise up the ranks of the Ultimate Dragon Fighting Championship until she'd made it to the big show. In UDFC 55, Lalin was pitted against Nednorth Cazren, a dark elf who had very large and pointy ears. The two matched up nicely through the first two rounds of battle, but in the third round things turned when Lalin flipped into her wolf mode and launched herself at Nednorth, catching the dark elf by surprise. Lalin snapped off one of Nednorth's ears during the exchange. This would have been a boon to Lalin's chance of winning except that the enormous ear got lodged in the werewolf's throat and she couldn't get it out. Nednorth went to reengage with Lalin, clearly agitated over the loss of his ear, but he stopped after noting that the werewolf had choked to death on it.

~

Baronin
UDFC 57

Baronin was a dark halfling who fought against Sir William Tellerington, a roaming knight who had served many kingdoms over his years. Tellerington was known for saying that he was terribly sorry for having to kill his opponents moments before his sword burrowed its way into their chests. Conversely, Baronin was known for getting under the skin of her opponents. She would incessantly poke fun at them and call them names. Her tormenting style of battle was a thing of legend. So when the second round of her fight against Sir Tellerington arrived, the knight had a sneer on his face. Apparently, he was not all that fond of being called "tin man" or "armor boy" or "steel-boot Billy." So when his sword cleaved its way into Baronin's side, she very clearly heard Sir Tellerington say, "I am *not* terribly sorry for doing this." She grabbed his boot as she hit the ground and motioned him to come closer. Being an honorable sort, Sir William Tellerington knelt beside the fallen Baronin. She winced for a moment and then smiled at him and, with her dying breath, she said, "Nice fight, Captain Pointystick."

~

Mark Beech
UDFC 61

Mark Beech was a dark elf who spent years studying the art of fighting dragons. When the day finally arrived for him to face one of the beasts, he was ready. It was at UDFC 61 and his opponent was the grisly creature named Wezindunia Ealumdrunan—or Wez, as her friends called her. At the bell, Mark ran towards the dragon, faked a step to the left, jumped over to the right, and swung up onto the dragon's back while pulling forth his blade in one fluid motion. But this wasn't Wez's first battle, and she seemingly knew precisely how to respond to this attack. With a shot, she launched straight up towards the clouds, causing Mark to drop his blade and instead hold on for dear life. When Wez got enough altitude, Mark passed out and slid off her back and began falling back to Ononokin. This would have been enough to end the match since the dark elf was incapable of flying, but Wez kept moving him back and forth until she had him targeted just so. Then she yelled to wake him up. It took him a moment to realize he was free-falling from a great height, but things got worse when Wez smiled at him and pointed. Mark followed the direction of her finger and saw the metal edge of the enormous UDFC 61 sign moments before it split him in two.

~

The Cassandra
UDFC 64

The Cassandra was an elf who had perfect balance, walked with a level of grace few had mastered, and was considered highly intellectual. She did have one flaw, though, and it turned out to be a fatal one. The Cassandra was not quite adept at tying her bootlaces. During the second round of fight number two in UDFC 64, one of her laces had come undone. She finished the round and came back to ask her corner to tie it back up for her, but it seemed that the hot dog vendor was nearby and the entire corner crew was famished. This left The Cassandra to fumble through the tying process on her own. She was apprehensive, but once finished fashioning a double knot, her spirits lifted and the bell rang signaling that round three had started. Feeling a sense of pride that was not typically attributed to tying one's own shoes, The Cassandra stepped purposefully toward her opponent and felt the pull of laces. She glanced down as she began to fall and noticed that she'd tied her boots together. A curse escaped her lips an instant before her head was crushed in by her own hammer.

~

Neil "Bruiser" Webber
UDFC 66

Neil "Bruiser" Webber was an undersized ogre with a chip

on his shoulder. He'd been fighting since he was young because the bigger ogres constantly pestered him. In UDFC 66, he squared off against a dark halfling named Dupree Littleknees who made Neil feel huge. The halfling was a cunning fellow, though Neil didn't know it until it was too late. At the sound of the opening bell, the dark halfling made chicken sounds at Neil, causing the ogre to run over in rage. Once he arrived, Dupree held up a hand and stopped Neil. He then pointed at a spot on the ground and Neil scratched his head and moved over to it. Dupree moved Neil around, getting things just right, until he finally nodded and winked at the ogre. Neil felt accomplished, though he wasn't sure why. The halfling then took out a pair of scissors and set about cutting a thick rope that was right next to Neil, but he wasn't getting very far. Trying to be helpful, Neil took the scissors from Dupree and snipped at the rope until it finally snapped in two. A gigantic piano plummeted from the top rafters and crushed Neil where he stood. It should be noted that Dupree was disqualified from the tournament, but he was given a consolation reward for his creativity.

~

Sandeelia Lloydwynn
UDFC 68

Sandeelia was known as a dark elf who would fight at the drop of a hat. One wrong look tended to spell doom for any poor soul in her path. This was especially true when it came to ogres, even the dumb ones. But she'd met her match in UDFC 68 when a mean ogre by the name of Gah faced her in the semi-finals. Gah had followed Sandeelia around for years, making no bones about the fact that he was madly in love with her. This gave Sandeelia even more ammunition to end the ogre in the ring because she was highly repulsed by him. At the start of the match, Sandeelia made solid progress, swishing her two scimitars expertly at Gah, adding to his already impressive scar ensemble. But when she dived forward and shoved both blades into his thighs, Gah didn't scream or yell. He grinned. You see, Gah was an ogre who felt no pain, and while Sandeelia's attack would certainly spell the end for Gah due to blood loss, she'd gotten within reach of his massive arms. He grabbed her, pulling her in and giving her a big wet kiss that stirred something inside, causing her to close her eyes and kiss him back. She'd never felt anything like that before. It was like a burning in her belly. Could it be love? It wasn't. When Gah had pulled her in for a kiss, one of her scimitars fell from his leg and stuck through her stomach. They both perished moments later. It should be noted that Gah continued pursuing Sandeelia in the Afterlife until she finally relented and married him. She figured she couldn't kill him in the Afterlife, seeing that he was already dead, but she could certainly make his eternity a difficult one. To this day their neighbors cringe at the amount of nagging that poor ogre endures after Sandeelia hands him a honey-do list.

~

Rob Rawl
UDFC 71

Rob Rawl was a human who spent most of his days in the portal stations acting in the role of scrag. He was tough, gruff, and in love with gold coins. In the semi-finals at UDFC 71, Rob found himself pitted against the wealthiest fighter the UDFC had ever known. Hubris Humphrey was a merchant who also happened to be a dark halfling. It was said that Hubris had attained his immense wealth through clever dealings, which became incredibly apparent during his fight against Rob Rawl. Rob had planned to destroy the little twerp in the ring and then mug him later in order to liberate a sizable chunk of change. But Rob's eyes caught sight of the massive change purse that Hubris had on his side and his heart skipped a beat. The purse was immaculate. It had deep brown leather that was oiled to a sheen, gold rivets and stitching, and it bulged enough to tell Rob that there were enough coins inside to pay a king's ransom. With a speed reserved typically for elves, Rob snatched the purse away and ran to the other side of the field as Hubris complained. But the halfling's aggravation turned out to be a ruse because when Rob unzipped the precious purse now in his possession, a flash of white light filled the air, costing Rob not only the match, but also his life.

~

Purple Kittiesocks
UDFC 73

It was rare for gnomes to participate in the Ultimate Dragon Fighting Championship, but Purple Kittiesocks was rather a rare-minded gnome. She was highly feared on the battlefield due to her strength of both mind and body. Plus, she fought dirty. During UDFC 73, however, she went up against Bigrin, a giant who was always smiling, even when he was unhappy. Purple knew full well how to defeat giants since she had knocked a good many of them in the shins over the years, but she'd made a misstep when choosing her outfit for the battle. She had decided on wearing a chainmail cape. This, in and of itself, was not a horrible idea, except that the one she selected was too long. When she went to swing her spanner wrench at Bigrin's shin, he jumped up and moved his foot behind her. During this exchange, one of the links in her chainmail got caught on the metal clasp of Bigrin's sandal. She tried to unhinge it, but Bigrin started running around the ring while looking for her, clearly not knowing that she was attached to his foot. A few crunching steps into Bigrin's search spelled the end of Purple Kittiesocks.

Thanks for Reading

If you enjoyed this book, would you please leave a review at the site you purchased it from? It doesn't have to be a book report… just a line or two would be fantastic and it would really help us out!

John P. Logsdon
www.JohnPLogsdon.com

John was raised in the MD/VA/DC area. Growing up, John had a steady interest in writing stories, playing music, and tinkering with computers. He spent over 20 years working in the video games industry where he acted as designer and producer on many online games. He's written science fiction, fantasy, humor, and even books on game development. While he enjoys writing lighthearted adventures and wacky comedies most, he can't seem to turn down writing darker fiction. John lives with his wife, son, and Chihuahua.

Christopher P. Young

Chris grew up in the Maryland suburbs. He spent the majority of his childhood reading and writing science fiction and learning the craft of storytelling. He worked as a designer and producer in the video games industry for a number of years as well as working in technology and admin services. He enjoys writing both serious and comedic science fiction and fantasy. Chris lives with his wife and an ever-growing population of critters.

CRIMSON MYTH PRESS

Crimson Myth Press offers more books by this author as well as books from a few other hand-picked authors. From science fiction & fantasy to adventure & mystery, we bring the best stories for adults and kids alike.

www.CrimsonMyth.com

Printed in Great Britain
by Amazon